# UNSAFE HAVEN

# UNSAFE HAVEN

Lucy Burdette

SEVERN
HOUSE

First world edition published in Great Britain and the USA in 2021
by Severn House, an imprint of Canongate Books Ltd,
14 High Street, Edinburgh EH1 1TE.

Trade paperback edition first published in Great Britain and the USA in 2022
by Severn House, an imprint of Canongate Books Ltd.

severnhouse.com

*British Library Cataloguing-in-Publication Data*
A CIP catalogue record for this title is available from the British Library.

ISBN-13: 978-0-7278-5082-9 (cased)
ISBN-13: 978-1-4483-0584-1 (trade paper)
ISBN-13: 978-1-4483-0583-4 (e-book)

*All Severn House titles are printed on acid-free paper.*

Typeset by Palimpsest Book Production Ltd.,
Falkirk, Stirlingshire, Scotland.
Printed and bound in Great Britain by
TJ Books, Padstow, Cornwall.

*For the Jungle Red Writers. Dear friends,*
*role models, and amazing writers*

# ONE

Tonight, Addy's worst enemy might be an irritable cop, just bored enough to be curious. She ducked into the station and melted into the waiting crowd, most of them jazzed up to celebrate the night before New Year's Eve. As she groped in her pocket for the change she'd been saving, she caught a glimpse of herself in the metal frame of one of the posters lining the stairs to the subway. White face, huge eyes, the dirty and oversized clothing of a runaway. She bought a one-ride MetroCard, slashed it through the reader, and clacked through the gate onto the platform, softly chanting the directions Rafe had made her memorize: *Subway from Harlem to Grand Central, shuttle to Times Square. N, Q, R, or W train to 33rd Street, PATH train to Hoboken.*

'Chicklet! What brings you out tonight?'

Her heart plunged, hearing her street nickname. It was Des, the dealer who worked the grid a couple of blocks away from Georgia's place. Addy always tried to stay far away from him. She'd seen what had happened to some of the other girls, who'd taken the samples he offered and then got hooked and desperate. Bad enough to service the *special* gentlemen Georgia introduced them to.

Des sauntered over and squeezed her chin with cold fingers, turning her face, forcing her to meet his gaze. 'Where you going, girlfriend?' He wore his hair greased back into a ponytail, a fringed vest, his eyes dark and mean like a hungry reptile.

Fear and the fetid heat of the subway tunnel pressed in, making her feel nauseous and crampy. She wrenched free, bolted to the trash can, Des on her heels, and heaved out the contents of her stomach.

'Whoa,' said Des, stumbling back. 'What you been drinkin', baby?'

Maybe if she ignored him, he'd leave her alone. At the very

least, she knew he'd tell Georgia tomorrow that he'd seen her. Maybe sooner. The subway car thundered through the tunnel and screeched to a stop in front of her. The people waiting began to shove forward. Without looking back, she drafted behind a tall man and flung herself through the doors, nearly landing on three girls dressed for a holiday party wearing Santa hats, spike heels, and loads of sparkly make-up.

'Dude, watch where you're going,' said one in a disgusted voice.

With no seats empty, Addy lurched from one pole to another and slumped in the far corner of the car, keeping an eye out for Des. Once it seemed he hadn't followed her, she dropped her gaze to the speckled linoleum floor. Which reminded her of the kitchenette in her mother's trailer in Waterbury. If only she had the kind of mother she could call when she was in trouble. The kind of mother who baked snickerdoodles to serve with a frosty glass of milk after school, who brought saltines and ginger ale when her kid was sick.

Fierce-hot tears stung her eyes and she rubbed them away and straightened her shoulders. Halfway there – she just had to make it to Rafe. Now that she was speeding away from Georgia and not quite as scared, her stomach hurt so badly she could barely think. She squeezed her eyes shut and tried to imagine the beach Rafe had told her about, where there was always a party. She fingered his phone number on the scrap of paper in her jacket pocket.

The subway car clattered through the Upper East Side and lurched to a stop at 42nd Street. She pushed out through the throngs – the people coming in as hurried as the ones going out – then made the transfer from the subway to the shuttle, and finally darted onto the F train. Almost there. At the next stop, she would take the PATH train that would cross the river and leave her in Hoboken where Rafe would pick her up and take care of her.

A bulbous-nosed man wearing a dirty blue cap with goofy earflaps staggered onboard behind her. He sat across from her and began to read a rumpled copy of the *New York Post*. A group of young men dressed in black clung to the pole nearest to her, taunting each other about how much they'd drink that night and who would nail the girls. The odors and noise of the car and the rocking motion made her feel as though she might vomit again. Or something worse – she was cramping, cramping. She closed her eyes, rested her head on her arms, folded them over her rounded lap, and breathed.

An automated voice announced they were approaching Delancey Street. In a flash of panic, she realized that in her haste to get away from Des in Harlem, and then to make it through the hordes of people underground at 42nd Street, she'd taken the wrong line. This train would deliver her to Brooklyn, not New Jersey. No one was waiting for her in Brooklyn. No one.

A painful stomach cramp hit and she doubled over and moaned. The earflap man looked up from his newspaper, drooled, and jabbered something unintelligible.

'Shut up, you crazy old coot,' yelled one of the boys.

She had to get to Rafe.

As she surfed through another wave of agony, she began to sweat. The earflap man, still watching her, grew more agitated. When the train ground to a stop, she grabbed the plastic bag containing her belongings and staggered out to the platform with a few other travelers.

'Carry on, brave soul!' the man called to her as the doors slid closed.

The walls of this subway stop were paved with white tiles trimmed in blue and black. She perched on a wooden bench as the pain washed through her belly, trying to focus on the designs on the walls – fish, a bowl of cherries, an enormous trout. It was after nine and there was no attendant in the fare booth. The small news shop was closed and barred. And no pay phone in sight to call Rafe.

Everyone else who'd gotten off had already rushed up the stairs and out into the night. The pain twisted her gut again. What if something was terribly wrong and she died right here in the freaking subway station? She thought about using the emergency phone tucked into a corner by the stairwell. Police and paramedics would come. She'd be taken to a hospital with clean sheets and drugs for the pain. She moaned at the thought of such welcome relief.

She spotted a restroom on the far side of the station – *Out of service, closed for cleaning*, the sign read, but the door was cracked ajar. She hobbled over and pushed the door open. The small bathroom stunk of urine. The trash can overflowed with dirty diapers, cigarette butts, and other unmentionables, and the sink was stained an ugly brown. Someone wearing a pair of ratty sneakers was slumped in the first stall.

The person snorted and a hypodermic needle clattered to the floor.

She rushed to the last stall, locked the door, stripped off her coat and sank down onto the toilet. The pains rode through her faster now, splitting her open. Oh, holy freaking god, the baby was coming. She clutched the filthy toilet seat, screamed into the padded recesses of the down coat. She needed help. Extracting the man's phone tucked in the bottom of her garbage bag, she turned it on. She'd tried this once before, but had frozen at the thought that his people might be able to track the phone and find her. Surely she could dial 911.

But then what? If the authorities came, they'd take the baby and make her go back to her mother's trailer in Waterbury, or more likely, another foster home. They wouldn't let a sixteen-year-old loose on the streets. And she couldn't return to Harlem. Georgia would kill her – literally – if she showed up without the kid. She began to sniffle, thinking of poor Heather, sleeping in their room. And Rafe, waiting for her in Hoboken. Waiting to start their new life, furious that she'd blown him off.

No. She would do this alone. And then keep going.

What seemed like hours later, after a terrible, searing contraction, she felt an overwhelming urge to push. Minutes later, she sagged to a crouch on the floor and the baby slid out. After a second wrenching wave, she pushed out a disgusting bloody pancake attached to the infant by a cord. She felt sick and weak and scared and empty, as if she'd lost something that belonged deep inside her. Blood everywhere and a salty, earthy odor like nothing she'd ever smelled. The child began to whimper.

What did doctors on TV do after a baby was born? Tie the cord and cut the kid loose, she thought.

She rustled through her bag and pulled the string from

the hood of her sweatshirt, tried to figure out what to do. She could tie it off, but she had no knife or scissors. Forget it. The baby began to gurgle, winding up and letting loose a miniature howl.

'Shhh, shhh, shhh,' she crooned as she picked up the creature and jiggled. 'You're here. It's me. We're OK.' They weren't, but why scare the kid so early by telling it how bad things were?

Bowlegged and pointy-headed, it looked like the star of her favorite movie growing up: ET. Ugly, but cute. Yanking a pink T-shirt from the garbage bag, Addy exchanged this clean one for the extra-large one she'd been wearing. She hobbled to the sink, wet the cleanest part of the old shirt, dabbed the baby's face, and swiped at the greasy white substance in the creases of its legs. A girl, she noticed, and then touched in turn each tiny but perfectly formed finger and toe. The kind of girl who might be called Emmeline or Maisy. Who might take ballet classes after school with her mother watching from the sidelines. Her eyes flooded with tears.

No, she could not afford to feel one more thing.

She wrapped the baby and the attached pancake in the discarded T-shirt and then her coat, knotting her into a tight bundle with the arms of the jacket. Then she wiped the blood from her own legs with her stained pants and stuffed them in the garbage can. She rattled the metal box on the wall until a maxi-pad dropped loose, and then dressed in clean underwear and her other pair of flannel pants. The baby watched, blinking rheumy eyes, taking little sips of breath. Would they turn hazel like hers? Have the same ring of brown?

Now what? She felt shocked and weak. She had no idea how to take care of a baby. And it was hard to imagine Rafe as a father figure. He'd never said they would raise her together. Why would he even want to, when he wasn't the father? If Georgia caught her, she would take the baby. Rafe had told her that she planned to sell it, Heather's too. After that, she'd be forced back to work. If she fought that, Georgia wouldn't hesitate to kill her. That's what Rafe had said. She'd be one more homeless teenager, found in an alley, dead of an overdose.

Probably had it coming.

# TWO

Elizabeth tore along Park Avenue, the street an Arctic wind tunnel. It felt too darn cold to walk the whole way as she'd planned. The putrid warmth of the subway beckoned. She hurtled down the stairs to the turnstiles, but by the time she found her MetroCard buried behind her American Airlines Visa and the notice of her next dental cleaning, the train's doors had hissed closed. It shot away, disappearing into its dark tube.

'Shit!' The heels of her black boots clicking against the cement, she paced the length of the platform, more pungent than usual with the stink of rotten food and the leftover traces of cologned New Yorkers who'd passed through the station earlier in the day. She heard a scuffling noise and leapt back, anticipating the appearance of hunger-emboldened rats. She perched at the end of one of the benches, away from the overflowing trash can and several other people who'd also missed that last train. She glanced at her phone. The service bars reappeared and a barrage of texts rushed in: sixteen new messages from her bridesmaids and girlfriends.

*OMG, Lizzie!! So sorry! What can I do to make things better?* That was from Erin, her second-best friend since freshman year in college.

*Elizabeth, he's a bastard – not good enough for you! Say the word, my Uncle Tony will take care of him . . .* From Annette, her cousin in New Jersey.

*We already have tickets to Connecticut, let's change them and meet up in Vegas . . .* That one from Holly, who had arranged all the parties in college.

In the messages that followed, the girls planned a weekend in Vegas to take the place of her wedding celebration. The outpouring of support should have made her feel better, but Elizabeth cringed at the idea of getting together to commiserate. She felt battered and lost, ashamed and depressed. An extended alcohol-soaked party with the women who were supposed to be standing up at her marriage was not going to help.

To be honest, the huge wedding with all those attendants had begun to feel as though it belonged to someone else. She wasn't the same person Kevin had proposed to eighteen months ago, right after he'd graduated. After two years together in college, she'd felt desperate at the prospect of being separated from him. So she was thrilled to accept his proposal. She'd finish her last year, then move to New York and start medical school. They'd get married in a big romantic ceremony on New Year's Eve, with all their closest friends in attendance.

What had he been thinking when he called it all off, two days before their wedding? Had he met someone else? Was there something wrong with her? Or was it him? For sure, she'd been preoccupied with her studies. And yes, they still had to figure out where they'd live and how they'd find time for each other. But was that enough to kill a marriage? Even when she'd pressed for an explanation, he hadn't been able to stutter out much more than that she was too perfect. How in the world could she fix that? She texted Jillian, her maid of honor, whom she planned to meet for coffee – and something stronger once they were thoroughly caffeinated. In truth, she only wanted the coffee, but she'd agreed to drinks to satisfy Jillian. She would beg her to call the girls off and let them know she needed some time alone. And then she'd retire to her studio to lick her wounds.

*Missed train. CU at the shop in 20.*

She opened Facebook and found Kevin's page. His smiling photo was like a surgeon's scalpel to the gut. And his new status – single, so quickly – twisted the blade. He wasn't wasting a moment mourning their breakup. How had she not seen this coming? She'd been busy dogpaddling through anatomy, biochemistry, histology, embryology – the subjects and exams pressed in on her like a series of rough ocean waves, carving away her confidence. How could she possibly learn all the things she needed to know? And none of this had really interested Kevin. Nor had her doubts about whether she'd survive the first year of medical school. Whether she wanted to survive was another question he didn't seem to want to hear.

She closed Facebook before she could be tempted to scroll through his photo albums, and clicked over to Find My Friends. At first she'd resisted turning on her phone's location service. Shouldn't they have some privacy, even if they were getting married? But eventually she'd agreed. They loved each other. They had nothing to hide. Everyone was doing it.

It seemed so silly now.

Kevin's superhero avatar was positioned in the Upper East Side of Manhattan – the Bullpen Sports Bar, Elizabeth guessed. Not far from his bachelor pad and one of his favorites on guys' nights out. Probably the bar he'd called from earlier, when he'd had the steel balls to ask for custody of their nonrefundable honeymoon trip to Disney. That had tipped her over – she couldn't sit in her tiny studio apartment, where her textbooks were screaming for attention, and where congratulatory flowers sent from her fellow medical students were dying, shedding a circle of sad pink petals on the desk. Maybe fleeing from her parents' home in the Connecticut suburbs had been a mistake. But every single thing in their house had screamed *wedding*. And her mother was distraught, desperate to find ways to help Elizabeth feel better.

Something rustled by the trash can again. She leapt up and tucked the iPhone into her purse. There'd been a sighting of rabid rodents in Central Park last month. This subway station was miles from the park, but she'd learned in Introduction to Epidemiology that illness could travel quickly when it came to homeless populations, whether furred or human. Another train squealed to a stop and she hurried aboard.

Addy shuffled out of the bathroom into the white- and blue-tiled subway station, clutching the swaddled infant and her plastic bag. She'd been tempted, so tempted, to leave the baby and run. How easy it would have been to tuck the bundle into the cabinet under the sink with the cleaning supplies, where someone – anyone – could have found her. But what if an addict like the one passed out in the next stall had picked her up? What if no one found her at all? Probably Addy would stink as a mother, like her own. But was she the kind of person who'd abandon a new creature to freeze to death? Then two tipsy girls had stumbled in wearing super high heels and furry coats, shrieking with giggles over the outrageous idea of using a disgusting subway bathroom, and the decision was made.

Back out in the station, she rested on the edge of a bench, exhausted and hopeless. The people crowding around her had the same loud and manic party energy she'd noticed earlier, making it hard to think. She had to meet Rafe. Couldn't let herself believe that he might already be gone. But first she had to do something with the baby.

A train whooshed by, then another screeched to a halt. The doors of the subway car remained closed. One woman waited to disembark, tapping a leather-gloved hand on the window. Through the glass, Addy's gaze locked onto the woman's face. She had enormous blue eyes and blonde curls and diamond earrings, like a princess. And she wore an expensive-looking gray coat – cashmere, maybe – and a gray beret, shot through with silver threads. Though she seemed sad, she didn't avert her eyes as most people did when they saw a homeless girl. Back when she'd first come to the city, after a few weeks on the street, Addy had begun to understand how they thought: *She's a druggie, a prostitute, a thief – she deserves what she gets.*

And she knew she looked awful tonight – worse even than usual – frightened and pale and way too thin, except for the bump in her middle where the baby had been, with streaks of blood on the coat and her sweatshirt. She looked at the helpless lump in her arms, then back at the woman on the train. She sent every ounce of sorrow and panic she was feeling through her gaze, then ducked away into the crowd.

As Elizabeth waited for the doors to open, she took out her phone and punched in 911, her finger hovering over the send icon. She clutched her bag tightly to her belly. The girl staring at her from the platform had totally unsettled her – it was almost as if she was pleading for something. But then her mother's cautious voice echoed in her mind: *Always be watchful in the city. That pitiful-looking girl could be bait for thugs waiting around the corner.*

The phone rang, causing her heart rate to spike – Jillian.

'Where are you?'

'Coming up the stairs, be there in a sec.' She jogged across the platform toward the exit.

'If you can't face Vegas, maybe you should go to Orlando on your own anyway,' said Jillian. 'Cancel Kevin's ticket and get out of Dodge.'

'Me? Disney World? What would I do, ride the teacups humming "it's a small world after all"?' Elizabeth asked, vaulting up the steps. 'Mr Frat Boy, my ex-fiancé, was the one who wanted to party with the other children.' She felt a twinge of leftover guilt, dissing Kevin. They'd promised each other, eons ago in college, that they wouldn't become one of *those* couples.

Light footsteps echoed behind her as she emerged into the night. Whirling around, she came face to face with the girl from the subway. The girl shoved a raggedy bundle into Elizabeth's arms. Reflexively, she grabbed it.

'Please take care of her. I can't,' the girl whispered, and turned to run.

'Wait! Wait! Who are you? What is this? Where are you going? Wait a minute!'

The girl seemed to hesitate, glanced back, and then took off. 'California.' The word floated over her shoulder and she was gone.

# THREE

A faint keening came from the soiled bundle Elizabeth was now holding. One tiny fist punched out. She stifled a gasp and peeled back the top layer – a baby. And absolutely brand new from the looks of it. Though they hadn't gotten to obstetrics yet, so what did she really know? The more she studied all the required subjects, the more she realized she didn't understand. A film of light hair stuck up the length of the baby's skull like a dog's hackles. Its face and neck were streaked with blood.

The child began to bleat pathetic squeaks. Elizabeth's eyes teared up and she held the infant against her shoulder and patted its back. Who in their right mind would hand a newborn baby over to a perfect stranger? She held up her phone with her free hand and pressed the on button – the bars that had lined up so nicely just minutes ago were gone. She banged the phone on her hip. Damn, damn, this was utterly bizarre. She looked around. A few cars whooshed by on the opposite side of the street, but the nearest shops were shuttered. Where were the authorities when you needed them? No one helpful in sight.

She ventured another peek at the bundle, moving a blue jacket sleeve away from the baby's face. Its lips moued like a tiny goldfish vamping through the glass wall of its bowl. Greenish eyes, but light like Kevin's. She wanted to find the girl, the mother. But first, she needed to figure out whether this baby needed medical attention. Tucking the coat around the child, she trotted west in the direction she thought the girl had taken, to the corner of Delancey and Norfolk. A small, wizened man was closing up his newsstand.

'Did a girl run by – wearing a blue sweatshirt and dirty UGGs?' Elizabeth asked. She pointed to her own boots, stomping her feet to keep them warm.

The man stared at her blankly, then grunted: 'No English.' He pouted and shrugged.

'Arrggh!' She shifted the baby into her left arm, darted across the street to the coffee shop on Orchard, and burst into the café. Jillian was seated against the back wall, sipping from an oversized white cup and reading her iPhone.

'You have to order here,' said the girl behind the counter.

Elizabeth waved her away and hurried across the room. She slid onto the bench beside her friend, placing the messy bundle between them and her phone on the table.

'What the heck?'

'Shhh,' Elizabeth warned. 'You can't imagine what just happened.' In a hoarse whisper, she described how the girl she'd seen on the platform had followed her out of the subway and foisted the baby on her.

'Oh my God, are you kidding me? Is the baby all right?' She lifted a corner of the coat's fabric and peered at the tiny face.

'I don't know,' Elizabeth said. Her shoulders and neck stiffened like a rock wall as she felt the tension of the last fifteen minutes settle in. She shucked off her coat, took a big breath, and rolled her head, first toward one shoulder, and then the other.

'This makes no sense,' Jillian said. 'Are you absolutely sure she didn't just want you to watch the kid while she went to the bathroom?'

'Who in her right mind uses the restroom in the subway? And even if someone did, she'd park her new baby with a stranger on the street? I don't think so.' As Elizabeth folded more of the slippery polyester jacket away from the baby's face, the earthy scent of blood wafted up.

'Oh my God, it's so small. Did you call the cops?'

'This just happened. I haven't had a minute to do anything. My phone had no bars in the subway, so I ran out to see if I could follow her. Gone.' She pulled the phone closer, overwhelmed by the bizarreness of the last half hour. 'Can you get me a cup of tea or something?'

While Jillian went to the counter to order the drink, Elizabeth dialed 911 and explained the baby's discovery to the dispatcher. 'I'm in the café on Orchard Street right now. It's too cold to take her outside.'

'We'll send an officer over. Paramedics, too.'

Jillian returned with the steaming tea.

'They're coming,' said Elizabeth, falling against the bright red fabric of the booth and fanning her face with her hand. 'I think I'm in shock.' She untied the sleeves of the jacket, and unfolded an old T-shirt wrapped around the baby, revealing a pink umbilical cord and the remnants of the placenta. 'Here's why she's bloody – she's just come out of the oven.'

'This is surreal.' Jillian took her glasses off, pinched the bridge of her nose, and then leaned over to peer at the baby. 'You're sure you'd never seen the girl before?'

Elizabeth shook her head, then tugged off the big scarf wrapped around her neck and covered the child. 'She was young, maybe around eighteen. Maybe younger. She was a mess, her hair uncombed, blood on her pants. They weren't really pants, more like pajama bottoms. And her eyes . . .' She shivered. 'She had this frantic look.'

The baby started to squawk, working herself up into a piercing cry. The couple sitting at the table nearest to them craned their heads to look.

'What's going on?' the woman asked. 'Is something wrong with the baby? Should we call someone?' And then other customers began to gawk, some of them standing up to get a better view.

'We've got this,' Elizabeth said, gesturing for them to stay away and feeling another flicker of anxiety. Was it hungry? She couldn't help with that. Hurt? 'Shhh, they'll be here soon. We'll take care of you.' She found a Kleenex in her purse and dabbed at the splotches of blood on the translucent skin. 'Shhh,' she whispered again, stroking the baby's soft cheek. The infant turned toward her finger and tried to suckle.

'Did the girl look scared? Maybe she was running from someone who she thought might hurt the baby,' Jillian suggested, settling her tortoiseshells back on her nose.

'Who?'

Jillian shrugged. 'Did she leave a note or any kind of identifying information?'

Elizabeth began to search through the recesses of the dirty coat. She reached into a pocket and pulled out a wadded tissue and an empty gum wrapper. 'I think I should wait for the cops – turn everything over to them.'

'Keep looking,' said Jillian. 'This is important.'

Elizabeth wiggled her fingers into the other pocket and extracted a piece of paper that looked like it had been torn from an envelope. The letter 'R' and a phone number with a Manhattan area code were printed on it in round, childish numbers, in pencil.

Jillian grabbed the paper and began punching the number into Elizabeth's phone.

'What are you doing?'

'Maybe this "R" knows who she is and where she's gone. This is all so tragic.' She put the phone to her ear. 'Every minute that goes by could be important.'

'Hang up. We don't need to know anything. They do.' Elizabeth stood to greet the police officers who'd just entered the café. She raised a hand and waved. 'Over here.'

A stocky woman with a blonde braid and a male officer with enormous shoulders wove through the tables, setting off a wave of chatter from the workers behind the counter and the few remaining customers.

'I'm Officer Ramsey,' said the woman. 'This is Officer Hernandez.'

'Here's the baby,' said Elizabeth, pointing to the bundle. The infant was still crying – pathetic, raspy peeps that broke Elizabeth's heart.

Ramsey gestured for Jillian to make room, then crouched down to take a closer look. She cupped the baby's head with one steady hand and folded the coat and Elizabeth's scarf away to examine the rest of her, wrapped in the faded pink T-shirt. 'A newborn, the umbilical cord and the placenta still attached. But she doesn't appear to be injured,' she said to her partner.

The baby scrunched up her face, lips quivering. Elizabeth could imagine that same pout when she became a teenager, told she couldn't stay out late or meet the boy she loved at the movies.

'She's probably hungry,' said Elizabeth, to cover her sadness. 'She's so tiny. And what a shock, to come out of the womb and end up in a coffee shop with strangers.'

'The paramedics are on the way,' said Ramsey. 'They'll take her to the hospital, make sure she's OK while we try to find the mom. Unless she belongs to you.' She stood up and stared Elizabeth down.

'Of course she doesn't belong to me,' Elizabeth snapped. The sadness she'd been feeling turned to outrage. 'If she was mine, I'd take her home, clean her up, feed her, and put her to bed. Not call the cops. And I sure wouldn't be sitting in a coffee shop right after giving birth. I'd still be panting in the delivery room cursing the guy who got me pregnant.'

Jillian laughed but the cops didn't.

'We need to let you know,' Hernandez added in a neutral voice, 'that there's a safe haven law in place for parents who feel they can't take care of a child. You've done the right thing, calling us.'

'Like she just told you,' said Jillian, all prickly now, 'it's not her baby.'

Jillian had always been the hothead of their crowd, sometimes getting into trouble by plowing ahead without thinking things through. But right now, Elizabeth appreciated her support.

The cops had Elizabeth review the last hour again – how she'd seen the girl on the platform, and then how the girl had followed her up the stairs, thrust the baby at her, and run.

'Did she say anything to you before she took off?'

Elizabeth massaged her forehead, wanting to be sure she remembered everything exactly as it had happened. 'I've had a horrible day and I wasn't paying attention – wrapped up in my own problems, you know? I was supposed to get married tomorrow.' She covered her mouth with her hand. Why had she told them that?

The two cops stared impassively, waiting for more.

'I asked her where she was going. She said California.'

'California?'

'I'm almost certain that's what she said. We were talking on the phone' – Elizabeth pointed to Jillian and then back at herself – 'about whether I should take my honeymoon trip alone. I wasn't focused on the girl.'

'You're saying you've never seen her before?'

'Never,' said Elizabeth. She pushed the scrap of paper across the table. 'We found this in the jacket pocket. Maybe it will explain something. I hope you find her. I hope she's not in trouble. What happens to the baby?'

'Children and Family Services will take over,' said Officer Ramsey. 'Until we find the mother and determine whether charges will be filed.'

'Charges?' Elizabeth asked.

'Child endangerment and abandonment.'

'What happened to your freaking safe haven?' Jillian muttered.

The paramedics stomped into the café and headed toward the police. Officer Ramsey explained what had happened. 'Nothing appears to be wrong with her that a bottle and a warm bath can't help. We'll work on the mother angle.'

The nearest paramedic removed Elizabeth's scarf, ran his hands over the baby's arms and legs, and then bundled her up in a clean blanket, leaving the coat with the police and returning the scarf, now spotted with blood.

Elizabeth watched them hurry out the door and strap the baby onto a stretcher in the back of the ambulance – the tiny form on the big gurney was the most heartbreaking thing she'd ever seen. Just watching, she felt chilled and alone.

'Will I be able to find out what happens to her?'

Officer Ramsey took a card from her wallet, scrawled a number on the back. 'That's my cell. Give me a call tomorrow and I'll let you know what I can.'

Elizabeth and Jillian left the café. 'Now for that drink,' said Jillian. 'I, for one, need it.'

Elizabeth buttoned her gray coat, stuffed the scarf in her pocket, and pulled the beret lower to cover her ears. The new mother must be freezing, without even the rag of a coat she'd used to wrap up her baby for warmth. 'I'm not sure I'm up for it. I feel like something's run me over. And I'm sick to my stomach.' That was the residue of an adrenalin rush. She glanced at her palms, brushed them together, a modern-day Lady Macbeth, only who knew what was on them? 'And I desperately need to wash my hands.'

'What are the options?' Jillian asked. 'Go home and mope? Just a quick one. I'll order while you wash up. And while we drink, we can text the girls and tell them you're not coming to Vegas, OK?'

She took Elizabeth's elbow without waiting for an answer and steered her across the street to The Delancey. The main bar was so loud that Elizabeth could feel the music piercing her ears, thrumming through her entire body. At least it was warm.

'One martini – you deserve it after the week you've had,' Jillian coaxed, pushing her through crowds of college students dancing, to two seats at the end of the bar. She patted her friend on the shoulder. 'You go wash your hands. I'll grab the drinks.'

By the time Elizabeth returned to her seat, the two martinis had been delivered, icy and enticing. She glanced at her phone, the screen filled with texts from her girlfriends.

Jillian fished an olive out of her drink and nibbled. 'What a night! What a day! That really sucks about Kevin. His timing is priceless. Cad of the year! How are you really doing?'

Elizabeth shrugged. 'Speechless, I guess. Numb. I had no idea he wanted out. None. I think I was too busy to notice. And that's scary. This changes everything. I thought we loved each other. Our life was all laid out, you know?' She stopped, swallowed the sob that had begun to well up and wiped her eyes on her sleeve. 'Let's not talk about him right now.' It really didn't matter that part of her felt relieved – the breakup had still been a shock. And she already missed Kevin; he'd left a hole in the fabric of her life. But for now, she needed to get a grip. Her troubles couldn't compare to those of the girl in the subway.

Jillian leaned in to give her a hug. 'I'm ordering more drinks.' She raised a finger to the bartender and called for a second round. The drinks came quickly and Elizabeth swallowed half of hers while Jillian chattered about the people in the bar, imagining stories about their lives.

'Where do you suppose that girl ran to?' she finally asked, when it became clear that Elizabeth wasn't interested in the strangers. 'Maybe we should try the phone number you found in her coat again.'

'There's no point,' said Elizabeth. 'It's police business. Besides, I gave the paper to Officer Ramsey.' The gin in the two martinis had hit her with a wallop. She felt woozy and exhausted. And creeping in behind that, completely humiliated. Kevin's defection seemed as though it had come days ago instead of yesterday – like a terrible dream she couldn't shake. Ditto for the episode with the girl and her baby. What kind of person left her child with a stranger? She hadn't realized she'd said this aloud until Jillian pointed at her iPhone just out of reach on the bar. Elizabeth picked it up.

'Let me see that for a minute,' Jillian said. She snatched it from Elizabeth and began to scroll to the outgoing calls. 'Aha!'

'Aha what?'

'Here's the number I was starting to call just as the cops came, remember?'

'Give it back,' said Elizabeth sternly.

'It's the only clue we have. And maybe it's someone who can help that poor mother. Someone who should know about the baby. Like you said, the girl was so young. She probably panicked. She probably had no idea she had options. The police will be fixated on who's to blame, you know that.'

She pressed the little phone icon before Elizabeth could stop her.

A male voice answered. 'Goddamit, Addy, where the fuck are you? Where are you calling from?'

'Hello?' said Jillian. 'Who are you trying to reach? With whom am I speaking, please?'

Which made no sense, as they had called him. Elizabeth signaled for her to hold the phone between them so she could hear too.

'Who the fuck is this? Where's Addison?'

'This is a friend,' said Jillian. 'If Addison is a young woman with a new baby, we're trying to track her down so we can help her. She had your number in her coat pocket.'

Elizabeth took the phone and cleared her throat. 'She needs medical attention. Obviously she was panicked about the baby, but she bolted as soon as she handed her over. The police took her little girl to the hospital. Now we'd love to get Addison the help she needs.' She hoped she sounded cheerful and helpful, rather than judgmental. Maybe he'd know where to look for the girl. Suddenly she wanted so badly for this story to have a happy ending.

A long silence. 'She had the baby?' The man's voice sounded furious, in an icy and frightening way.

This phone call was a terrible idea.

'Apparently,' said Elizabeth. 'I don't know that for sure. What I mean to say is she had a baby with her. Are you the father? Do you know how to get in touch with her?'

'Yes,' the man said after a long pause. 'I'm the dad. Where was she headed?'

Obviously he didn't know crickets about the situation.

Jillian leaned closer.

Elizabeth frowned and shook her head. But too late.

'Florida,' said Jillian. 'What is your name please? So we can get in touch if we see her?'

The line went dead.

'Florida?' Elizabeth asked.

Jillian laughed. 'I wasn't going to tell that moron what she really said, was I?'

# FOUR

Addy burst off the PATH train in Hoboken and searched the station for Rafe. Not there. She was too late. She pushed through the exit turnstile and trotted up the stairs, heart pounding, feeling the blood leak between her legs as she ran. The street bustled with commuters heading home late, or back into the city for a night of carousing, but there was no car waiting for her, no friendly – or even irritable – shout hello. She reached for her pocket, forgetting for a minute that she'd left her coat, wrapped it around the baby, handed the whole package to the woman at Delancey Street. And Rafe's phone number was in that parka.

Her stomach cramped and her heart squeezed in despair. Shivering in the sharp wind, she shuffled back down the stairs into the station and sank onto a bench, her head cradled in her arms. A wave of fatigue and hopelessness overtook the fierce energy she'd been feeling, leaving her weak. She laid a palm on her forehead – hot. She was starving and feverish and so tired.

What now?

Rafe had told her the phone was a throwaway. No way to trace it. She didn't dare call his apartment, even if she could find that number. Maybe she could try to reach her roommate Heather on the hall phone tomorrow.

But what now? The idea of turning herself in – to whom? – floated into her mind. If only she had a place to spend the rest of the night. She would be able to think more clearly after some sleep. And breakfast. And a bath. She could smell herself – sweaty from the painful exertion of the birth, and saturated with the warm, earthy scent of dried blood. She felt a rush of hopelessness, thinking of Rafe, hours down the road, crossing New Jersey on the way to California. He'd told her they had to leave instantly – she couldn't be late. Georgia would be angry enough to kill them both.

'It's always sunny there, babe,' he'd told her. 'Have you ever seen the Pacific Ocean?' Of course she hadn't. 'We can go to the beach every day. Fucking bars everywhere – free beer and live music. The town has a couple of gentlemen's clubs – a girl as pretty as you will have no trouble getting a job. Waiting on tables or something. In no time, we'll be able to afford our own place.'

Over the past month, she'd kept the vision of the beach in her head, while she hunkered down at Georgia's, waiting for the night they'd run. Most of the time, Georgia had kept her locked in the house. Business was dead for her anyway. Her special *friend*, the father of the baby, had lost interest when he realized she was pregnant – by someone else, Georgia had told him. The girl had made a stupid slip-up, nothing he should be concerned about. She'd tried sending Addy over two weeks ago when he refused the other girls, but the sight of her seemed to make him angry and mean. Or maybe it wasn't her – he'd been on the phone screaming at people the whole time she was there. And she'd been so nervous about stealing the man's phone and hiding it for Rafe, as he'd suggested once he heard about her pregnancy.

'Georgia is going to try to double-cross that man,' he'd said. 'We'll help him out. He is the baby's father, right?'

She'd do anything for Rafe, even lifting the man's phone. She hadn't let herself think about the clubs he'd mentioned. The 'waitressing'. He loved her, right? That's what he'd told her. He wanted a new life away from Georgia too – with her.

She could strip if he needed her to. She felt tears slide down her face.

'Excuse me,' said a gruff voice.

She stiffened, kept her head in her hands. Through the cracks in her fingers she saw polished brown leather shoes, creased trousers, a knee-length tweed coat.

'Are you all right?'

Addy wiped her cheeks on her sleeve. Straightened her shoulders. Tried to look cool, like she needed nothing from nobody. Not pathetic like she felt. She'd met rich men like this through Georgia – they didn't care about her.

'I was supposed to meet someone here,' she said, training her gaze on his chest. Her voice came out in a whisper. She cleared her throat and spoke louder. 'My boyfriend. I must have gotten mixed up on the time.'

The man looked at his watch, ran a gloved hand through his wiry gray hair. 'It's awful late for a young girl to be out here alone.'

'I'm nineteen,' she said, adding three years to be safe. 'I'll be fine. He'll be along soon.' Her teeth had started to chatter. She clutched her arms so he wouldn't see her shake.

'Can I give you a ride? I had a late night at the office; I'm on my way home. My car's right up the block.'

He pointed to the stairs and flashed her a smile. Good teeth, nothing creepy in his face. He looked tired but sincere. How could catching a ride with him be worse than staying here? He was right: it wasn't safe.

'OK,' she said. 'My boyfriend said he'd meet me at the rest stop on the New Jersey Turnpike if we got our signals crossed. But you can drop me off anywhere that's convenient for you. I'll hitch the rest of the way.'

A slight frown creased his forehead. He reset his wire-rimmed glasses further up the bridge of his nose. 'Which rest stop?'

'New Jersey,' she said, mentally kicking herself as soon as she said it. He would realize she had no idea. 'I forget the name of it. Right over the bridge. Maybe Secaucus?'

'The Alexander Hamilton?'

She nodded. 'That's it.' It didn't matter. They hadn't actually

made a backup plan. She just needed to go. To get moving.
Somewhere. So she wouldn't have to think about what had
just happened, and what was to come.

'I'll take you,' he said. 'That's not far out of my way. You
shouldn't be hitching a ride at this time of night.'

She didn't argue, sensing he was on the verge of driving
her to the nearest police station and marching her in if she
didn't let him help. She trailed him to the parking lot outside
of the PATH station, holding back in case he pulled something
unexpected. She heard the beep of his keys and the lights
flashed on a forest green BMW. He nodded and smiled,
holding the door open to the passenger side. She slid into the
car, which still smelled new. He instructed her to put on her
seatbelt and flipped on her seat warmer, then tried to make
small talk on the twenty-minute drive. How unusually cold it
was for December, the snowstorm last week, how much he'd
enjoyed the latest *Star Wars* movie. But she said nothing,
feeling the blood seeping through her Kotex, her flannel pants,
and probably staining his tan leather bucket seat. She felt her
eyes drooping; her stomach growled.

'My daughter got into some trouble when she was about
your age,' he said, glancing over at her as they pulled off the
highway.

She sat up taller, waiting for the next freaking shoe to drop.
For him to explain how much she and some rich girl with a
real father had in common.

He guided the BMW off the ramp and stopped in front of
the food court at the rest stop. He put the car in park and fixed
a steady gaze on her. 'She suffered a lot because she didn't
dare tell us. She thought we wouldn't understand. We suffered
too, watching her struggle.' He sighed and tapped his fingers
on the gearshift. 'We didn't know how to talk to each other.
The problem wasn't as bad as she imagined it was – if only
we'd known earlier, we might have been able to help.'

Addy pinched her lips together, looked down at her hands.
What did he know about her life? She wasn't some kid
from a privileged home who'd flunked a final or got caught
smoking cigarettes outside the school. If she called home,
guaranteed her mother would be stinking drunk. And so, so

angry. Assuming the telephone company hadn't cut off her service again. She was the kind of mother who started drinking in the morning and never let up until she staggered to bed. The kind who invited leering men to 'meet' her girl when the cash in the flour tin ran low.

'Are you sure I can't phone someone for you? Maybe drive you home?'

Teeth clenched to keep from chattering, she shook her head firmly. 'Thank you very much.' She grabbed the door handle, ready to bolt.

He stuffed a handful of twenty-dollar bills into her fist and her eyes flooded with tears.

'You take care of yourself,' he said. 'Call home. Call your mother.'

As if.

# FIVE

R afe hung up and bellowed out a string of curses. His plan was in the crapper – Addy had totally blown him off. And somehow she had managed to pop out the kid in the last eight hours, turn it over to the cops and head to Florida. If he could believe the cow who'd called him. Why the hell hadn't she met him where they'd planned? He'd waited there for an hour but she hadn't shown up. He couldn't wait any longer – Georgia would be on his tail, hard. He lurched off the highway at the next rest stop, parked under a streetlight, and then copied the woman's cell phone number and texted it to his friend, Mitch, who was a whiz at tracing anything. For the right price. While waiting, he checked for voicemail on his other number.

A message from Georgia sounded as angry as he'd ever heard her – and she was the queen of foul moods. Thank God he'd had the sense to quit that job. And then double-cross her. Just like she thought she could double-cross the senator. Working for her, he had been nothing more than a glorified

errand boy, assistant pimp, and security guard. And poorly
paid for the risks he took, too.

'The girl's gone. Addison. Did you have anything to do
with this? I swear I'll track you down and rip you to pieces
if she doesn't turn up soon.'

And she would hack him up, she wasn't exaggerating. But
first she'd have to find him. He deleted the message with
another blast of swear words. His second phone beeped: a fast
reply from Mitch. The cell phone was registered to Elizabeth
Brown, who lived at East 26th Street in student housing
for the NYU Medical School. And Mitch had pinpointed
where she'd been when she called Rafe earlier: the bar at The
Delancey.

Those dumb women had sounded tipsy and way too helpful.
People were so stupid, assuming they were safe and private,
when all the while their fancy GPS was broadcasting their
whereabouts to the world. Which was the reason he carried
only cheap disposable phones and switched them often.

But why hadn't Addy herself called? He'd given her the
number. Why would she give it – and her coat – to strangers?
And bizarre as it seemed, she'd believed him when he'd said
that he loved her. He'd been very patient, cultivating her
trust, describing the imaginary house he'd buy for her by the
water. He'd done it so well that she was convinced they'd
rise, phoenix from the fucking ashes, out of the pit of drugs,
violence and prostitution they were both mired in. She
believed they'd find a happy ending. He shook his head at
the absurdity of it. In the end, she saw him as a boyfriend,
and maybe even a father.

He saw dollar signs. The kid was worth a lot more than one
under-aged prostitute would ever be: hundreds of thousands.
Or so Georgia boasted. He didn't have the same connections,
but he knew damn well that a white infant could be sold easily
enough if you could find the right desperate parents. He had
the proof in his bank account – a big deposit from a rich guy
firing blanks who'd spend buckets to keep his wife happy. The
man would go batshit crazy when he heard the baby had
disappeared. But selling the baby was only part of the plan.
Once he'd heard about Georgia's blackmail scheme, he knew

he could persuade Addy to help. He'd make a fortune squeezing Georgia's mark himself.

First, he had to find Addy and convince her to reclaim the kid before Georgia got to either of them. Once he had her safely back, along with the phone he'd persuaded her to steal, he'd call Georgia's dupe and get the ball rolling.

He texted Mitch and instructed him to track down the medical student and squeeze her for more information about Addy. How had that woman gotten his number anyway? He'd find out once Mitch located the student and got her to tell him exactly where Addy was headed. He'd intercept her as soon as he had the coordinates. Though why would she say she was going to Florida? If she'd decided to run from *him* too, she wouldn't get far.

# SIX

W hen the phone rang at six-thirty the next morning, Elizabeth woke with a pounding headache and a furry tongue. She waited through several rounds of the 'Chapel of Love', remembering how happy she'd been when the countdown to the wedding was thirty days, and she'd had the bright idea to download that ring tone. Now the notes stabbed like ice picks to the soft parts of her brain. Who would be calling so early? When she couldn't stand the noise one more second, she flung the covers back, marched across the room to the counter where she'd dropped her purse last night, and snatched up the phone. The screen said *unknown*. Was it possible that Kevin was calling sheepishly from a friend's place to apologize? He was certainly capable of misplacing his own phone. She shouldn't talk to him after what he'd done, but she accepted the call.

'Elizabeth Brown? This is Olivia Lovett with the *New York Post*. I'm calling about the abandoned subway baby who you turned in to the police last night. Could you please describe what happened in your own words?'

'Do you realize it's six-thirty on a Saturday morning?' Elizabeth punched the off button and returned to bed, her heart revved into overdrive and head pounding. Now she'd never get back to sleep. How did this person get her name? The Dixie Cups sang out a second time. Elizabeth stabbed *decline*.

A text message buzzed in. *Someone is going to tell the story, I swear I'll do it right.*

She dialed Olivia Lovett back. 'What do you want from me? And how did you get my number?'

'I realize it's early and I'm so sorry to bother you. But the NYPD spokesperson released the news of the subway baby last night. I suspect you might be getting a lot of calls because it's an amazing story. I'm a reporter with the *Post*. I figured you'd probably want the details about the baby told accurately. And then maybe we could help find the mother. If that's what's best for her, of course.'

'Who gave you my name and number?' Elizabeth hated the idea of more reporters calling.

'I'm not able to say. A reliable source.' A pause. 'But believe me, I really want to help the girl.'

Would it hurt to find out what she knew? Elizabeth had woken a dozen times throughout the night, thinking about the young mother, and worrying about the man they'd called. He'd sounded so angry. She sighed and tucked her feet and knees back under the covers. 'Fine. Go ahead. Ask your questions. I can't promise I'll answer.'

'Did you know this girl? Any thoughts on why she abandoned her daughter? Any idea why she chose to give the baby to you? Any ideas about the father?'

Elizabeth brushed her hair away from her face, her foggy mind shrinking from the onslaught of questions.

'No, I didn't know her. I'd never seen her before in my life. I assume she chose me because I was a woman who didn't have the look of a serial killer.'

'Could you describe the mom for me?'

Elizabeth bristled. 'Why in the world would I tell you anything more?'

'Because it's a heartbreaking story. Delivering a baby in the subway, alone? Can you imagine anything worse? Why did this happen? What is she running from? If we can draw a picture in the readers' minds of this lost, desperate girl, maybe we can get her the help she needs. Maybe someone will have seen her somewhere and will call or text it in. Google my byline if you want. I've written a whole series on homeless kids, and a lot of good has come from those stories. I'll call you back in five minutes,' she added briskly, and hung up the phone.

Elizabeth searched for the reporter's name, and as she'd said, her credits included a series of what looked like thoughtful pieces about troubled teens. And then some follow-ups about how the kids had gotten some special schooling and decent family placements after that publicity, and a leg up on brighter lives. Maybe the reporter wasn't just blowing smoke, trying to get a jump on a juicy story. Maybe helping tell this girl's story the right way, to the right person, made sense.

'It all happened so fast,' she said, when the reporter called back. 'Brown hair, hazel eyes with this striking rim of brown around the edge of the green, maybe seventeen years old? Hard to say because she was small and had on baggy clothing. And she looked so exhausted, so wrung-out. She left her coat wrapped around the baby and ran off wearing only a sweat-shirt. I think it was blue and gold, with some kind of faded college logo on it.'

'Do you know about New York's safe haven law? Did the cops say anything about whether you qualified as a safe haven? Did you have a chance to discuss this with her?'

'Oh for God's sake, we didn't have a discussion about anything,' Elizabeth said. 'She handed me this bundle and ran.'

'So she said nothing to you at all?'

'She asked me to take care of the baby, as she wasn't able to do it herself,' Elizabeth said, her voice hitching a little, remembering the fierce poignancy of that moment. A poignancy that she only truly recognized looking back, once some of the shock had receded.

'Any idea who she is, where she lives?'

'She said she was going to California. I wouldn't swear that was the truth. Even if it was true, I doubt she'd make it. She had nothing with her – no purse, no suitcase, no backpack, nothing except for a black plastic bag.'

'And has anyone contacted you about this girl? Aside from me, of course.'

Elizabeth paused, a sinking feeling filling her gut and closing her throat. 'A man called last night looking for her,' she said. 'He claimed he was the father.' She couldn't bear to tell the actual truth – that she and Jillian had reached out to him. In the cold, gray light of morning, that phone call felt like a huge mistake. If only they hadn't had those second drinks . . .

There was a silence.

'How did this man get your number?'

Now Elizabeth wished she'd never agreed to say anything. What did she really know about this woman's intentions? She stayed silent.

'I'd be careful about this kind of thing,' Olivia said finally. 'It sounds like the girl was scared to death and frantic to get away from something. We don't know what kind of trouble she might be in. Maybe it was as simple as a girl with a baby she couldn't handle, but maybe there was something more. Do you have the man's name or number?'

Elizabeth said nothing.

'I don't like that this man has *your* phone number, you know? Maybe think about changing numbers or at least screening calls, and blocking your number when you call out. And definitely alert the cops if you notice anything off.'

Now she felt reckless and stupid to have allowed Jillian to use her phone to call that guy. She should have grabbed the phone back and erased the number from her log. Instead of helping the girl, had they made things worse? Flickers of fear nibbled around the edges of her mind. Even a third-grader would have known better. 'OK.'

'I'm going to poke around, see what I can turn up. And I'll keep you posted. Thank you for your time.'

The reporter hung up before Elizabeth could ask if she'd learned anything new about the baby or the girl. She slumped back against her pillows, feeling sad for both of them. And a little sorry for herself, too, she had to admit. And underneath all that, uneasy.

Through slitted eyes, the wreckage of her studio apartment came into focus – roses from her fellow med students, now shriveled and browning, clothes everywhere, the mini-kitchen cluttered with coffee cups and cereal bowls. She'd left New York in a flurry of excitement after taking her last exam of the semester – no time to clean up as she pawed through her drawers to pack for the days she'd be at home in Connecticut and then on her honeymoon. On the back of the door, the empty hanger that had held her wedding dress clanked against the hook as the forced air heater banged into action.

She rolled out of bed, started a pot of coffee, dropped the dishes into a sink full of soapy water, threw the flowers in the trash, and checked her email. Notes from her mother and her aunt – she'd read them later. And the bridesmaids' plan to descend on Vegas the next day was gathering steam. They meant well, but she knew how it would go: At first, they'd be oozing sympathy. Then they'd probe for details of Kevin's rejection so they could pile onto the hate fest. Then she'd begin to feel a subtle pressure to cheer up. And she'd end up constructing a front of optimism that would only highlight how badly she felt inside.

She wasn't ready to share with them her confusing mixture of feelings: her sadness about losing Kevin – at least the *old* her missed the *old* Kevin – the humiliation of being dumped so close to the wedding, and her mounting relief, the sense that she'd dodged a toxic matrimonial bullet. All through college, he'd been her best friend, the one she would have talked to about this mess. That friendship was gone now, too. She tapped out a group message that left no room for misinterpretation.

*So very sorry about the trouble and expense I caused. Appreciate your support so much. I will talk to you very soon. But no party in Vegas for me. Happy New Year!*

While the coffee brewed, she paced around her studio apartment, which hardly allowed for much pacing.

'It's like a cruise ship cabin,' her mother had exclaimed in September when her parents came to deliver a lamp and a small table from Connecticut.

'An inside cabin,' Elizabeth had answered with a grin, pointing out her sliver view of the air handler on the next building.

'Cabin with an obstructed view!' Her mother had laughed. 'You're not going on a cruise,' her father had said. 'You don't need a view. You're in medical school.'

'It's a joke, Dad,' she'd said. As if she hadn't realized she was in medical school. As if a knot of anxiety didn't cramp her stomach every time she headed off to work on her cadaver, or attend anatomy class. The pressure was incredible – already some of her fellow students were panicking about the board exam, a year and a half in advance. Her father was an old-school emergency medicine doctor – he believed the students' training shaped them as future physicians. Training meant nothing if they didn't suffer along the way. She felt sorry for his residents at Yale. They'd learn plenty, but they'd pay dearly in hours of sleep and stress on their families, their health, and their social lives.

She poured a cup of coffee and tried to think of how she could distract herself from the empty week stretching in front of her. She definitely couldn't spend it here in this room – her claustrophobia was mushrooming like ash from a volcano. But if she went home to Connecticut, the drama accompanying the unraveling of the wedding would be impossible to avoid.

She paged through her rented copy of *Williams Obstetrics*, and skimmed the introductory section on giving birth, under-lining important phrases. There was no end to the list of complications that could have occurred with the subway baby. What if it had been a breech presentation, or Addy had suffered a ruptured uterus, pre-eclampsia, or failure to progress? Those were all possible, even common with first-time mothers, espe-cially young ones. A miracle, really, that the girl and her baby had survived without any medical help whatsoever. How did she stand the pain? Elizabeth doubted that the girl had attended Lamaze classes to learn the tips that might have helped her struggle through labor.

She tapped her pen on the desk for a few minutes, then dialed the number of the precinct and asked to speak with Officer Ramsey. A short time later, the cop came to the phone.

'Hi, it's Elizabeth Brown. I'm the one who turned in the baby yesterday? Turned in isn't quite the right description, but you know what I mean. I wondered if there was any news on the case? Did you find the mother? How's the baby doing?'

'Nothing new here,' the officer said briskly. 'The baby's in pediatric intensive care at the NYU medical center. No word on the mother. We checked the subway station – it appears she did give birth in the restroom. We found signs of blood in one of the stalls and some bloody clothing in the trash.'

'That poor girl. What will happen to the child if you don't find her mother?'

'Foster care and then hopefully adoption. Assuming the mother doesn't show up. Sounds like she couldn't have provided much of a home. But either way, with a start like this, the poor kid's already hobbled. I don't imagine the girl got regular prenatal care.'

Elizabeth thanked Officer Ramsey and hung up. Should she have told the cop about Olivia Lovett? Or last night's call to the angry man? She took a fast shower and dressed in gray wool slacks and a blue sweater. Then she pinned her hair up, put on the short, white jacket with her name written in blue script over the pocket, and clipped on the hospital photo badge identifying her as a medical student. She pulled on her wool coat, hat, and gloves, and went out into the hallway to call for the elevator. The conversation with the policewoman had left her feeling enormously sad. She couldn't imagine how she could help the teenage mother, but at least she could see for herself how the baby was doing.

In the newborn ICU, Elizabeth stopped at the nurses' station. A brusque woman with a gray topknot and teddy bear scrubs looked up from her computer. Elizabeth explained her story about how she'd been involved with the infant, adding: 'I'm a first-year med student at NYU. I'd really love to see her. Is that possible?'

'Sorry,' said the nurse, returning her attention to the computer screen. 'No can do.'

Elizabeth grimaced. This didn't seem like the kind of woman who'd respond to an emotional plea. 'I know it's against the hospital protocol. I was just hoping to take a quick look. I feel so sad for her. And as a professional, I can't help wondering how that baby is doing today. You know, after what she went through.'

'Sorry,' said the nurse again, without even making eye contact. She got up and headed down the hallway, pushing a medication cart in front of her.

A petite, redheaded nurse who'd been making notes on an iPad at the other end of the nurses' station looked up and smiled. She came over to the counter and peered at Elizabeth's badge. 'You're the one who found her?'

Elizabeth nodded. 'I feel so helpless. Is she OK?'

'She's doing quite well, considering how she came into the world. And Bridget' – she cocked her head in the direction the other woman had disappeared – 'she's very strict about following the rules. As she should be. There have been incidents where estranged spouses or even perfect strangers tried to steal a baby.' She dropped her voice to a whisper. 'Come with me.'

They trotted down the opposite hallway and into a room filled with bassinets, each containing a small baby, and stopped in front of a cubicle labeled 'Baby Girl Doe'. The child was swaddled in a flannel blanket with pink bunnies on it and wore a white knitted cap. She opened her eyes and managed to work one tiny hand out of the blanket and reach for Elizabeth, almost as if recognizing her.

'She's precious,' said Elizabeth. 'Look at those fingers.'

'She appears to be full term,' said the nurse, 'or very close. Even though she's little.'

'Her mother was petite, too,' said Elizabeth. 'Shorter than me, with narrow hips. Almost looked like a boy from behind. I hate to think of her laboring in that bathroom by herself.' She shook her head to clear the image. 'How can you tell the baby's full term?'

'Have you studied the Dubowitz scale?'

Elizabeth shook her head. 'Not yet. Maybe I've heard of it in passing? There's so much to remember.' She groaned. 'I study and study but it seems impossible to cram everything in.'

The nurse smiled sympathetically. 'It'll get easier when you're actually doing clinical work. We use the scale to measure the baby's age. It's considered accurate plus or minus two weeks of gestation.' She pointed at the plastic ID bracelet around one tiny wrist. 'First, we look at the creases in the palms of her hands and her feet – more creases, longer gestation. Another factor is cartilage in the outer ear.' She folded the baby's left ear and let go. 'You see how it sprang back into place? More cartilage, longer gestation.'

The baby wiggled her free hand in the air and made small squeaking noises. Then she opened her eyes again. Elizabeth would have sworn she looked right at her.

'A younger baby wouldn't have that kind of muscle tone,' said the nurse. 'She's probably thirty-six weeks or more.'

Elizabeth sighed. How did a mother make the choice to leave this tiny being with a complete stranger? The alternatives must have felt far worse. Was she really on her way to California? 'The mom hasn't come in?'

'No one's asked to visit,' the nurse said. 'Well, other than you.'

# SEVEN

E lizabeth left the hospital, questions about the girl whirling through her head. Where had she fled to? How did she feel today about abandoning her newborn baby? Elizabeth felt sick, imagining what it might have been like in that disgusting subway bathroom. The girl must have been desperate, to deliver alone and then foist off the child on someone she'd never seen before. She tried to remember whether she'd seemed frightened – more frightened than the experience of the birth alone might have caused. Regardless of the reasons, she had looked panicked for sure.

Elizabeth made her way to Bellevue South Park, a block from her apartment building. The swings, the looping slide, and the concrete chess tables were covered with a two-inch layer of snow, which meant fewer people enjoying the park this morning. She found a bench in the sun, swept off the snow, and sat, face tipped up to the weak light. A squirrel chirred angrily and then scampered up a nearby oak.

She took off her gloves and rubbed her hands together, startled for an instant at seeing her ring finger naked, where Kevin's diamond had perched for over a year. Then she remembered that she had stuffed it into the pocket of the jeans she'd been wearing when he'd come to her childhood home two days ago to deliver the news: he couldn't go through with the marriage. She'd return it to Kevin, she supposed. She didn't have the sheer nerve of one of her fellow medical students, who had suffered from a broken engagement earlier this fall. The day after her fiancé bailed, she'd listed the ring on eBay, where it sold within the week. Auctioned to the highest bidder, the proceeds spent on new clothes and a trip to Paris with her mother. Her ex-fiancé had been livid. But helpless. Hadn't it been a gift? Besides, the money was gone and so was the ring. No amount of guilt-mongering would make a difference.

How did she get here? And where was she going? She let herself wallow in regret for a few minutes. They'd had everything worked out, she and Kevin. She'd finish medical school, take a residency nearby, and then join a pediatric practice while they started a family. She did sometimes wonder how Kevin the middle school English teacher would handle a wife who was a doctor, who might appear to have more status than he did. He certainly wasn't cut out to be a househusband. But once this semester had started, she'd been too busy to worry about anything but what she was supposed to be learning. Too busy to pay attention to the warning signs. And yes, they'd been there; she could look back now and see them plainly.

Her phone rang and she answered before the Dixie Cups could start to sing again. Too late she remembered the reporter's warning. Luckily, it was her mother.

'Honey, is everything OK? You sound a little down. I'm so sorry about the wedding. I know you said you needed a little space, but I got worried when I didn't hear from you yesterday. Your father insisted I wait to call until this morning. He said that's what you'd asked for and we should respect it. I knew he was right, but still – you'll always be my baby.'

Her voice was shivery and weak, like she was on the edge of crying herself, making Elizabeth feel guilty that she hadn't called to reassure her earlier.

'I'm fine. I'll live. Just barely.' Elizabeth tried to laugh. 'I mean, obviously, if Kevin didn't want to marry me, it's better to find out now. I'm mostly sorry about all the work you've done, and the money . . . I left you with a gigantic mess.' Her words were starting to wobble too.

'Aunt Susan is here,' her mother broke in. 'So I'm not by myself. She loves a challenge, so she's been making lots of calls and handling details. And the food is delicious. The caterers delivered it here yesterday. The veggies weren't going to keep so we sent almost everything to the Women and Children's shelter in New Haven, like you suggested. But I did pack some lemon chicken up in little containers for your freezer. When classes start up after next week and you're too busy to cook, you'll be able to pop them into the microwave and presto – there's dinner.'

'Thanks, Mom.' Could anything be more pathetic than a freezer full of the food from your failed wedding reception?

'When are you coming back home? We'd love to have you visit. Just us chickens . . . Your father went back to work this morning, thank God,' she added. 'If I heard one more time how he would tear Kevin limb from limb if he ever darkened our door again . . .'

She couldn't possibly go home. Not yet. Everyone would be so kind, but the news was still raw. She wasn't ready for the endless post-mortems, the hashing through of Kevin's problems, the search for signs and symptoms. Not ready to keep reassuring her mother that she was bouncing back just fine. But her mom wasn't likely to stop asking as long as Elizabeth remained hunkered down in New York, within easy striking distance of her mothering.

'Thanks for the offer,' she said. 'I'll probably come in a couple of days, at least for a short visit. The girls want me to fly to Vegas – they keep saying why squander a perfectly good vacation just because Kevin turned out to be a cretin?' Which wasn't really fair to Kevin, but she thought her mother needed to hear some spunk.

'That's my girl! I'm so relieved to hear you say that. I can't bear to think of you hurting. Is someone flying out with you? Do you want me to come along?'

'Mom, I'll be fine. You've got Aunt Susan there, and besides, some time alone will be good for me.'

'Are you sure? Phone me when you get in OK?'

Elizabeth ended the call, paged through the ring tones offered by her phone, and switched from the Dixie Cups to David Bowie's 'Changes'. She felt a little bit bad about allowing her mom to think she was actually going to Vegas, but it would keep the panicked phone calls at bay.

A man she didn't recognize strode across the playground and sat beside her on the bench. Dark wavy hair, brown eyes, bushy eyebrows, tight jeans and a down jacket. Nothing obvious that would make the hairs on your neck stand up, but hers did all the same. The park was empty – why crowd her?

'Elizabeth? I'm a friend of Addison's. The girl you met last night. I need your help in finding her – she's in trouble and she needs our assistance right away.'

Elizabeth stared, her heart pounding like a trapped bird, trying to picture him as the man on the phone. The voice didn't match, not quite. 'I'm sorry, who are you?'

'I'm a friend of Addy's,' he repeated. 'We were supposed to meet up last night and she didn't show. You called me, remember? You wanted to meet face-to-face.'

The details of the phone conversation that she'd suppressed came back in a rush. But this man's voice definitely sounded different. And she certainly hadn't arranged to meet anyone. Even deep in a haze of martinis on an empty stomach, she would not have agreed to that.

'I'm sorry,' said Elizabeth, reaching back into her pocket to grab her phone and gathering her coat around her. 'I don't know anything about her. How do you know my name?' She glanced around, suddenly feeling chilled and alone. The solitude of the park that had felt like a godsend earlier was now simply frightening.

'That's easy,' he said, throwing his head back and laughing. 'Reverse directory, it works every time.'

Even if that was true, how did he know she'd be here in this park at this moment? She had to get away from him. Could she beat him to her apartment building if she got the right head start? Or would the sudden movement whet his appetite the way a fleeing antelope tempts a lion? Forget it: she was out of shape and hungover – she could only think to keep talking and hope another human being came along. She fingered the screen of her phone, wondering if she could manage to dial 911 without looking. She should have called the cops the moment he hit the bench. She thought of the reporter's warning and another tremor of fear tightened her neck and shoulders. She should have told Officer Ramsey what they'd done the night before.

'Last night you said you were the baby's father,' said Elizabeth.

A pause. 'Right. I am. Did you say she was on her way to Florida? She shouldn't be traveling alone. She has medical problems . . . related to the birth.' His voice was soft and sympathetic, but his eyes were hard like marbles. If he knew that much about Addy, he should have known where to find her. How would he possibly know about medical issues related to childbirth if he hadn't talked to the girl?

'I don't know anything more,' Elizabeth repeated. 'I'm sorry, I can't help.'

She clenched her free hand into a fist and scooted forward off the bench. As she struggled to find words that would sound firm and dismissive but noncombative, she heard a faint pop.

The man next to her slumped to the ground.

# EIGHT

Elizabeth slapped her hand over her mouth to keep from screaming and tried not to panic. Or puke. *Think like a doctor.* A heart attack? She reminded herself about the steps of CPR and crouched down, prepared to start chest compressions. As she nudged the man onto his back, she saw the perfectly round hole in his forehead. The pop had been a gunshot. A feeble attempt at CPR would not help. And she could be next in the killer's sights.

'I'm going to get you medical assistance,' she said, just in

case the man could hear her or sense her leaving. Then she
shot up and bolted out of the park toward her apartment
building, punching 911 as she ran, praying she wouldn't
be mowed down by the same sniper. Her fingers trembled
so she could hardly hit the numbers.

'Someone's been shot,' she yelled into the phone, once
she'd reached the safety of the lobby. 'A man in Bellevue
South Park. I was sitting right next to him.' She started to
hyperventilate.

'Stay on the line and tell me exactly where you are.'

The dispatcher talked to her for the next five minutes until
two police cars with sirens wailing and lights flashing roared
down the street that bordered the park. A few of the inhabit-
ants of the apartments were gathering near the bench where
she'd been sitting. The uniformed police who'd arrived first
herded the onlookers back. Then the paramedics pulled in
and a phalanx of uniformed professionals circled the man
who'd been shot. From the lobby of her building, Elizabeth
saw a stocky figure stump in her direction. Officer Ramsey.
She opened the door and waved her in, grateful for a familiar
face.

Officer Ramsey brushed her ponytail over her shoulder, her
eyebrows lifted in surprise. 'You again. You're the one who
called in the shooting?'

Elizabeth sniffled and nodded and then described the conversation she'd had with the swarthy man before he was mowed
down. As she finished, she glanced down at her gray coat,
noticing red speckles.

'Oh my God,' she moaned. 'His blood.'

The room spun and she started to sink to the floor. The
policewoman caught her arm and guided her to the brown
vinyl bench positioned beneath the wall of mailboxes in the
lobby.

'Put your head between your knees. And breathe.' Officer
Ramsey patted her back.

She kept her head down until the dizziness passed, then
leaned back against the wall, fighting to keep her breakfast.

'How are you feeling?' Officer Ramsey knelt down to her
level.

'Better.' She smiled weakly. 'I do wonder how I'll ever make it as a doctor if I faint at the sight of blood.'

'Blood spatter from someone who's been shot two feet from you is not your ordinary blood,' said Officer Ramsey.

Elizabeth looked out of the window: a swarm of uniforms was spreading across the park. The man who'd been shot was being loaded onto a gurney and from there, into the waiting ambulance.

'Are you ready to answer some questions?' asked Officer Ramsey.

'Fire away,' said Elizabeth, then flinched. 'I'm sorry. I'm usually not this pathetic. It's just . . . the last few days have been one shock after another.'

The policewoman nodded. 'Start at the beginning. You know this man how?' She pointed out the window to the park.

Elizabeth sighed. 'It's complicated. But I really don't know him. I can tell you who he claimed he was.' She described how Jillian had saved the man's phone number in her iPhone and then how they'd called him the night before. Officer Ramsey's face tightened as Elizabeth talked.

'I'm embarrassed to say we'd been drinking martinis – we probably told him more than we should have.' She glanced down at her feet, then met Officer Ramsey's eyes. 'I'm sorry we called him at all.'

'Was the fellow on the bench the same man you spoke with last night? Did you recognize the voice?'

'I don't think it was him. I've never seen this man before. Of course I've never seen the man on the phone either, but the man in the park sounded different. On the other hand, he knew all about the baby and that poor girl. Addison, he called her. Addy. I don't know how he found me – I certainly didn't tell him who I was or where I live. He claimed I'd agreed to meet with him, but I hadn't.'

'For the right element, tracking down a cell phone is not difficult,' said Officer Ramsey. 'I don't suppose you have one of those locator apps installed?'

Elizabeth gulped and nodded. 'All my friends use it. Makes it easier for us to hook up for drinks and so on.'

Officer Ramsey rolled her eyes – the universal sign of one

generation finding it hard to understand another. Though Elizabeth would have sworn that they were ten years apart at the most.

The policewoman shook her head. 'Tell me again about the girl and the baby. Maybe you'll remember something that didn't occur to you last night.'

Elizabeth repeated the story about the girl staring at her in the subway, and then how she'd startled her on the street by shoving the baby into her arms and running.

'I went to the neonatal ICU this morning,' said Elizabeth. 'The baby's doing fine. But according to the charge nurse, no one's come to see her. No one's asked about her.'

Officer Ramsey frowned. 'Why were you asking questions in the hospital?'

'I felt bad about the baby,' Elizabeth said, feeling the heat of embarrassment rush into her cheeks. 'Responsible. Here she is, hours old, and she's been dumped by her mother and nobody cares.' The memory of the reporter's call surfaced. 'Except for one reporter who tracked me down this morning.'

'You talked to a reporter?' Ramsey looked horrified and Elizabeth hurried to explain.

'She seemed legitimate. I researched some other articles she'd written. She seemed to really care what might happen to Addy. But I doubt I gave her enough information to write anything,' Elizabeth added, and then felt a surge of anger. 'And by the way, who leaked my name to the press?'

'I don't know about that,' said Officer Ramsey. 'It wasn't one of us.'

Elizabeth glared at her. Was this the truth? 'I doubt my information will lead to anything,' she said, trying to reassure herself more than anything else. 'Most people don't care about a runaway in trouble. Especially if she's poor and homeless.'

'Maybe you haven't seen the headlines in the *Post*,' said Officer Ramsey. 'Your reporter didn't waste any time. Plenty of people care. Our phones have been ringing off the hook.'

'About what?'

'People wanting to adopt the baby, tips about seeing the mother anywhere from Pennsylvania to Georgia, offers to start college funds, you name it.' She stared at Elizabeth and gestured toward the park. 'Don't talk to anyone else about what happened, clear? If this shooting is related to the girl and her baby, there are some dangerous people involved. And now you are associated with both the girl and the crime.' She waited until Elizabeth nodded. 'Did you notice anyone else in the vicinity of your bench?'

'No one,' said Elizabeth. 'In fact, I was just thinking how unusually quiet it was when that guy sat down. After the gunshot, I'm afraid I was too rattled to see anything.'

'Did he seem worried, like someone was following him?'

Elizabeth shook her head as a second police officer cracked open the door and peered in. 'When you're finished, we're patrolling the area. EMT says it looks like a professional hit. No identifying information on the body. He was carrying a throwaway phone. Anything new here?' He raised his eyebrows at Elizabeth.

'Not really. We're wrapping things up.' Officer Ramsey nodded and replaced her notepad in her uniform pocket. 'Is there someplace else you can go for a couple of days? Someone you can hang with? Just in case?'

In case of what? She didn't even want to think about who else was lurking. Or who shot that man and why. It probably had nothing to do with her. Elizabeth tried to smile. 'I was going on my honeymoon. But we never made it to the ceremony. Now I think I'll just go home to my parents' house in Connecticut for a couple of days.'

'Good idea. And it won't hurt to check in with the police in your hometown. Let them know what's going on. They can contact me if they like. I doubt someone would follow you up there, but . . .' She shrugged and handed Elizabeth another business card, then headed outside. She turned as she reached the door. 'Sorry about the wedding,' she said, flashing a quick grin. 'Can't live with 'em, can't live without.'

'Thanks.'

Once Officer Ramsey had jogged off to join the other police combing the park, Elizabeth checked her mailbox – empty – and took the elevator to the twenty-third floor. She texted her mother about the change in plans and then turned off the ringer. She didn't want to talk to any more reporters or hear any more bad news.

In her apartment, she sponged the specks of blood off her coat with club soda, and then began throwing clothes into her suitcase, replacing the sexy silk negligee she'd bought for her first full night as Mrs Preble with a flannel nightgown. Even without her wedding band, she reminded herself again, her life was a thousand times better than the girl being stalked by a man insisting he was the father of her brand-new baby. Who was now shot dead in the forehead by some other thug. What was the truth behind it all? Did the unknown shooter know that Elizabeth had lied about Addy going to Florida? What were the chances that the girl would actually make it to California on her own with no money and no friends? Slim to none.

Her hands began to shake so hard, she had to take a minute to lie down and breathe. Getting away from New York no longer felt optional.

# NINE

Addy woke feeling groggy and sick. Her neck ached from slumping forward to snooze on one of the rest-stop tables. She felt feverish and weak, and she hurt down there, cramping like crazy. She hobbled to the bathroom, tried to scrape a few spots of dried blood off her flannel pants, washed her face, finger-combed her hair. And she still looked like something a rat terrier had dug up and dragged out of a tunnel. She extracted one of the twenties the man had given her last night and shoved the rest into the bottom of her plastic bag.

Back in the food court, she bought a cup of coffee and a chocolate donut and watched the crowd bustle by, mostly commuters she guessed, from their purposeful but joyless expressions. Or maybe people on their way to visit relatives they'd rather not see. She searched all the faces, looking for

Rafe. He wasn't here, she knew that. But she was so tired and it would be such a relief to see him, that she'd almost convinced herself that he really had told her he'd meet her here, at the rest stop in New Jersey, like she'd insisted to the man who'd given her a ride. Pulling that man's business card out of her sweatshirt pocket along with the change from the rumpled twenties, she ran a finger across the shiny, raised black type. He was a lawyer, specializing in trusts and wills. Nothing that could help her, not anytime soon. Probably never. She didn't own anything that anyone else would want. Other than a baby – or so Rafe said. He'd told her early on that if she ran away with him, and didn't want to raise the kid, he could find it a great family. No one would blame her, he'd said. But now it was way too late for that.

When an hour had passed she decided to risk calling Georgia's rooming house. If she was lucky, she'd get to talk to Heather, tell her she was alive and well. And see if she could find Rafe's phone number somewhere. If she was unlucky and got Georgia, she'd hang up fast. She padded into the souvenir shop near the restroom and studied the prepaid phones. Was it worth spending twenty bucks when no one in the world would know how to reach her? When there was only one person she wanted to call?

Spotting a payphone attached to the tile wall, she plunked three quarters into the slot and dialed. A high-pitched voice answered. 'Hello?' Judy, a new girl, scared like a rabbit most of the time and already strung out on crack and meth.

'Judy? Can I speak to Heather? It's Addy.'

'Addy. Oh my God, you are in so much trouble,' Judy whispered. 'Georgia is so angry. I have never, ever seen her this pissed. Oh. My. God. Did you hear about Heather?'

'What about her?' asked Addy, her heart beating like a trapped animal, not sure at all that she wanted to know.

'Dead,' the girl whispered. 'I saw them take her out early this morning. It was still dark. Oh my God, her face was like, covered with a sheet and everything. They loaded her into a blue van—'

'The police came?'

'No, it was that beater minivan that Rafe used to drive—'

'Was Rafe driving?' She felt a burst of hope.

'No, and Georgia said she's going to kill him too.'

'Dead of what?' Addy asked, clutching her throat and sinking down the wall until the metal phone cord was stretched taut. 'What happened to Heather?' She kept her focus on her friend, refusing to think of Georgia hurting Rafe.

Judy was crying now; Addy could hear the muffled sobs. 'Suffocated,' Judy said. 'Georgia acted so sad when those men came to pick her up. She told one of them carrying the stretcher that Heather smothered herself with her own pillow.'

'Bullshit!' Addy exploded, springing to her feet. A woman walking by with her two children scowled in her direction and hurried them past. Addy lowered her voice. 'No one smothers themselves. Georgia killed her.'

'Bingo,' said Judy. 'I heard Georgia screaming at her last night and lots of banging. Then later she came out of the room and told us other girls that you'd both gone into labor. That she was going to take you both to the best hospital in New York City. That she had wonderful adoptions lined up for yours and Heather's babies and then you'd be back. She said you couldn't wait to get back home. But then I saw Heather leaving . . . dead . . . and no one knew where you were.'

'Home!' Addy spat, then watched the glob of spittle trickle down the wall. 'Wonderful adoptions? What pipe was she smoking?'

'Addy, where are you? I'm scared.'

'Listen,' Addy said. 'You know Rafe—'

'Gotta go,' Judy mumbled, and the call went dead.

Addy held the receiver to her chest, willing herself not to cry. Poor Heather. She never should have left home. Even if her mother was too strict and super religious and didn't want her dating until she was thirty, and even then not without a chaperone until she actually got married. They used to laugh and laugh about that – wouldn't her mother just lie down and die if she could see how things had really turned out.

She could hardly bear to think for long about Heather. She'd been too sweet and too dumb to survive on the streets. And now Addy felt responsible for her death. She'd still be alive

and bubbly and eating Cheerios every hour of the day and
night if she – Addy – hadn't skipped out. If she'd warned her
how to handle Georgia – how crazy angry she'd be once she
realized Addy had disappeared. And Addy hadn't even said
goodbye. Killing Heather and her baby right along with her
made no sense at all. But that was Georgia – once she lost
her temper, anything could happen. She was quite capable of
destroying whatever – whoever – was in her path.

She dropped the receiver and let it bang against the wall.
Her head sank to her fists as she leaned against the tiles and
wept. When she could no longer stand the tinny voice of
the operator instructing her to please hang up, Addy slung the
phone back into its cradle and bought another coffee. Then
she planted herself at a small table by the window, strewn
with trash and newspapers from the previous diners.

Lulled by the hum of the people around her and the noise
of two teens playing video games, her mind drifted back to
the dark hole that was Heather. Georgia was ruthless and
vindictive. She'd never said anything about selling their babies
– not to them – but Addy was a first-rate eavesdropper. She'd
overheard her making arrangements with some sleazy lawyer
for Heather's baby, assuring him there'd be no problems with
signing the waiver of parental rights. Of course there wouldn't
have been a problem, because Heather would never have seen
it. Georgia must have been insanely pissed to kill Heather's
baby and lose all that money. But her anger made sense because
Addy had run away, and Rafe had betrayed her too. She realized that Georgia wanted her baby and the phone she'd agreed
to steal. And Georgia was prepared to kill for them. She wasn't
completely stupid, though it sure felt like that right now.

When she couldn't bear to think about Harlem anymore, her
thoughts veered back to Waterbury and home. She imagined
her mother's angry face, wrinkled up like an apple forgotten
and rotting at the back of the refrigerator. She'd explode into
a thousand pieces if she knew she was a grandmother. Maybe
her mother was born sour or maybe she turned bitter when
Addy was born. Addy had *ruined* her life, she always said, as
if she wasn't quite capable of spoiling things for her own self.
Her mother's boyfriend, Duke, hated her too, because she

reminded him every day that her mother had had men before him. Duh. Give her mother a six-pack and a shot of something stronger and she'd drop her XXL cotton panties for anyone. And still she blamed Addy for her misery. Like, double duh, how did she think Addy got conceived – just jumped into her womb like the immaculate freaking conception? The thoughts kept coming at her like a vicious game of four-square, only she was in the middle and the mean kids were pelting her.

She pushed aside the crumpled bags and napkins on the table and spread open a grease-stained copy of the *New York Post*. She skipped past the headlines on terrorism in Europe and Africa and the continuing stream of homeless refugees – who could bear to read about that when there wasn't a damn thing anyone could do to help. In the metro section, she noticed a picture of the New York University Hospital. Above it a headline screamed: 'Girl Gives Birth to Infant in Delancey Street Subway Bathroom'.

Her heart nearly stopped cold, and then picked up and began to pound faster and faster. She glanced around, was anyone watching? She felt beads of sweat pop on her forehead, sluice along her hairline, and drip onto her neck. The article was part of the morning police report. She smoothed out the paper and began to read.

> *An unidentified young woman gave birth to a live infant in the Delancey Street subway station last night after 10:30 p.m., a police report said. The girl thrust the infant into the arms of a passing stranger, identified by an anonymous source from the Metro police as Elizabeth Brown, a first-year medical student at the NYU College of Medicine.*
>
> *Ms Brown called the police from a coffee shop on Orchard Street, where the child was examined and then taken to the New York University Hospital. Ms Brown reported that she had never seen the girl before.*
>
> *'We hope the mother will come forward,' said a police spokesperson, who was unable to confirm that this incident would be covered by the Safe Haven law. The Safe Haven law was passed in order to 'decriminalize*

*the act of abandoning an infant, as long as the baby was*
*left at a specified safe place and an appropriate person*
*was informed'. The spokesperson declined to comment*
*on whether this instance of the subway baby would fall*
*into a safe place category. Anyone with information about*
*the mother should contact . . .*

Addy's eyes glazed with tears and she crumpled up the newspaper and left the table, jamming the wad of paper into the
trash can as she passed. She had to make a plan. But what
plan? Heather was dead. Georgia was in a killer rage. Rafe was
gone. And she certainly couldn't go home. The thought of
starting over somewhere else, where she knew no one, made
her nauseous and scared. Only one hopeful thought surfaced:
if she could find this Elizabeth Brown, she could find her coat.
And in the pocket of that coat was Rafe's phone number. He
wasn't perfect, but she was sure that he loved her.

Addy took a turn around the food court, looking for someone
to approach for a ride. After watching and listening for half
an hour or so, she settled on a pair of truckers who appeared
to be husband and wife. They were arguing about whose fault
it was that they'd missed the turn to the city and accidentally
begun the trek south on the 'Jersey F'ing Turnpike'. They
seemed grumpy but not mean – teasing each other about who
was dumb and who was dumber. Not arguing the way her
mother used to with her boyfriends, when someone usually
ended up getting belted. And with two in the truck, wasn't the
chance of any funny business decreased? Most men would
not molest a girl with their wife right there. In the privacy of
a hotel room, well, that was different.

The truckers sounded surprised when she approached them,
but seemed to buy her story about being left behind accidentally by her church youth group. 'I left my purse on the bus
with my money, and my phone has died,' she explained. 'By
the time I got back outside, the bus was gone.' She added that
if she could get to New York, her sister would make sure she
ended up where she was supposed to be.

'I know you're thinking I should call my mother,' Addy
said with a shy smile, looking right at the woman. 'But she

died of cancer last year. My sister's kind of taken over. Anyway, she won't freak out the way Mom would have. She's a first-year medical student,' Addy added for a touch of realism. 'She lives in their dorm towers, right by the NYU medical school.'

'You mean near the hospital?' asked the man, pulling on the tip of his red beard.

Addy had no idea if there were dorm towers by the hospital, but it was as good a guess as any. The image of her baby floated into her mind. She was in that hospital somewhere. Addy bit her lip hard and blinked back some tears, which probably added another element of realism to her story. This couple would have no way of knowing what they really meant: that she was a hopeless loser, a bad person.

'Give us just a minute, let's see if we can figure out how to help you, OK, honey?' the woman asked.

Addy backed away from their table, but stayed near enough to eavesdrop.

'We can't just leave her here,' the woman murmured.

'We have no idea who she is or what she's capable of,' the man replied.

'We can't leave her. There are two of us, and we're a lot bigger than she is,' the woman said.

He finally nodded and waved Addy back to the table. 'Awfully sorry about your mother,' the bearded man said. 'I guess we can take you. As long as you don't mind riding in the sleeping loft.'

'I'm happy for any ride at all,' she said, as they gathered up their belongings.

She followed them out to the parking lot, where the wind whistled across the pavement, knifing right through the thin cotton of her sweatshirt. Which made the image of the swaddled baby push into her mind again; she pushed it back as quickly as it had come.

When they reached the truck, the woman opened the passenger side door and turned to look at her. 'Are you sure you're all right, hon? You look awfully pale. Have you had anything to eat today?'

'I'm fine.' She forced a smile. 'Lots better now that I found you guys.' Leaving her UGGs on the floor of the cabin, but taking her plastic bag with her, she struggled up to the sleeping loft. The space was filled with a nest of faded sleeping bags – old-fashioned cotton plaid, the kind that quit working as soon as they got wet. The cabin smelled a little like pipe tobacco and sweat – not unpleasant. All of this reminded her of her grandfather before he had the stroke and her mother checked him into a home for feeble old men. She noticed several plugs in the truck's console, one containing a charging iPad, and another a Samsung phone.

'Would you mind – if it wouldn't be a problem – could you charge my phone? I must have left the charger lead on the bus.' She knew it was almost out of juice. And if she needed to make an emergency call, it was her only option.

'Of course,' said the woman, exchanging a glance with her husband. Addy handed her the BlackBerry she had stolen, which was stashed at the bottom of her bag. After hearing the cheerful chirp indicating that the phone was connected, she burrowed into the top sleeping bag, listening to the couple banter about football and where they'd find dinner and the bummer of having to drive over the holidays.

From the snatches of conversation that drifted up to the loft and penetrated Addy's sleepy haze, she realized that her destination was not really on their way.

'Imagine our daughter hitching a ride with no coat on New Year's Eve,' said the woman in a soft voice. 'Unbearable.'

'This isn't the kind of phone a teenager carries,' the man said. 'Could very well be stolen.'

'She isn't going to tell us the truth,' the woman answered. 'She doesn't know us from Adam. Love to hear her story, but I'm sure she isn't telling.'

*You got that right,* Addy thought.

Gradually she heard more of the noises of the city – the blaring of taxi horns, the screeching of brakes, the clatter of construction. Then the truck's gears downshifted and the rig roared to a stop. From her perch, she could see through the windshield that they were idling in front of the hospital where she'd told them she could find her sister.

'Here's the hospital,' said the driver. 'Is this the right place?'

'This is it, exactly right!' Addy said.

The woman in the passenger seat swung the big door open and got out.

Addy slid down from the loft and pulled on the dirty UGGs.

'Look, we've got an extra coat and a hat. You take them – they're not the height of fashion, but better than nothing, right?' The woman grinned and pressed a faded tan car coat into Addy's hands, added a fleece hat on top, and then returned the phone to her. Addy thanked them and hurried off before they could hug her or suggest waiting until she had made a safe connection. In her experience, overinvolved adults usually wanted something from her. No matter how much they expressed their concern.

The wind cut through her sweatshirt as soon as she'd hit the sidewalk, and she pulled on the coat – at least four sizes too big – and hustled into the warmth of the hospital lobby. She edged behind a small oasis of green plants in the center of the space in order to get her bearings. Approaching the information desk was out of the question; the official channel was unlikely to be helpful in locating Elizabeth, and might even raise suspicions. Who could she ask? Doctors rushing by? Too busy, and also likely to meddle. Patients? Too sick and too sad. She spotted a trio of what looked like medical students sipping coffee on a bench to the right of the lobby. She screwed up her courage and approached them, pleased to see that her instinct had been correct. Their names were written in blue script above the pockets of their short white coats, with *medical student* added underneath.

When there was a lull in the conversation, she said, 'I'm thinking of applying to school here for next year's class. Where do most of the first-year students live?'

That was a conversation stopper. Obviously she didn't look like anyone's idea of a medical student candidate.

But the cheerful blonde girl with rosy cheeks must've felt sorry for her. 'No dorms, sadly, but most of us start out in the studios in the tower on 26th Street.' She paused, her eyebrows rising slightly, as if to say she didn't believe in Addy as a future medical student. 'Are you looking for anyone in particular?'

Addy almost spit out Elizabeth's name, but stopped herself,

worrying that they might know her. Might get to her before she could and warn her about a strange girl looking for her. Maybe they'd even read the article in the *Post*. And if they had, maybe they'd make the connection between the pathetic new mother described in those paragraphs and Addy herself, still bloody – though she'd washed most of it off in the rest-stop bathroom – and still pale, draped in an enormous coat that couldn't be hers. And then maybe they'd feel compelled to call someone and start a troubled ball rolling with consequences she couldn't even imagine. Or afford.

After an uncomfortable pause during which Addy said nothing, the girl spoke again. 'It's a couple of blocks south. You'll recognize it by the pocket park outside with a playground. Can we help—'

Addy cut her off with a quick thanks and headed back out into the brisk wind. It was starting to snow again too – big wet flakes that looked like they'd stick together and pile up on top of the filthy gray layer that was already on the ground. She pulled on the blue fleece cap, which smelled faintly of coconut shampoo. If she didn't find Elizabeth, she'd have to find somewhere to spend the night. Outside was not an option. Not that finding Elizabeth would solve the problem anyway. But it was almost as if in handing the baby over to this stranger, she'd tied an invisible cord between them.

She trotted the two long blocks to the student apartments, and stopped short when she saw the yellow crime scene tape flapping from the bench in the park grounds. Her stomach lurched as she spotted a cop car idling on the far side of the playground. Two uniformed police were tromping around the perimeter of the taped-off bench, flashlights out though it was the middle of the day. Cops equaled trouble for an underage runaway. She ducked behind a big oak, wishing she'd reacted more quickly. She could taste the chocolate donut and that second bitter cup of rest stop coffee. If Elizabeth Brown hadn't exited from the lobby at that moment, rolling a small suitcase behind her, Addy would have bolted. She'd know her anywhere – the silvery hat and matching coat and those perfect blonde curls.

Elizabeth was moving fast, and Addy followed her, serpentining between cars so the cops wouldn't catch sight of her. After that, it wasn't hard to keep enough people between them to prevent her sensing Addy's presence. The city felt packed and claustrophobic. Elizabeth ducked into the doors leading to Grand Central Station, and Addy followed, hurrying behind her to the big central hall, bustling with people, half of whom had stopped to crane their necks at the constellations painted on the expansive blue ceiling. Elizabeth purchased a ticket at the window labeled New Haven line. Addy considered buying one too, but she only had the change from the sixty bucks the man had given her the night before. And that might have to last a while. She'd figure it out. She followed Elizabeth into one of the tunnels, watching her bump her suitcase down the stairs and then duck into the third car of the waiting train.

'All aboard for New Haven,' a rotund conductor yelled.

Luckily for her, the train was mobbed with last-minute escapees from the city, probably heading to suburbs for their New Year's celebrations. Addy found a seat about ten rows behind Elizabeth. The ride would give her the time to decide what to say and if she would say it. For all she knew, the *Post* article could have been a sham, with Elizabeth acting as decoy – a way to draw Addy in and then file legal charges. But then why would she leave New York?

She had no reason really to trust this woman. She might be just as likely to turn Addy in as give her Rafe's number. But the man last night had been kind. And so had the truck drivers. Maybe her luck would hold. Besides, there was no one else to trust.

The train pulled away from the station. Once she saw the conductor approaching, she slipped into the restroom to wait until enough time had passed. The sour stench of urine brought her spinning back to the Delancey Street station bathroom and a kaleidoscope of painful memories pushed into her head. Her body felt different – battered and lighter, without the baby she'd carried inside and then held for a few moments, whose trusting eyes she'd met. At least she was safe and out of Georgia's hands. She leaned her forehead against the stainless-steel door and breathed those images away. On the way back up the aisle, she palmed a yellow and white ticket that belonged to a woman who was rustling through her luggage on the overhead rack. Back in her own seat, she planted the receipt in the slot in front of her.

As the New York, and then Connecticut towns rushed by, the scenery changed from the faded high-rise brick buildings around 125th Street to marinas and sweet downtowns all decked out in Christmas finery. Places where it probably cost more to live than she could earn in a lifetime or even imagine. Although she was desperately tired and the train car was over-heated, she tried not to doze, so she wouldn't miss Elizabeth getting off. She kept her focus on the silver-threaded hat, wondering what a girl like that was listening to through the buds in her ears.

The conductor announced the New Haven station, the last stop on the line. 'The Shoreline East train will be located directly across the platform on track ten,' he said.

Up ahead, Elizabeth wrestled her suitcase down from the overhead rack, exited the car, and trotted across the platform to an older train waiting there.

As Addy stepped off to follow her, the conductor of the new train hollered, 'Shoreline East to StateStreetBranford-GuilfordMadisonOldSaybrook,' running all the names together like that big word in *Mary Poppins*. 'Supercalifragilisticex-pialidocius,' she used to sing until her mother screamed for mercy. Which never took long. This time she bought a ticket on the train to the farthest town, not knowing where Elizabeth would disembark.

As the train chugged through the shoreline towns, Addy saw the marsh out to the right, frozen and gray. In the far distance, the Sound was dotted with small islands. She could imagine herself living on one of those, alone. She'd plant a little garden, and she'd fish, so she'd never have to return to shore. As they approached the town of Guilford, the engineer sounded a lonely blast of horn. Elizabeth once again grabbed her suitcase and stood near the door, bracing against a pole to keep her balance, looking back down the length of the car. Addy slunk down in her blue seat, pulling the ugly cap low on her forehead.

Once the town's name flashed past and the train ground to a halt, Elizabeth exited. Addy slipped out behind her, hovering in the cover of the brick structure that contained the stairs crossing the tracks to reach trains going in the opposite direction. A large dark blue Mercedes was waiting in the passenger pick-up area, plumes of white exhaust puffing into the frigid air. Two older people got out when they saw Elizabeth make her way across the platform to the parking lot. The man driving reached her first, hugged her briefly and grabbed her bag. The woman pulled her into a long hug, held Elizabeth's cheeks between her gloved hands, and stood on tiptoes to kiss her forehead before finally letting her go.

Addy's heart plummeted. Elizabeth wasn't a solitary lost soul like her. She was part of a family, a rich family with a mother and father, a family who loved her enough to pick her up and welcome her home.

This was as far as she'd thought ahead. She didn't belong here, that was clear enough. She slumped down on the first step, head in hands. The frigid cold of the metal seeped instantly through her flannel pants. For right now, Elizabeth Brown was a dead end, like everything else in her life.

# TEN

'Oh honey, we're so glad you decided to come home,' said Elizabeth's mom, Videen, craning around the headrest to meet her daughter's eyes. 'We're happy to talk about your feelings and the wedding and Kevin as much as you're willing. Or feed you and leave you alone, if that's what you need.'

Elizabeth's father grunted from the driver's seat, making a rolling stop in the center of Guilford and heading left toward Sachem's Head. 'I'd just as soon wring that asshat's neck as talk about him.'

'This is about our daughter, what she needs,' Elizabeth's mother started.

'That isn't actually why I came home,' Elizabeth broke in, chewing on the ragged cuticle around her thumb and gazing out over the reeds in the marsh, brown against the patches of ice and snow on the frozen ground. 'Kevin is the least of my worries.' The bare bones of the whole story spilled out – the girl, the baby, the shooting in the park. 'The officer who responded both times suggested getting out of town would not be a bad idea.'

Her father braked to a neck-snapping halt on the road that crossed the marsh, leading to the Sound on one side and the West River on the other. Both parents turned to look at her.

'Are you in danger? Was this person shooting at you?' her mother asked.

'I don't think I was the target at all,' said Elizabeth. She knew they'd be upset by this turn of events, and she'd been right.

'Goddammit, Elizabeth, how do you get into these situations?' her father asked.

'She didn't get into a situation,' her mom snapped back, her voice thin and sharp like the frosty marsh grasses. 'Kevin was a situation. This is different. You heard her. The girl handed her this baby out of nowhere. What was she supposed to do, leave it in the subway?'

'Are you in danger?' her father asked this time.

Elizabeth sighed, clutched her arms around her chest, feeling the fierce and frightening possibility of that question. 'I don't know. From what little the man had time to say before he was shot, he was looking for the mother of the baby. And somehow, he got my name and came looking for me, thinking I'd know something about her whereabouts. Which I don't.' She couldn't bear to tell them just yet about the phone call Jillian had made. It wasn't *somehow* that he'd gotten her name, it was their own doing, their own foolishness.

'Who was this man? Why were they after him? And who are *they*?' her father asked.

Elizabeth's parents exchanged a worried glance. Her father spoke again. 'I say we go to the police. Tell them what happened. Just in case someone has followed you out here.'

Her mother's lips quavered, but she nodded in agreement.

'It's probably overkill,' her father added, patting his wife's hand awkwardly. 'She's safe and sound with us. But it can't hurt to let them know. We'll go right now, so they understand the seriousness of the situation.'

Elizabeth squeezed her mother's shoulder, feeling the bird-like bones – she'd always felt enormous in comparison. 'It can't hurt, Mom,' she said. She felt torn between the powerful urge to pretend nothing in the past week had happened, and the sinking feeling that something hideously awful still lurked.

Her father made a K-turn in the road, then barreled back through the downtown, still cheerfully strung with holiday lights, to Route 77, where the police station was located fifty yards north of Interstate 95.

The waiting area had brick walls, a tile floor, and what felt like air-conditioning on full bore, despite the tip of December Arctic blast. Inside, a young cop with rosebud lips tapped on a computer behind a glass window. Elizabeth's father rapped on the glass until the cop slid it open, then explained (demanded, really, Elizabeth thought) that they needed to speak to a detective. He wanted the cops to be aware that their daughter could be in danger.

The rosebud-lipped cop looked at each of their faces in turn. 'Detective Meigs is on duty, but he's on a call. Take a seat and he'll speak with you when he's finished.'

Elizabeth and her mother sat as instructed. But her father frowned for a moment and she tensed up, fearing he was going to make a scene, insist on immediate attention. He should know from his years of hospital experience that patients who behaved like demanding idiots often mysteriously ended up with the longest waits.

But instead he sat in the chair on the other side of her and began to scroll through the messages on his phone. Her mom took her hand and began to run her fingers over Elizabeth's. 'You've ruined your manicure.'

'At this point, I don't suppose it matters. My plans for New Year's Eve and New Year's Day are pretty much kaput.' She tried to smile, look like she was OK. Her mother could use some reassurance. On top of the failed wedding, the idea that her daughter had been shot at was probably over the limit of what she could bear.

'We have no plans either, but we've certainly got champagne. And we could get out the games,' her mom said in a voice full of faux cheer. 'You always did love Bananagrams. Aunt Susan loves it too. Are any of the girls coming out for the weekend?' Her voice was pleading, as though the problems could be shuffled aside if company filled the house.

'I told them I needed some space.' Elizabeth disengaged her hand from her mother's grip. 'And really, Mom, you absolutely don't need to entertain me. And we don't need to try to pretend everything is normal. I don't think that's even possible, do you?' She patted her mother's thigh, covered in simple but expensive houndstooth checked trousers. Then they sat without talking, studying the photos of the most-wanted criminals that had been posted on the opposite wall.

Several minutes later, a burly man with reddish curls tinged with gray pushed open the door into the waiting area. He introduced himself as Detective Meigs.

'I'm Doctor Harry Brown, and this is my wife Videen, and my daughter Elizabeth,' said Elizabeth's father in his stentorian doctor's voice.

The detective shook each hand and ushered them down the hall to his office. Stacks of paper covered all but a narrow swath of the desktop and one of the chairs in front of it. He scooped up the pile on the second chair and dropped the papers on a file cabinet, partially obscuring a photograph of him with his arm around a big-boned brunette and a black Lab. In a second photo, the same brunette was hugging a disdainful teenager, who leaned away from the woman. Meigs surveyed the office, seeming to realize that squeezing three people into the mess was going to be an insurmountable challenge.

'We'll go to the conference room,' he said, and led them further down the hall. He settled them into a small room with a plain wood table and six chairs. He looked tired and rumpled, wearing a pale blue shirt and a dark plaid blazer. His tie was definitely too wide for New York fashion, but at least it served to partially obscure what appeared to be a coffee stain on his chest. He deposited a yellow legal pad and a pen on the table in front of him.

'How can I help you?' He chose to look first at Elizabeth's father, which ticked her off. 'The desk sergeant said something about your daughter being in danger?'

All three of them started to speak at once. Elizabeth waved both parents away. 'I'll tell it if you don't mind.'

She rifled through her red leather bag and found the New York City policewoman's business card. 'This is the contact information from the officer I was dealing with in the city. I'm sure she would be happy if you reached out to her. In fact, she said you could.' She handed him the card and put her phone on the table.

Then she explained about the girl thrusting the infant into her arms, how she called the authorities from the coffee shop, and how the baby had been taken away. 'I went to see her in the hospital this morning. The whole thing seemed so sad, you know?'

Videen's face mirrored the sadness that she felt.

'But earlier this morning, I had a call from a reporter at the *New York Post*. She told me there'd been a police report about the so-called subway baby. That's what they're calling her. An anonymous source identified me. She said I would be swarmed with reporters, which I have not been. But she promised that she would tell the story fairly if I gave her an exclusive interview, and she would get help for that girl if possible.'

'I hope you told her to stick it where the sun doesn't shine,' said her father, clenching both of his hands into fists.

'Do I wish I hadn't talked to her? Yes, I do. But she sounded like a caring person,' said Elizabeth, refusing to look away from the detective. 'And I did my research. She was not lying. She's been writing a series on homeless girls that has resulted in a lot of good for many of them. Some of them refuse help, and there's not much to be done after that.'

She fidgeted, feeling uncomfortable, wishing she didn't have to tell him about the drunken phone call in front of her parents. Her mother would freak out and her father would be reduced to his least appealing default position, anger and blame. But this detective would probably call Officer Ramsey and the truth would come out anyway – it might as well come from her. But then Detective Meigs saved her with a question.

'Let's start at the beginning,' he said, tapping his pen on the yellow pad. 'You were going up the subway steps when this young woman came toward you out of nowhere and gave you a baby. A newborn.'

Elizabeth nodded. 'We made eye contact while I was actually in the car waiting for the doors to open. She must have followed me with the baby. I didn't realize the infant was brand new until I got to the coffee shop and unwrapped her. The placenta and umbilical cord were still attached.'

'Why did she choose you?' Detective Meigs asked.

Elizabeth felt herself bristling, as if he was making an accusation. As if somehow her story wasn't holding together for him. And she felt the sharp attention of her parents on either side, her mother quivering with anxiety, and her father apoplectic. He had always been like that, confrontational when he might have been supportive, when anything bad had happened to her over the years. Her mother had tried to explain it away: that he felt his responsibility for his daughter so keenly he could hardly bear to see her in pain. She wasn't so sure. If she'd been his biological daughter, would he have behaved the same way?

She took a cleansing breath, then chose her words carefully. 'I can't get in her head, of course, to know what she was thinking. But I must have been the most responsible or maternal-looking person in the subway.'

'Who else was nearby?' the detective asked.

A good question. Elizabeth closed her eyes and forced herself to reimagine the scene. 'Some teenage girls who looked like they'd started drinking long before they got to the party,' she said. 'It was after ten o'clock. I also noticed a small pod of older folks who, sad to say, seemed a bit confused. They were studying the subway map near a bench.' She smiled an apology at her mother, who hated assumptions that the elderly were incompetent, and who certainly would have stopped to help them. 'And some young men with the low pants and the big hair.'

She gestured to show what she meant, that style she would

never understand. Which she supposed moved her one step
closer to old fart range. Another thing Kevin accused her of
when he wanted to go out and she had to study.

'And why might this man who was shot have assumed you
knew the whereabouts of the girl?' asked Meigs.

'Of course she doesn't know—' started Videen.

'Please let her tell me,' said the detective, flashing a perfunc-
tory smile at her mother.

Elizabeth sighed. 'The article in the paper, for one. But for
another, we called a number last night and spoke with someone
who claimed to be the father.'

'A number?' Meigs asked. He'd lost the slouch that he'd
started the interview out with. Now he was focused, laser-eyed,
on her face.

Her words tumbled out in a rush as she explained how
they'd spoken to this man in the bar. 'It was a horrible idea
and I realized that as soon as we heard how angry he was.'

'Back up a minute,' said Meigs. 'Where did you get the
number and who were you calling?'

Elizabeth sighed and covered her eyes with her hands. 'It
was on a slip of paper in the pocket of the coat that came
wrapped around the baby. My friend had punched it into my
phone just before the police came. I was kind of in shock.
My friend figured this guy might have a clue about the girl.'
She dropped her hands to the table. 'Instead, he seemed furious
to hear she'd had the baby.'

Her parents and the detective stared at her, and then he
pointed to her phone. 'Can you find this number now?'

She scrolled through the list of her recent calls until she
found the number and read it out to him. The detective jotted
the digits on a yellow pad. 'Chances are his phone was a
throwaway, assuming he's part of a criminal element.'

'A safe guess,' said Elizabeth's father, 'considering that the
man sitting next to my daughter was executed.'

'No one's tried to contact you since that incident?' Meigs
asked, ignoring her father.

'Other than the reporter, no one. And to be accurate, I talked
with her before the man was shot.'

The detective stared at her phone, which she'd placed back

on the table, then looked up at her. 'If you get any unusual calls, texts, anything, or notice anyone in your neighborhood who is not familiar, I want you to call the emergency line immediately. Here's my cell, in case you think of other details or have any questions.' He passed her a card with his name and several numbers on it and rubbed his fingers over the stubble on his chin. 'I will follow up with Officer Ramsey, but with any luck, these people have lost interest in you and are tracking the girl instead.'

The car ride home was completely silent. Not the usual state of affairs – ordinarily, her mother would have kept up a steady stream of chatter. News about her best friend Teresa, how much she'd enjoyed Elizabeth's Christmas gifts, and so on. But now she seemed too shocked to speak. Elizabeth was relieved to see Aunt Susan's car in the driveway. At least there would be one person in the house who wasn't appalled about her bad judgment – that would come later when Videen filled her sister in.

'I'm going into the office,' said her father as the women got out of the car.

'But it's New Year's Eve,' said Videen, leaning over to look at her husband, who remained in the driver's seat.

'And your point?'

Videen slammed the door shut and he roared away. She shrugged. 'He's had a lot to take in this week,' she said.

'Haven't we all?' Elizabeth muttered, following her mother to the front door, which was decorated with a silver wreath studded with tiny stuffed birds and twinkling white lights. A candle winked in each window of the house, all the way up to the attic. Tasteful, yet festive, as befitted an old New England town. Her mother double locked the door behind them.

Aunt Susan met them in the hallway and enveloped Elizabeth in a big hug. 'How are you holding up, sweetheart? Let me put on the kettle and we girls can chat.' She hustled back into the kitchen and Videen followed. Elizabeth stood staring at the living room. The white carpet and upholstered couches were barely visible under the stacks of wedding gifts. And the coffee table was covered with wedding flower centerpieces

– white and pink roses with evergreen and ivy and even a few sprigs of mistletoe, as she and Kevin had chosen eons ago.

'Red zinger or English breakfast tea?' called Aunt Susan.

'I need caffeine,' said Elizabeth. 'And sugar. I'll be there in a couple of minutes.' She dropped her overnight bag in the hall and waded into the sea of gifts. She felt short of breath and drained. Everything would have to be returned and regretful notes sent to all the guests who'd been inconvenienced by booking expensive holiday tickets that most likely weren't refundable. Why in the world hadn't they planned to elope? Why had she said yes in the first place? No, that wasn't fair. They'd been so happy in the beginning.

Videen appeared in the doorway. 'We'll help with all this, honey. Come to the kitchen and relax with us for now.'

But once the three of them were seated at the table, inhaling Christmas butter cookies and sipping tea, Videen began to report the blow by blow of what had unfolded since they cancelled the wedding, including several ugly phone calls with Kevin's mother.

Kevin's mother had turned out not to be Elizabeth's number one fan. He came from an Irish Catholic family and his mother had been horrified to hear the wedding was taking place in the Congregational Church. Not to mention disapproving of her future daughter-in-law's plans for a big career. Mrs Preble had stayed home to raise seven children and interpreted any major deviation from that path as personal criticism. 'At least choose something less demanding that leaves more time for your family,' she'd suggested more than once. 'Couldn't you study nursing or work in a pharmacy? CVS right in town is always looking for help. As a doctor, you'll be on call night and day. What if your own children are sick?'

'I bet she was secretly relieved when Kevin called the wedding off,' Elizabeth said. 'Or not so secretly.'

'Anyone would be thrilled to have you as a daughter-in-law,' said her mother, reaching across the table to squeeze her hand. 'I thank God for you every day.'

Then came a moment of silence. There was more, Elizabeth knew it. Though it might sound ridiculous, she could tell by the tone of the silence when her mother was holding back.

'But . . .' she said.

'But the truth is, seeing as her own son chose to call the wedding off, she could have been more generous.'

Now Aunt Susan took her sister's hand and squeezed.

'Are they covering any of the expenses?' Elizabeth asked.

'Kevin said they would make us whole. Reimburse us for half of anything we had to pay out.'

'Not really,' said her mom. 'In her opinion, Kevin didn't want the big wedding to begin with. She felt that since he was pushed into it, he really shouldn't be responsible for the bills. She claims that she tried many times to suggest scaling our production back, but we wouldn't budge.'

'Our production?' Elizabeth felt herself building up a head of steam, anger so pure it felt white-hot, as if anything she touched would sizzle and burn.

'Let's not talk about that anymore,' said her mother quickly. 'Let's think about dinner. How does lemon chicken sound? With wild rice?'

Leftover wedding food.

'Grotesque,' said Elizabeth, 'that's how it sounds. Grotesque, grim, and utterly pathetic.'

'Let's put the rest of that in the freezer,' suggested Aunt Susan, 'or maybe the trash, where it belongs.' They all three burst into laughter. 'I'll cook something. What are you craving?'

'Macaroni and cheese,' said Elizabeth. 'Comfort food.'

'On New Year's Eve?' Videen asked. 'Your father will have a heart attack.'

'If he had been here, he would have had a vote,' said Elizabeth.

'The grocery store will be mobbed,' said Videen.

'I'll go, I don't mind,' Elizabeth said. 'Give me a list and your keys.'

'By yourself?' her mother asked.

Elizabeth gave her a look.

'OK, then, at least be careful.'

Elizabeth drove back toward town in her mother's car, first detouring down Whitfield Street to the water. She parked and got out of the car, pulling her coat tightly around her stomach (newly toned and spray-tanned for the wedding), the wind whipping her scarf and knifing through her jeans. The hardware on the flagpole clanked briskly. She imagined the flag raised to half-mast, in memory of her marriage, dead before it got started. When her tears had frozen to her cheeks and eyelashes, she returned to the car, remembering how the wedding planning had begun.

Two days after Kevin proposed, after she'd hashed through her parents' concerns about getting married during her first year of medical school, her mother had suggested they visit Angie's Alterations. 'No job is impossible for Angie,' her mother assured her. So they packed up her mother's wedding gown – the same narrow tube of soft white satin edged with heirloom lace that her grandmother had worn down the aisle – and drove to the tailor. Her beaming mother explained that they wanted the dress altered to fit Elizabeth.

The seamstress unpacked the antique gown from its pre-servative wrapping and laid it out on her sewing table. She pulled on a pair of white cotton gloves and walked around the table, studying the dress from all angles, touching the lace, fingering the satin. 'It's beautiful,' the woman said. Then she peered at Elizabeth's mother – petite and bird-boned – and back at tall Elizabeth, with her peasant legs and solid hips and shoulders of a seaman. Not exactly a fair assessment, but in comparison to Videen, she'd always felt like she had the physique of a longshoreman.

'I have to be honest. I can't make this work,' said the seamstress as she stripped off her gloves. 'I could use the lace to trim a new gown. We could find cream-colored satin and reproduce the style.' She narrowed her eyes and looked Elizabeth over. 'To be honest again, this is not the style I'd choose for you.' Then she smiled and tried to crack a joke. 'Are you sure you two are related?'

'Related by choice and by love,' her mother had answered. But the excitement in her eyes had dimmed. They packed up the gown and headed two towns east to a luxury bridal boutique recommended by several of Videen's friends who had daughters getting married. Sometimes the universe was sending a powerful message that a person should not ignore.

Elizabeth drove to the Big Y grocery store, which was

absolutely as crowded as her mother had warned. She picked up a hand basket and wove through the other shoppers, quickly choosing the cheeses, the pasta, the milk, and the butter that Aunt Susan needed, plus a bunch of broccoli and a half-gallon of Tillamook butter pecan ice cream for good measure. Her father would have preferred chocolate but her mother was deathly allergic. She could have gotten both, but she didn't feel like accommodating him.

On the way out of the store, she noticed someone set up to beg at the intersection of Route 1 and the entrance to the Big Y/Walmart complex. Often homeless veterans stationed themselves there, or women who promised to work in exchange for money to feed their kids. But this time it was a thin girl with brown hair, dirty UGGs, and a car coat that looked twice her size. She must be freezing. She was holding a hand-lettered, brown cardboard sign that read:

STRANDED & HOMESICK
PLEASE. ANYTHING HELPS.
MERRY CHRISTMAS. GOD BLESS.

My God, it was Addy.

# ELEVEN

Addy had hitched a short ride from the station to Route 1 with two teenagers who'd gotten off the same train. When they'd dropped her in front of the Big Y grocery store in Guilford, she'd asked about ways to make a little cash. They'd pointed out the spot near the entrance to the complex where people sometimes panhandled.

'You can find some cardboard in the trash bins out back to make a sign. And either lift a magic marker from Walmart, or if your nerves aren't that good, they might loan you one at the service counter,' said the willowy girl with shiny brown hair and a friendly smile.

'If anybody asks how old you are, you're nineteen,' said the boy, putting his arm around the girl. 'The cops in this town are sticklers for underage. They'd just as soon take you into the station as look at you. Right, Caroline?' He squeezed his girlfriend's waist and laughed.

'And we're having a little party at my house later,' Caroline said. 'It's right near the green. You're welcome to come.' She reached for Addy's hand and scrawled the address on the inside of her wrist in blue ink. 'And not to worry – no parental units will be in attendance.'

So Addy made the sign and planted herself at the entrance and the dollars started to trickle in. Everyone seemed to feel a little sorry for a young woman out in the cold on New Year's Eve. She felt like death itself, and probably looked like it as well. Behind her, snowplows had pushed the snow into gray piles pocked with gravel. She heard a crunching noise – someone stumping over the ice piles. It scared the crap out of her when a woman tapped her on the shoulder.

'Addy,' the woman said in a soft voice. 'I'm Elizabeth. We met in the subway yesterday.'

Addy dropped her sign, grabbed her plastic bag, and started to back away, her first instinct to bolt. Yes, she'd come looking for this woman, but the reality of seeing her here, in her town, in her life, was a different thing altogether. And how did she know her name?

'It's so darn cold out,' Elizabeth said. 'I wondered if you'd like to come home, take a shower, get something to eat. Then I'll bring you right back if that's what you want.'

After a little more talking, Addy agreed. This was why she'd followed her up here, wasn't it? A chance to get Rafe's number back and figure out where to meet up with him and get started on their new life. Elizabeth was her only link. And she seemed cool. Not full of pity or too pushy with questions about how she'd got here or what she was looking for.

Once she was settled in the passenger side of the fancy Mercedes with its heated seats, Addy's stomach began to somersault. She hoped she wouldn't be sick on the expensive leather. This was a monster mistake. How had she let herself get talked into it? Suddenly, going to the princess's house felt all wrong. But then, what had felt right over the past year?

At the beginning of the ride, Elizabeth tried some friendly chatter, but Addy felt like a block of wood, or even granite, unable to participate. She wanted to ask whether the baby was still in the hospital, as the newspaper had said, and if she was okay, but her voice felt frozen. She kept her gaze on her hands. Her fingernails were bitten to the flesh, and the nail polish Heather had applied last week was partly scraped off, only patches of blue remaining. Her eyes welled with tears at the thought of her friend. She couldn't keep her mind from flashing to Georgia, holding a pillow over her friend's face, Heather thrashing to get away. How terrified she must have been.

After several quiet minutes, Elizabeth turned on the radio, tuned to a station Addy didn't know; orchestra music, she supposed. What was the point of listening to music without words? They drove through the center of the seriously cute town, with a chocolate shop and a bookstore and a coffee shop and an old-fashioned hardware store that her grandpa would have loved.

'It looks lovely all decorated, doesn't it?' Elizabeth asked. 'Like something from a cozy mystery book or a holiday musical.' She took her eyes off the road and glanced over at Addy, who continued to look straight ahead. 'It's not much further,' she said. 'Technically, you could walk to town from our house, though I've never seen my parents do that. Of course I used to meet my girlfriends here all the time when I was about your age, before I got a car.' She glanced over at Addy, her forehead furrowed. 'Sorry, I'm going on like an idiot.'

They pulled into the driveway of a big white house with a wreath on the door, candles in each window, and twinkling white lights on the fir tree near the driveway. Like something out of one of the sappy old movies her grandma liked to watch every Christmas. Except for this past year, Addy always watched along with her.

'Come on in,' said Elizabeth. 'My mom's home, and so is her sister, Aunt Susan. My father went back to work.'

Addy noticed that her voice got quicker and her lips thinned as she mentioned her father. What was the story there? She had no way to even guess, no insight into fathers. Hers had split before she was even born. She pulled the big car coat close around her body. One thing was clear: she didn't belong here. She didn't look right or smell right or know how people talked and acted when they lived in a town like this. This was a different Connecticut than the one she grew up in.

Elizabeth grabbed a grocery bag from the back seat and ushered Addy up the sidewalk to a door beside the garage. 'We rarely use the front door,' she explained, seeming a little embarrassed. 'This way we can leave our coats and boots in the laundry room and not track anything onto the carpets.' She grinned and shrugged as if they both understood the weird demands of mothers. 'We're home,' she warbled, once the door closed behind them.

'Did your father decide to join us after all?' A tiny woman with neat brown curls and pink lipstick appeared as they shucked off their winter gear. 'Oh, goodness,' she said, placing her hand to her mouth. 'Looks like we have a guest.'

'This is Addy,' Elizabeth said, 'the young lady I told you about.'

Addy's stomach lurched again. Exactly what had she told her?

Elizabeth's mother's lips formed a perfect pink O as she looked Addy up and down – the grubby sweatshirt, greasy hair, socks with holes. And then behind her a second woman appeared, with the same pointy nose and Cupid lips, only her curls were streaked with gray and she was a few inches taller.

'Welcome,' said Elizabeth's mother. 'Come right in. This is Addy,' she said to her sister. 'The girl from New York. This is my sister, Susan.'

'Hello,' Addy said stiffly. 'Thank you.'

'What fun to have company on New Year's Eve,' said Aunt Susan in a chipper voice. 'I bet you'd like something to eat and drink. My specialties are hot chocolate and grilled cheese. How does that sound?'

Addy's stomach growled in response and the three women shook with laughter, as if she'd told the funniest joke ever. As if she even knew how to say something funny anymore. The last year had squeezed the joy out of her. Maybe those few early days had been fun – after she'd caught the bus out of Waterbury to Manhattan and believed that she'd find a good life in the city. She'd felt drunk with freedom. It had been scary though – really scary – to be on her own for the first time in sixteen years. The drunken bums terrified her, ranting and groping. And the women dressed like prostitutes with shorty shorts and gobs of make-up were worse, talking about how much her cherry would be worth. It didn't take long to figure out what *that* meant.

And that was why she'd agreed to go along when Georgia found her crouched in the Port Authority bus station restroom and offered to give her some supper and a place to sleep for the night. Next thing she knew she'd agreed to sleep with one man and give the money to Georgia. As payback, Georgia explained, and then they'd be even. If there had ever been a point when she'd believed she could return home, she'd crossed the line right there. Pretty soon that one man turned into a series of tricks that all blurred together. And then Georgia had introduced her to Les. An important man, Georgia told her, so she needed to be on her best behavior, so he'd think she was something special. For a while, she'd be seeing only him. And then she'd ended up pregnant. When she figured this out, she'd expected Georgia to be furious. Instead she'd been pleased, very pleased. Rafe had pulled her aside one night when he was on security duty and whispered why. *Blackmail. But I can get you out of here. And we can take the money from Les instead of her.*

She needed to remind herself that at first she'd thought Georgia had meant to help her. It was not so different from what was happening now, relying on people she barely knew. She'd have to stay alert – things could turn sour fast.

'The powder room is right here,' said Elizabeth's mom as they walked through the hall that led to the kitchen. 'Why don't you wash up while we fix you a bite? Elizabeth used to love grilled cheese sandwiches – that should tide you over until dinner. You're welcome to take a shower later. I'm sure we can find some clean clothes. And we're serving homemade macaroni and cheese for supper. Elizabeth insisted! Gosh, that sounds like a lot of cheese, so let's get you some fruit too.'

As Addy headed toward the bathroom, she couldn't help pausing to stare at the piles of gifts in the living room. Boxes everywhere – papered in gold and white with glittery bows and cascading ribbons. *Happy New Year, Happy New Life!* one of the decorations read. *Wishing You Happily Ever After, Elizabeth and Kevin!* said another. And the dining room and coffee tables were completely covered with flower arrangements, which explained the faint, almost rotten smell of roses.

'Wedding presents,' said Elizabeth grimly, stopping beside her. 'I probably didn't get the chance to tell you I was supposed to get married tonight. They'll all have to be returned because the SOB bailed out.'

'Sorry,' said Addy. She'd only ever seen this many presents on television.

Elizabeth faked a smile. 'It's for the best, really. Who wants to marry a guy who isn't sure he loves everything about you?'

Addy shrugged. She doubted Rafe loved everything about her – that was too much to ask. But he loved her enough to want to help her escape from Georgia's and start a new life with her. Wasn't that enough? Whatever money he earned from her and the baby, he planned to share it with her. To Georgia, she meant nothing. She went into the bathroom, catching sight of herself in the mirror, shocked again at how shabby and pale she looked. After using the toilet, she washed her hands with lavender soap, splashed water on her face, and dried everything on a length of toilet paper so she wouldn't mess up the carefully folded Christmas towels. By the time she got to the kitchen, the three women were seated at the table, with mugs of tea steaming in front of them. At her place, set with a red placemat and a pretty white dish with holly around the rim and a napkin decorated with dancing reindeer, she found a perfectly grilled cheese sandwich, a heap of fruit, and a glass of milk.

'Don't be shy,' said Elizabeth's mother. 'Dig in. And please, call me Videen.'

'And me Susan,' said the aunt. 'And we've got tons of cookies and the hot chocolate I promised when you're done with all that.' She pointed to a plate in the middle of the table, mounded with homemade sugar cookies shaped like bells and candy canes, and gingerbread men, and some round ones covered in powdered sugar that she'd never seen before. When they had Christmas cookies at her mother's house, they came from the local supermarket. The women sipped their tea and chatted about little things to pretend they weren't watching Addy eat.

'Addy,' Susan said, 'Elizabeth said you came up from the city today? Do you have relatives up here?'

'Not that I know of,' said Addy, hunching her shoulders against more questions.

'Sweetheart,' said Videen, when Addy had finished the sandwich, 'I think we should take you to the doctor to be checked out. I know it's New Year's Eve, but I've had the same gynecologist for thirty-five years. If I can't pull some strings by now, when could I?' She let out a nervous, tinkly laugh. 'Or if you'd rather, we can go to the urgent care center at exit fifty-nine. It's only a mile away. I can't imagine there'd be much wait this afternoon. Tonight, maybe, but not right now.'

'I'm fine,' Addy said, keeping her eyes down and picking at the fruit. 'Thanks for the offer, but I'm good,' she added through a mouthful of cantaloupe. 'I appreciate your hospitality.'

Her grandmother had been a stickler for thanking hosts – she'd be proud of Addy for that. And horrified about how the rest of her life was turning out. Once her mother had shacked up with Duke, they no longer went to her grandmother's apartment for Sunday suppers. Addy spoke to her on the phone often in the beginning, but as her plan for fleeing Waterbury took shape, there had been less and less to say. She had thought of sending her grandma a postcard from Manhattan. She'd even written one out – 'Wish you were here', along with a big heart on the back, and on the front, a collage of all the cool places a tourist would want to visit. But that would only make her grandmother worry. And what if she gave it to her mother and they had the cops track her down from the postmark or whatever? In the end, she'd torn it into pieces and thrown it out.

Elizabeth's mother took Addy's hand. 'Where is home for you?'

'Mom, she'll talk about it when she's ready. Don't push her,' said Elizabeth.

But Videen continued. 'Things must have been terribly hard for you, if you decided to leave home.'

Addy grimaced and pulled her hand away, weighing whether and how to answer. Maybe she could say just enough to stop any more questions. 'My mother hooked up with this cretin. There was barely room in our palace for two.'

'Palace?' Elizabeth asked.

'That's white trash speak for trailer,' Addy said. 'Standard single wide, not much insulation, hot in the summer, cold in the winter. I slept on the couch, aka the living room.'

None of the women spoke for a moment.

'So your mom had a boyfriend. Sometimes it can be hard to split your love,' said Elizabeth's mother, smiling gently and reaching for Addy's hand again.

'It wasn't her love we were splitting, it was his. Or it would have been if I'd stayed,' she said, pulling away from Elizabeth's mother and clenching her hands in her lap.

Videen's brows furrowed. 'Oh honey, you're safe here with us. And maybe we can help you sort things out with your mom. Make sure she understands how you feel.'

Addy watched Elizabeth's face as she listened to her mother. Everything about them was so genteel on the outside, but she could tell that Elizabeth was upset with these questions.

'Mom, could I speak to you privately for a moment? It's a wedding detail – boring,' she explained to Addy and Susan, adding a big eye roll for emphasis. The two of them got up and moved into the hall.

Aunt Susan chatted about her cookie recipes and then pointed to the little TV on the counter that droned in the background. 'I'm a CNN junkie,' she said. 'Politicians are so whacked-out, I can't stop myself from watching. These dudes will fight over anything. And if no one's in Washington because of the holiday recess, CNN shows the reruns of the highlights. And the politicians all start their sentences with things like: "The American people think . . ." However they imagine they know what I'm thinking, they are almost always wrong.' She grinned. 'I bet they don't have much insight into your mind either.'

Addy nodded to be polite, though Susan might as well have been speaking in Eskimo; meanwhile, she strained to hear the private conversation in the hall.

'I know you like to think the best of people,' Elizabeth was saying to her mother, 'but are you listening to her? Her mother treated her terribly.'

Elizabeth's mother's lower lip trembled. 'I understand that she might have felt she had to leave, but I'm trying to help her explore all the possibilities. Running away, and getting pregnant, and then giving away a baby to a stranger is an extreme reaction.'

'But not so uncommon,' Elizabeth said, pointing to her own chest. 'You've always said that my biological mother made the choice she thought was best for me. Addy did the same for her baby. And besides, you're going to scare her off, pressing so hard when she barely knows us. If we ask too many questions – or the wrong questions – this girl will bolt. I'm dying to find out why Addy left her baby so abruptly – why would a mother push a newborn into a stranger's arms? – but we have to wait her out. And I'm scared for her.'

'And I'm scared for you,' Elizabeth's mother said.

Elizabeth nodded and, out of the corner of her eye, Addy thought she could see the two women hug.

'I know.' Elizabeth touched her mother's face. 'But please, give her the chance to trust us before we ask her anything more.'

Addy had felt alone many times over the past couple of years, but this was maybe the worst. These people might be arguing, but they at least were family. Leaving home – that was terrifying. Discovering she was pregnant – sickening. Having the baby in the subway – hideous. Giving it away – impossible. And showing up at the PATH train to find no sign of Rafe – unbearable. The list was long.

But this somehow felt worse, because she was being forced to face how freaking far from normal her life had become. The little bit she'd let Elizabeth and her mother know was reflected back at her in their horrified expressions, distorted and ugly like a funhouse mirror. She needed to get out.

The two women returned to the table, their faces tight enough to shatter into pieces.

'Sorry about that,' Elizabeth said. 'There are so many ridiculous details to unwind with this stupid unwedding.'

'I was wondering,' Addy said, 'if I could have my coat back?'

Elizabeth blinked. 'Your coat? Are you chilly? We can turn up the heat. The coat's out in the laundry room on the peg where you hung it.'

Addy shook her head, tears welling in her eyes.

Elizabeth's eyes widened and she touched her fingers to her lips. 'You mean the one wrapped around the baby?'

Addy nodded.

'I gave it to the police – or the paramedics, to be more accurate.' She bit her lip and paused for a moment. 'You know the baby's fine,' she added. 'I went by to see her in the hospital this morning. She's beautiful. And you were so brave to do that alone.'

'You don't have the coat?' Addy fought to keep from bursting into tears.

'Sweetheart, I'm sure we can find a coat that will fit you better than the one you were wearing. And be warmer too,' said Videen. 'I haven't been diligent about sorting out our old clothes. We've got boxes and boxes in the attic.'

Tears began trickling down Addy's cheeks. She hated to look weak but she couldn't help it.

'Maybe there was something special about that particular coat?' asked Aunt Susan.

Addy wiped her wet face on the paper napkin beside her plate, darkening the fur of the dancing reindeer. She cleared her throat; it felt like the opening had tightened smaller than a pencil so she could barely breathe. 'There was a phone number in the pocket.'

'Oh my gosh,' said Elizabeth. 'I never thought. The paramedics took the whole bundle, baby, coat, and all. But we – that's my friend Jillian and I – found the paper first, and tried to call the number later last night, thinking the person at the other end might know how to get in touch with you. I was so worried.'

Addy felt the first real flicker of hope she'd had in days. 'Did you talk to him? Do you have it, the number?'

'I don't think he's a nice man,' said Elizabeth's mother, 'not from what Lizzy told us.'

'I'm so sorry,' Elizabeth said, gesturing for her mother to stay quiet. 'He's dangerous. You could be in serious danger.'

'No,' said Addy. 'That's Rafe. He loves me. He'll keep me safe.'

But Elizabeth shook her head. 'I was sitting on a park bench this morning and a man came to sit next to me, asking about you. He said he was the baby's father, but before I could ask anything else, he was shot dead.' Her face whitened as she explained. 'I gave the number to the cops earlier today after the shooting. And then we stopped at the Guilford police station here in town and gave it to their detective, too. But after all that, I got scared and deleted it from my phone.'

'What did he look like?' Addy asked, shaking uncontrollably. Could Georgia have killed him so quickly? Was Rafe really dead?

'What shooting? What are you talking about?' asked Aunt Susan.

Elizabeth explained the events of the morning again, and how the man had dark hair and brown eyes.

Addy couldn't focus on the conversation after that, feeling so hopeless about losing her one connection to Rafe. It couldn't have been him who was shot, it couldn't. Lots of men had dark hair. And Rafe's eyes were blue, anyway. It had to have been someone else, someone who'd been sent by Rafe to help find her. Because he cared about her. She just needed to call and talk to him. But she couldn't go to the cops and ask for the number, no way. Snapshots of Rafe warning her exactly where and when to meet him went whirling through her mind until she got dizzy and thought she might puke. She stared at the little television to take her mind off her problems. She tried to imagine Elizabeth's mother watching funny reruns and laughing as she prepared the dinner for her family every night. But now it was tuned into Susan's news station, something about a disagreement in Washington.

She thought her eyes might bulge out of their sockets when Mr Les came on the screen. Even only a couple of inches high on the TV, it was hard to miss him. He was tall and handsome and he carried himself with a swagger, like some of the boys in high school back when she used to go to school. The kind who were sports stars and used their fame and good looks to get girls to go all the way under the bleachers. Addy stopped listening to Elizabeth describing the shooting to her aunt, her eyes glued to the program on which a woman was interviewing three men about a health insurance bill. They were arguing, talking over each other so none of the words were clear. Seeing him, remembering the nights she'd spent with him, made her skin crawl and her stomach churn. She couldn't look away. She was pinned to the screen like a butterfly specimen, terrified but unable to escape.

'Who is that?' she asked Susan, who was watching her watch the TV.

'Oh, those are our senators, the worst of the worst. I don't believe a word that comes out of their mouths.'

'Do you mind if I take that shower?' Addy asked abruptly. 'I feel sick . . . really . . . sick.' She clutched her stomach and tried to steady herself, but her breathing was ragged. She felt weak and dizzy.

'Of course, sweetheart,' said Elizabeth's mother, her voice filled with concern. 'Take some deep breaths – that's right.' She got up from the table and put a calming hand on Addy's shoulder as her breathing evened out again. 'Where are my manners?' Her nose wrinkled as if she had only now noticed that Addy didn't smell so great. 'I bet Elizabeth has some things in the attic that might fit you. You might have to roll up the pants. Give me a minute to dash upstairs and root around.'

Minutes later, Videen came back with a pile of clothing including a beautiful pink cashmere sweater, fleece sweatpants with elastic around the ankles, a knitted hat, leather gloves, and a pair of gray UGGs that looked like they'd hardly been worn. 'Here you go, I think you'll be a lot warmer with these things. Lizzy's feet must have grown two sizes the year she had to have these. And I brought a package of sanitary napkins too. In case you need them.'

She gestured for Addy to follow her down the hall. Then she pulled two plush yellow towels from a neat linen closet, added them to the pile, and directed her to the guest bathroom.

Addy locked the door and turned on the shower, hot as she could stand, and shucked off the clothes she'd been wearing. Not thinking of all that had happened, of Mr Les . . . she wouldn't let herself dwell on that. Squeezing a blob of shampoo from one of the expensive-looking blue bottles, she soaped up her hair into a beehive of bubbles and let the hot water beat on the knots in her shoulders. By the time she emerged from the shower, smelling like a hair salon she could never afford, she'd decided she couldn't stay here. They were asking too many questions. Nothing but trouble could come of this. And they didn't have what she needed most of all – Rafe's phone number.

She left the water running, toweled herself dry, and dressed in the clean clothing. After pulling the hat over her damp hair and grabbing the plastic bag containing her few clothes and Mr Les's phone, she pushed open the window over the toilet and slipped outside into the bushes.

Now she was on the run again with nothing but a few dollars. No plan. No one. The only thing she could think to do was go back to the grocery store where the town kids hung out. Though that was probably right where Elizabeth would come looking – if she bothered. But Georgia would be hunting her down for sure, and she'd proved that she could kill without warning. Maybe if she went back to town, somebody would invite her somewhere. It might cost her, but what were the other choices?

Or . . . wait. She'd already been invited. She checked her wrist. The inked address was faint, but still there. Caroline had said she lived near the town green, and Elizabeth had said the green was within walking distance.

# TWELVE

Elizabeth waited at the kitchen table with her mother and her aunt, sipping tea, wishing it was whiskey, and hoping she could coax Addy to stay overnight. It wasn't likely, she suspected, as the girl seemed overwhelmed by everything in their suburban life, including her mother and aunt – even watching the TV. Which made total sense, given where she'd come from and what she'd been through. And she seemed really disappointed about that dreadful Rafe. Distraught when she'd heard about the shooting. Was it possible he was a better man than he'd sounded on the phone, or on the bench next to her? If that was really him. She sighed, knowing wishful thinking when she saw it. Addy wasn't safe from whomever was tracking her, that was the frightening truth. Somehow, they would have to convince her to stay here, at least for now.

'She's taking an awful long time with that shower,' said Aunt Susan. She got up to add a pinch of salt into a pot of water that had begun boiling on the stove, and then stir in the dried macaroni.

'She's probably got a lot to wash away,' said Videen.

'That's not very supportive,' Elizabeth said, shooting a death glare at her mother.

'I meant the grit of the city and that dreadful subway bathroom. That's all.' Videen got up and joined her sister at the counter. 'How can I help?'

'How about if you grate and I'll start the white sauce?' Susan said. 'We're all a little unnerved about this poor girl turning up out of nowhere, aren't we? And the man shot right next to you, my God . . .'

Elizabeth stood up and crossed the room to squeeze her mother's shoulders. 'Sorry to snap.'

'It's OK. You've been through a lot this week.' Videen began to grate a pile of cheddar with the Monterey Jack and fontina cheeses that Susan had asked Elizabeth to buy at the grocery store.

'My top secret recipe,' Susan said with a laugh. 'You are sworn to secrecy.' She began to whisk the white sauce, using a big chunk of butter, spicy mustard, flour, and whole milk. Once all the ingredients were ready, she mixed the cheeses in, and stirred until the sauce was thick and pale yellow. Then she added the cooked macaroni, poured it into a buttered glass pan, and finally coated the top heavily with seasoned bread-crumbs and a generous layer of fresh Parmesan.

'What else are we serving?' she asked.

'A big green salad, green beans with slivered almonds from the reception, and more Christmas cookies. I told the bakery to send the cake to the homeless shelter in New Haven,' Videen said, checking Elizabeth's face for disappointment. 'I hoped you wouldn't mind.'

'Are you kidding? The only thing better than that would be delivering that cake directly to Kevin's face. I doubt the bakery would have done that,' Elizabeth said with a hollow laugh.

'Then we're good for now, until the doctor gets home. I've texted him about his ETA, but he hasn't answered.'

'Dad's in the doghouse again,' said Elizabeth to her aunt, adding a chuckle. 'You can tell when Mom calls him "the doctor".' She had to bite back the comment that almost followed: Would Kevin have called her 'the doctor', too? It would have been too pathetic to make that slip in front of her mother and her aunt.

The two women sat down and Videen glanced at the clock hanging over the sink. 'Elizabeth set the record for long showers when she was a teenager, but half an hour seems excessive. And her panicked breathing just before she went for the shower . . . What if her iron levels were so low from the birth that she passed out? Do you think we should check on her?'

Which Elizabeth knew meant 'you should check on her'. It might have been annoying but by now she was beginning to worry too. She got up and went down the hall to the guest bathroom. She could hear the water on full blast, and steam had begun to billow under the crack of the door. Elizabeth tapped on the white wood.

'Addy? Is everything OK?'

No answer. Now she began to fear the worst. Maybe the girl *had* lost so much blood during the delivery that she was weak and had fallen in the shower. Maybe she had some kind of raging infection. She was very pale. Maybe she'd fallen onto the drain and the water was creeping up the tub, stained a pale pink and close to drowning her. Like her mother, Elizabeth had always been a bit of a worrier, but becoming a medical student had exaggerated those tendencies. Nothing was incidental in medical school; all signs and symptoms led to the possibility of a dreaded disease.

She tapped louder. 'Addy?' She tried the knob but the door was locked.

She returned to the kitchen. 'Mom, I think we should break in. She's not answering. Maybe you were right: she fell and hit her head.' She shrugged, trying to show that she didn't really believe this. But she could see that her mother and aunt were feeling anxious too.

'I'll get the key,' her mother said. She hurried into her bedroom and returned with an old-fashioned skeleton key that she handed to Elizabeth. 'You should go in. You know her better than we do.'

'I hardly know her at all,' said Elizabeth. But she took the key, fitted it into the slot, and jiggled it until she heard the key on the other side drop to the tile floor. The door swung open. Clouds of steam mushroomed out of the bathroom. No one was in the shower. Addy's clothes, the old ones, lay in a heap on the floor. And the window over the toilet was open. Icy air from outside rushed in.

'She's gone,' Elizabeth said, turning to her mother and aunt, and clutching her stomach. 'She didn't even have a coat.'

'I hate to say this, but I hope she didn't steal anything,' said Aunt Susan, then retreated into the hall as she caught the fury on Elizabeth's face. 'She looked that desperate, that's all I mean. As well she might be . . .'

While her mother slammed the window shut, Elizabeth slipped into a pair of old garden clogs and dashed outside to see if she could catch the girl and talk her out of running. But even in the early darkness she could see the faint but distinctive footprints of the UGGs as they circled the house, marched down the snow along the driveway, and pointed into town. And it had started to snow again, big lazy flakes that looked like they wouldn't mind floating down all night and sticking hard to the frozen ground, creating havoc for New Year's travelers.

She nipped into the laundry room, brushed the snow off her head and stamped the slush off her clogs. 'No luck,' Elizabeth said when she returned to the kitchen. Then they reviewed the entire conversation, everything from the point when Elizabeth had coaxed her into the car at the grocery store to the moment she went into the bathroom.

'I can't think of anything we said that might have been offensive,' said Susan. 'We tried to make her feel at home, though I agree that was a stretch. This couldn't have felt like any home she's ever experienced. But still, were we enough to scare her off?'

'A night like this, she could freeze to death,' Videen said, her voice tight with worry. 'I feel terrible about all this. She asked to take a shower right after we were arguing in the hall.'

Elizabeth nodded. 'It's possible she heard us and had her feelings hurt. But I also think she was clearly upset that I didn't have her boyfriend's phone number. Besides that, we told her a man was shot right next to me,' she added with a shiver. 'Possibly this Rafe. I'm scared. You're scared. She probably is too.' She let herself feel it for a moment, the sheen of her own fear, like a layer of black ice hidden under the new snow.

'Maybe we should call the Guilford detective and let him know that Addy was here but now she's disappeared again.'

'Let's give it a little time,' said Elizabeth. 'I'm going to take the car, drive through town and see if I run across her.'

'And maybe check the Big Y, too,' said Videen. 'At least that would be familiar territory. How alien she must feel in this world. Just be careful driving!'

'Lock the doors behind me,' Elizabeth said as she pulled on her boots and coat. Then she settled into the driver's seat of her mother's car and turned on the heater. Poor Addy must be freezing. She drove slowly along the road that bisected the marsh, looking for a small dark shape, and remembering how she'd told Addy that it was an easy walk to town. But she'd meant in summer, when the air was balmy and the fireflies blinked like miniature lighthouses and her friends waited on the green to gossip and strike disinterested poses for any boys who might be driving by.

Seeing no sign of the girl, she kept driving, circling the green, where another handful of stores had turned out their lights, leaving the town looking more abandoned than festive. Then she continued north to Route 1 to the Big Y grocery store. They were most likely to stay open late on New Year's Eve. And maybe Addy had found a hiding space and hunkered down there for the night. She parked the car and ran to the entrance, where the electric doors whooshed open to a display of drooping poinsettias in pots covered with red foil whose price had been slashed to ninety-nine cents. She searched up and down every aisle and then went into the ladies' bathroom, looking under the stalls, surprising one old lady who shrieked in dismay.

Feeling discouraged and worried, she returned to her mother's car and fired up the engine. At least the girl wasn't hungry; at least her stomach was full for now. And she was clean. And she had warmer clothes, except for a coat. She leaned her forehead against the steering wheel. The truth was that she felt awful about Addy disappearing. Somehow, she and her family had failed to understand her. They had failed to bridge the gap between her life and theirs. How could they have? But they should have tried harder. She'd been too busy squabbling with her mother about how to help Addy. She wasn't thinking clearly after the events of the past few days. The shock of seeing all those gifts, all the detritus of the wedding, hadn't helped a bit. Still, she should have stepped outside her own pain to think about Addy, whose problems were much more serious.

By the time she got home, the small white Christmas lights on the tree and over the mantel had been turned on. The kitchen was perfumed with the smell of the cheesy casserole baking, and her mother and aunt were finishing the salad. They both looked up expectantly.

Elizabeth shook her head. 'She's vanished.'

'Oh honey, you did what you could for her.' Her mother crossed the room to give her a hug, which felt almost worse. Everything she had, including the support of her family, reminded her of what Addy was lacking. 'Your father will be home in half an hour. Then we should talk to the detective.'

'We can wait until he gets here if you want, but I should be the one to call. Dad doesn't have a clue about what's been happening.'

'You're right,' said Videen, slumping into a kitchen chair. 'He isn't going to be happy about this either.'

'Who is? I'm going upstairs to unpack and sort through my email,' Elizabeth said. She picked up the small suitcase she'd left in the hall when she first arrived, and trudged upstairs to her childhood bedroom.

She pushed the door open with one foot, dreading the sight of her wedding gown inside the closet even more than the alarming display of gifts. But it wasn't hanging from the top of the door in all its lace and satin glory as she'd expected. Someone – her mother probably, maybe with an assist from Aunt Susan – had had the foresight and kindness to put it away where Elizabeth wouldn't have to face it. She needed to remember to thank her mom – Elizabeth might have been the one dumped at the altar, but her mother was shouldering a lot of the fallout, both actual and emotional. She'd thank her father too – they'd all been humiliated, but he was the one who'd ended up paying for the disaster. If she ever got married for real in the future – a big if – she'd insist they elope.

She dropped the suitcase on the floor and her backpack on the desk and pulled out her laptop. Maybe through the wonders of Google she could find a clue to Addy's background that might help explain where she'd run to. Even if she only knew her first name. She plugged the computer in and fired up the screen. While she waited, she scrolled through the text messages piling up on her phone. Sixteen from her girlfriends. Four of those were from Jillian. She'd deal with all of that later.

She sat down at the desk and began by Googling the shooting in the park near her apartment. Almost instantly an article from the Associated Press came up.

> *Man Dead in Bellevue South Park*
> *Associated Press. Last updated 5:30 pm. December 31.*
> *New York, N. Y. – Authorities say one man is dead after a shooting in Bellevue South Park earlier this morning. Police say the victim was shot from a distance while talking with a medical school student who resides in the nearby apartments. Yesterday this witness turned a newborn infant over to the New York City Police Department, stating that a teenage girl had handed the baby to her outside the Delancey Street subway station. Police are investigating a possible connection between the baby and the shooting.*
> *The victim has been identified as Mitchell Spignola. Police are asking that any witnesses in the case please come forward.*

A headshot of the man who'd sat next to her on the bench accompanied the news. So it wasn't Addy's Rafe after all – unless this was an alias. At the time the photo was taken – a mugshot? – this man had short dark hair, a small gold hoop earring in one earlobe, and the top of a blurry blue tattoo of a snake climbing out of his T-shirt and up the side of his neck. She shivered, remembering the horror of that moment. And the moments of fear that had come before it. If Addy's boyfriend was involved with this man, she was in a lot of trouble. They all might be. Why was finding Addy so important that someone had been murdered for trying to locate her? Everyone knew where the baby was, so why bother with Addy?

She typed the man's name, Mitchell Spignola, into the Google search bar, but came up with nothing. Next she Googled 'New York Safe Haven laws'. She was still bothered by the question of whether Addy would be in legal trouble for leaving the baby if the authorities found her.

The first link to surface was the website of the man who'd pushed for the adoption of Safe Haven laws in New York City.

He'd been an EMT for many years, and after finding one too many abandoned, dead infants, had developed a way for desperate new mothers to turn their children over without penalty. He reported that many of these women denied the fact of their pregnancy right up to the moment of birth, even to themselves, or disguised their condition and then delivered their infants in secrecy. Without prenatal care or professional assistance at the birth, both the infants and their mothers were at risk.

Elizabeth forced herself to imagine this girl hunkered down in the subway restroom, wracked with the pains of labor. Why hadn't she called for help? Was she afraid of her mother's anger? Or was she in some other kind of trouble? Where exactly had she run from? Was the man she and Jillian called later that night really the father as he claimed? It seemed more and more unlikely. What was the connection with the man who'd been shot? Why hadn't she kept her own baby?

Finally her mind pushed into her own dark space: her biological mother. Her parents had always been clear that she was adopted, but didn't discuss the matter any further. When Elizabeth was ten, she'd finally asked Videen, the only mother she'd known, why she'd been given away as a baby.

'Your mom knew she couldn't take care of you, give you the family that you deserve,' Videen had replied. 'And your father and I wanted a child so badly. We never stopped hoping . . . and then you came along. When they put you in my arms, it was the happiest day of my life.'

Elizabeth could picture her mother's tremulous smile, the look in her eyes that had begged her not to ask any more questions. And when she'd reached her teens, and found her parents unbearably restrictive and old fashioned, she'd only ever imagined using the sharpest weapon in her adolescent arsenal: 'You're not my real mother.' She would never have had the nerve to say it.

Her phone rang. Olivia Lovett, the reporter. Elizabeth's fingers felt cold as granite as she fumbled to answer.

'I'm out in your driveway. I wondered if it would be OK if I came in to talk.'

# THIRTEEN

Addy took a left out of Elizabeth's driveway and walked along the river, feeling the damp cold all the way through the borrowed clothes to her skin and down to her bones. She passed large boats wrapped in white plastic like hulking carcasses. The people in this town must be loaded with money. Their houses were mostly covered with white clapboard, windows and doors hung with green spruce wreaths and red bows, rather than the crazy blowup Santas, abominable snowmen and blinking icicle lights that she would have seen in her city. She couldn't help wondering, did her mother help her grandmother with her decorations? Or did her house remain dark through this season, without Addy there to haul the boxes down from the attic? The thought of her grandmother alone, in her tiny drafty apartment, hoping for a phone call, brought the sting of tears to her eyes. She wanted so badly to see her again, but could she ever bear to tell her about the things that had happened since she left? She couldn't.

She trudged past a few freshly painted red barns. They looked like barns that rich people used for show, not the faded working buildings outside the center of her town, where you could shop at the feed and seed or the IGA market, or have a cup of strong coffee at the corner shop and come out with a powerful smell of bacon permeating your clothing.

Finally she reached the town green with its tall Christmas tree set in the center, colored lights strung in neat loops and a white star perched on the top. But the tree was surrounded by a flimsy red fence corralling the snowman, reindeer, and angel figures inside. Protecting them from what? Everything in this town seemed perfect and safe, overseen by a perfect white church at the far end with four tall columns and a steeple decorated like a gingerbread house. Even the statue of a soldier in the center of the green carried his own decoration, a green wreath with a red bow, this one beginning to brown around the edges. *Antietam*, his inscription read.

The wind picked up, whistling through trees standing bare and black against the gray sky. If it were a warmer day, she would sit on the bench facing the center of the green to get her bearings and weigh her options, which were few. But it wasn't warm, so she just kept slogging through the snow until she came across the street name that Caroline had written on her arm. She turned left, looking for the house number. These homes were smaller, but cute and snug. A large black mailbox told her she was at the right place, though the outside lights weren't on except for the colored Christmas lights, and there were no cars in the driveway. It didn't look like a party.

She crouched in the bushes near the drive, studying this small white cape house, which was minimally decorated for Christmas. The railing along the steps to the front door was strung with big, old-fashioned colored bulbs, half of them burnt out. A fir wreath hung on the door, its needles tinged brown and beginning to shed, and the red ribbon at the bottom fading to rose. Not quite as shabby as her mother's trailer would have looked, but not perfect like Elizabeth's family's place either. The residents of this house had tried to dress up their home for the holidays, even if they weren't quite able to carry it off.

She moved a little closer and hovered in the shelter of a large holly bush beside the concrete stairs leading to the front stoop, stomping her feet quietly. She was freezing. The walk from Elizabeth's house to town had been longer than she'd imagined, and her wet hair had frozen into an icy sheet by the time she'd reached the road. Then it had taken some searching to find the address that matched the one scribbled on her wrist – she certainly wasn't going to draw attention to herself by knocking on doors and asking strangers for directions. As she peered around the bush to look again for any signs of a party, an automatic floodlight blinded her. Either she had to summon the courage to knock or she had to move on before a neighbor reported a prowler to the local police.

She took a deep breath, crept up the stairs, and banged

the doorknocker. If a parent or anyone other than Caroline answered, she would run. She heard the thud of footsteps inside the hall and her heart pounded in response. Every muscle tensed and she could almost feel the blood coursing through her veins; she was ready to fly if necessary.

The door swung open and Caroline's friendly face appeared, first looking surprised, then wary. She was wearing tight jeans, a messy ponytail, and a plaid flannel shirt several sizes too big that had been buttoned wrong so it hung askew.

Addy pulled off her hat and mustered a smile. 'We met at the grocery store? You invited me over? I'm Addy.'

'Addy! I didn't recognize you at first. You must be freezing to death – you look like a popsicle, poor thing. We weren't sure you'd come.' Caroline grabbed Addy's hand and drew her inside. The hallway was paneled in dark wood, as though she had landed in a cabin in the woods. To the right, a set of worn carpeted stairs led up to the second floor.

'Party's up in my room,' said Caroline, waving her to follow.

As they reached the top of the stairs, Addy could hear the beat of music, and the muffled sound of kids laughing. And almost certainly she smelled both marijuana and patchouli.

'Don't worry,' Caroline said, 'no adult types are home. Nor are they expected.' She grinned as she pushed open the first door off the landing. 'Everyone, this is Addy. Addy, meet my friends.' A chorus of sleepy hellos came from the kids around the room, and someone handed her a beer.

The bedroom was cozy small, big enough for Caroline's canopied bed, a desk by the window, a bureau, and a tall bookcase. And crowded with teens – maybe ten, she guessed – mostly lounging on the floor. Once Caroline closed the door and replaced the towel along its bottom, the only light came from a collection of flickering candles. A haze of smoke – cigarettes, incense, pot, and hash, Addy thought now – hung in the room. In the combination of thick smoke and dim light, their faces seemed almost blurry. Addy waved away an enormous glass bong; the one thing she'd learned over the last year was to stay on her toes, on guard. Because terrible things could happen at any moment. And did. Besides that, she felt so tired, so battered.

Caroline pointed to the boy in her bed: 'You met Randy earlier at the store.'

Addy watched her slide back onto the bed where Randy was waiting. 'I missed you,' he said, covering Caroline's face and neck with sloppy kisses. 'Where have you been?' He began to unbutton her flannel shirt and push it off her shoulders, leaving only a white lacy camisole in its place. Caroline giggled as she batted his hands away. 'Come on, dude, it's ten degrees outside.' She pulled the yellow flowered quilt up to cover them both to the neck.

'Did you just move here?' asked one of the boys slouched against the bookshelves lining Caroline's wall. Addy slid down to the floor beside him, noticing the titles on the shelves. Caroline was big on Harry Potter and mysteries – or she had been at some point. Addy couldn't remember the last book she'd read. Or even the last time she'd seen more than one book at a time, except in a library. Maybe at her grandparents' house, and that would have been a full set of old Encyclopedia Britannicas, bought for a low price because it had been missing volume M.

'I'm just visiting,' Addy said, hoping her disinterested tone would discourage more questions.

'Visiting from where?' the boy asked.

'New York City.'

'Cool! I love the city. Maybe you could show us around when we come in one day? The times I've gone in with my parents they've only taken me to museums. Bor-ing. Oh yeah, and the Statue of Freaking Liberty. The waves were so friggin' rough that day, half the people on the boat were puking their guts out before we got there.'

'Sure,' said Addy. She felt the gulf between them yawn wider, certain he'd never believe the *tourist destinations* where she'd spent the last year. She guessed he was a little older than she was, but not wiser at all.

One of the other kids – a thin girl with waist-length yellow hair – cracked the window an inch or two to let in some fresh air. 'Are you sure your father isn't coming home? It feels kind of weird to be here.'

'He's working the whole night,' Caroline said.

As the smoke cleared a bit and Addy adjusted to the dim light, she saw there were more kids in the room than she'd first thought. The girls around her were entwined with boys, whose main goal seemed to be loosening and removing as much clothing as they could get away with. The girls were laughing and pushing their wandering hands away, but then kissing them so it started all over again. It all seemed like a game to them, a game they found fun.

Addy felt her face get hot. She dug her fingers into Caroline's soft blue carpet, unsure where to look. This public pawing was not like her own experience with men, if these boys could be called men. In her world, everything happened once the doors were closed and locked. Every once in a while Georgia would have a customer who asked her to send out two of the girls at a time. The company on the way to the hotel and back was welcome, but the time in those rooms – unbearable.

Back at Georgia's place, the girls never spoke of those nights again. But a night like that bonded them tightly; she would have done anything to protect those girls. She would never have left one of them alone with a man like that. Like she shouldn't have left Heather. She pressed her hands to her face, wishing she'd never come. But then where else would she go?

'What's it like to live here?' Addy asked the boy who loved the city, to get her mind off what was going on around her. And the memories that had come flashing in.

'It's cool,' he said. 'If you like boring.'

He grinned, a goofy smile like the black Labrador retriever that lived up the street from her grandmother.

'But this is fun, right?' He took her hand and began to trace the curve of her arm with his fingers. She pulled away and stood up.

'Any chance I could get another beer?' She slugged down what was left in the brown bottle she still held and set it on the windowsill, feeling queasy. She didn't want another beer, she just wanted him to leave her alone. But she took the can that someone handed her and sat again, this time leaving more space between herself and the boy.

'I've got the munchies,' said a girl across the room. She

had beautiful, shiny chestnut hair and a red cashmere sweater. 'What do you have in your fridge, Caroline?'

Caroline's head appeared from under the quilt. 'Go ahead and take a look. We haven't been to the grocery store in a while though. There's a half bag of Oreos in the freezer. Or how about we order pizza or Chinese?'

'Not Chinese,' said the girl. 'My mom says they use actual I kid you not dog meat at the Happy Garden. Disgusting.'

'I'll call Antonio's,' said the boy who was with her. He pulled out his phone and ordered six pizzas. 'Three meat lovers, one sausage and peppers, one plain cheese, and one veggie all the way.' He looked around at the other kids. 'That should cover it, right, Randy?'

'Yep,' said Caroline's boyfriend. 'Do you think they'd deliver a couple of cases of beer?'

Caroline smirked. 'There's not a single one of us that's legal. And New Year's Eve? They will definitely be carding. But my stepdad hides a big bottle of rum behind the cereal. Why don't you bring that up along with the cookies?' she said to the girl with the munchies.

The boy who had ordered went around to the others, collecting money for the pizza. Addy had never been with a group of kids who had had the money or the guts to order whatever they wanted and have it delivered to someone's parents' house. Kids in her hometown might get an older kid, home for the holidays, to buy a couple of six packs of cheap beer. But then they'd go off into the woods to drink them, maybe build a fire to keep warm while they gulped them down.

Randy rolled on top of Caroline, kissing her in a way that made Addy even more nauseous. He slid the thin straps of the lacy camisole off Caroline's shoulders and pushed them down her arms. Addy, probably along with the rest of their friends, saw a flash of her breasts. Then he began to hump her under the covers, struggling to get his pants down, or so it looked.

Caroline tried to twist away. 'That's enough,' she said.

He leaned in to kiss her again, his hands roaming her chest.

'I said, cut it out,' said Caroline, this time with a note of what Addy thought was panic in her voice.

Flooded with a sudden rush of adrenalin, Addy shot up from her seat on the floor and flew over to the bed. She grabbed the kid by his pathetic man-bun ponytail and pulled him off her new friend. 'You heard her – we all did. She said that was enough.' She didn't even recognize the sound of her own voice, fierce and rough and angry.

All the kids in the bedroom fell silent, and Caroline pulled on the plaid shirt, not meeting anyone's eyes.

'That's one way to kill a buzz,' muttered the kid as he sat up, batting off Addy's hand. 'Why did you invite her here anyway?'

Addy backed away from the bed and began to gather her belongings.

'Come on, she didn't mean anything by it,' Caroline said, coaxing him to return to bed. 'I'm OK,' she said to Addy, adding a smile, 'it's just Randy. He gets carried away. Please don't go.' And she sent Addy a beseeching look that reminded her of one of those girls in the hotel rooms and the bond they shared. She sat back down on the floor.

# FOURTEEN

Elizabeth ran down the stairs and peered through the peephole in the front door. The woman on the stoop did resemble the photo of Olivia Lovett that she'd seen in the *Post* – black hair, thin pink lips, a delicate nose. But after the last two days, she was feeling jumpy. 'Can I see your license?' Elizabeth looked over her shoulder at a white car with NY plates parked in the driveway.

'Sure.' The woman dug in her purse, a leopard-patterned, soft-sided bag – a tragic fashion faux pas, her friend Jillian would have said – and held the license up to the peephole.

Elizabeth unlocked the door and cracked it open, keeping the chain in place. 'Sorry, I don't really know you.'

'Understood,' said Olivia, her expression sympathetic. 'No problem.' She shivered on the stoop, her faux mink hat covered in a layer of snowflakes. 'Do you mind if I come in for a minute? It's about Addy. I'm worried.'

Elizabeth hesitated, then took a step back and opened the door wider. She'd let her in to hear her out, but nothing more. Olivia stomped the snow off her boots and stepped inside, taking care to stay on the rug rather than drip on the wideboard oak floor.

'Who is it?' asked Videen from the kitchen. 'Teresa said she might stop over to give you a hug, but I'm surprised she came out in this weather.' Her expression changed from welcome to worry as she came down the hall.

'I'm Olivia Lovett,' said the reporter, reaching around Elizabeth to pump Videen's hand. 'I work for the *Post* and I spoke with your daughter earlier today. About the homeless girl with the subway baby.'

'About Addy,' said Videen, her face shaded with concern. 'She isn't here any longer.'

Olivia pulled her hat off and shook out her hair, her eyes lasering in on Elizabeth's face like a hound on scent. 'So she did follow you out. I had the feeling she might. But how did she know where to find you?'

'Wait a minute,' said Elizabeth. 'How did *you* find me? Why are you here?'

'Like I said, I'm concerned about Addy,' said Olivia, ignoring the question. 'Not only her physical and mental well-being, though those are a worry too. I believe she's in danger.'

Elizabeth and her mother exchanged a glance. 'We don't want more publicity,' Videen said. 'My daughter was already put in grave danger because of your reporting.'

'I'm so sorry about the scare this morning,' Olivia said. 'I don't think you're in danger, though I could be wrong. And I'm quite sure Addy is. I know you'll want to help if you can.'

'I suppose we can give her a cup of tea if she's traveled all this way,' said Videen. Then, alerting to the sound of a bass rumble in the kitchen and Aunt Susan's answering murmur, she added, 'Uh-oh, your father's home. He'll be starving and grumpy, I'm sure. I'm sorry, but we're about to take the macaroni and cheese out of the oven.'

'I'd love that,' said Olivia. 'It smells divine in here. I don't cook myself, but I definitely eat. Luckily takeout food abounds in the city.'

Her mother met Elizabeth's gaze and shrugged. She didn't have it in her to be rude enough to turn even this pushy woman away into the cold and snow. Olivia brushed past her and followed Videen toward the kitchen before Elizabeth could protest that her mother hadn't meant to tender an invitation.

If the dinner at her family's kitchen table wasn't the oddest meal on record, Elizabeth thought it certainly made the top ten. Her mother fluttered around like a demented butterfly, unable to keep herself from trying to make Olivia Lovett feel at home, though Elizabeth was quite certain she didn't want her here. But her grandmother's training in being hospitable to strangers won out. And her father, who'd been told the minimum, looked ready to explode at the idea of having a reporter from the *New York Post* at their table, sharing macaroni and salad – not a shred of meat to be found – on New Year's Eve.

And really, why was Olivia here? She hadn't made this very clear, and Elizabeth couldn't help feeling stalked.

Partway through the meal, her father's fork clattered onto his plate and he glared at Olivia. 'Explain to me again the story that you are chasing, and why in the world you think you're going to find insight about it in my home, with my family, on New Year's Eve.'

But Olivia just grinned, as if she'd seen a lot worse than this crabby suburban doctor. And she probably had. 'I thought Addy might try to find Elizabeth and tail her out here if she read the police report, and it sounds like I was right.'

'Surely you didn't arrange to plant my name in that article so she would follow me here?' Elizabeth asked. 'And put my entire family in danger too?'

'Oh my goodness, certainly not,' Olivia said. 'I had nothing to do with that. I'm just not surprised that she turned up. She's the one these people want.'

'What people?' Elizabeth's father shouted. 'Where? What are you talking about?' He stared around the table.

Elizabeth bit her lip and said quietly, 'Addison was here for an hour or so. We gave her a sandwich and let her take a shower and then she vanished. She was looking for her boyfriend's phone number. Which I no longer have.'

They glared at each other.

Olivia smoothly changed the subject. 'This mac and cheese is out of this world. One of my pet peeves about New Year's is how everyone thinks the food should be fancy-dancy and three times as expensive to match. And who wants to stay up till midnight anyway, to kiss some toad you wish you'd never agreed to go out with? So you drink more cheap champagne and then start off the first day of the year with a massive headache and who knows who in your bed?'

Videen looked horrified, but Aunt Susan let loose a gale of laughter. 'You called it. New Year's Eve has to be the worst date night for single gals ever, after Valentine's Day, of course.'

Olivia held up her hand for a high five and they chuckled together. Then Olivia held a hand up to Elizabeth.

Elizabeth shook her head, not eager to join this club of perennially single women. Aunt Susan had been married and divorced and didn't seem interested in taking another plunge. Olivia looked to be in her early forties, but no ring on her finger. She wished she'd figured out earlier that her relationship with Kevin wasn't going to go the distance, rather than embarrassing herself and her family in front of just about everyone they knew.

'I'm dead serious,' Elizabeth's father broke in. His face had turned red enough that the web of broken veins on his nose showed through the skin. 'Why are you here?'

'So here's the thing,' said Olivia, her face serious now too. 'Because of the shooting in the park, I think we can safely assume that someone's after Addy, and they will stop at nothing until they get her. I don't know the why exactly, or who the someone is, but the more we know, the safer she is. Not to mention the baby. And the safer your daughter will be, too.'

She looked the doctor right in the eyes, and then nodded in Elizabeth's direction, as if to say, *we are all in this together, protecting your precious daughter.* Elizabeth felt a buzz of fear course through her, followed by a quick vision of the man who'd been shot. Why had she insisted Elizabeth wasn't in danger, but then changed her tune? She took a gulp of wine, stood up, and began to clear away the empty dishes.

'You will excuse me if I'm having some difficulty believing your appearance is related to my daughter's well-being, rather than the possibility of landing a big tabloid story,' said her father.

Which was lurking in Elizabeth's mind too, not that she would have said it so bluntly.

'What could she possibly have that's worth anything?' Elizabeth asked, looking up from arranging plates in the dishwasher. 'Addy showed up here in those exceptionally dreadful clothes, carrying a plastic bag with not much in it. The baby is either in the hospital or with a foster parent, so that can't be it.' She felt her shoulders tighten, now flashing on Addy's tiny infant wrapped in the first godawful coat, even worse than the car coat she'd worn to Connecticut. 'Maybe she knows someone's secret?'

'Either she knows something, or she has something. That's the way it looks to me,' Olivia said. 'The bad news is, someone else wants it too, because why else would they shoot the man who'd been talking to you?'

Elizabeth froze. She knew this, of course, but it hadn't been said that way, aloud, before. Someone very ruthless was after Addy. And Elizabeth was an important connection to the girl.

Her mother came over to stand beside Elizabeth and put a hand on her wrist, squeezing gently and murmuring: 'The police will figure it out.'

'For the last time,' said Elizabeth's father to Olivia. 'Why are you here?'

'I'll tell you.' Olivia brought Elizabeth's parents and aunt up to date on what she knew about Addy's case so far, which was not much, really. She described the articles she'd written about other homeless girls and how some of the outpouring of support had been way beyond what she'd expected, showing the burst of intense warmth that had convinced Elizabeth to take her call early Saturday morning. A decision she now regretted.

'Some people are only glad it's not them on the streets, or even worse, their daughters,' said Olivia. 'Others unfortunately assume these girls brought their troubles on themselves.'

'Blaming the victims for their horrendous circumstances,' said Videen. 'We even see that sometimes at the local food pantry.'

Olivia nodded. 'It's not a simple matter of pulling up your bootstraps and finding a job and dragging yourself out of the muck. Sometimes a difficult family background is a greater weight than we lucky people could ever imagine. We're all born with varying degrees of privilege – or lack of it.'

'In Addy's case, maybe more bad luck than anything at all,' said Aunt Susan. 'Her mother sounds like a disaster, and she never mentioned her father, did she?'

Elizabeth's father broke in, his hands gripping the edge of the table as he addressed Olivia. 'You seem like a nice lady. But be careful you don't take everything this girl says as the truth. There's always another side to any story. She could very well be a druggie or a thief, sussing this house out for her compatriots and bamboozling three lovely but gullible ladies.' He waved his hand at his family. Elizabeth saw her mother pinch her lips together – even if she agreed at some level, she would not appreciate his rudeness.

'We're not idiots, Dad,' Elizabeth broke in. 'Though you might not realize that about me from looking at the mess in the living room. I know I've made some mistakes lately, but none of us appreciates being called gullible.'

Her father growled in response. 'If I so much as see that cretin on this property, he's likely to find a set of strong hands around his neck.'

Elizabeth shook her head and shot Olivia a grimace. 'My ex called off our wedding—' She stopped, suddenly imagining the details of her personal life folded into one of the reporter's stories.

'Then you're probably better off without him. If I could, I have a few more questions,' said Olivia. 'You mentioned Addy showed up here looking for Rafe's phone number, correct? And then she had something to eat and went to take a shower.'

'She left rather abruptly,' added Susan.

'What were you talking about right before that?' Olivia opened her small laptop.

Elizabeth met her mother's eyes, and then shifted her gaze back to Olivia. 'No taking notes on this. We'll talk if you're trying to help Addy, but not for another story.'

Olivia nodded slowly and closed the laptop. 'Go ahead.'

'We were arguing a little bit,' her mother admitted. 'My daughter thought I was being hard on the girl, and I probably was. Pushing too hard to understand why she ran away and why she handed her new baby to Elizabeth – someone she'd never seen in her life! It's mind-boggling, really.'

'And I was trying to entertain her in the meanwhile by talking about what was on the TV,' said Susan.

'Which was what?' Olivia asked.

'Reruns of important moments in Washington over the past year.' She let loose a peal of easy laughter. 'It's ridiculous – those senators can be such idiots. For most people, seeing them once would be plenty, but I'm a news junkie.' She took a sip of her wine. 'Now that you bring it up, that is the moment when she asked about a shower. And she said she felt sick. She looked panicky . . . her breathing wasn't right. We all thought her reaction was related to the argument, but maybe not.'

'What exactly were you watching?' asked Olivia again, leaning forward, fingers fidgeting on the table as if she wished she were typing.

'It was a panel of senators grilling someone about the healthcare crisis. I can't imagine she would have been inter-ested in that subject. Though she did ask about them.'

'What about them?'

'She just asked who they were and I told her they were senators.'

'Do you happen to have anything here that belongs to Addy?' Olivia asked.

Elizabeth wondered whether she planned to sniff them like a search and recovery dog.

'We have the clothing she was wearing when she arrived. She left it behind when she bolted out the window.' Videen's cheeks colored a ruddy pink. 'More specifically, I already put it out in the trash. The clothes were filthy and worn thin, and honestly, smelled to high heaven.'

Elizabeth's father broke in, glowering at Olivia. 'Where are you spending the night? With the way the snow was coming down on my way out from New Haven, you should probably get to where you're going.'

Elizabeth didn't admire her father's abruptness, but she had to admit this woman made her uncomfortable. Question after question after question, drilling down until she found . . . what?

'I have a reservation at the Comfort Inn,' Olivia said.

He pushed his chair away from the table and stood. 'I'm going to show our visitor out and lead her to town so she doesn't slide off the road and end up in the marsh.' He pulled Elizabeth into a quick hug, then strode out of the kitchen and down the hall before she could see his face. Disappointment, anger, sadness – it was probably all reflected there.

Olivia shrugged, said goodbye to the women, and followed him out. 'I'll phone or text you if I hear anything about Addy,' she called back.

Elizabeth finished stacking dinner plates, feeling sick to her stomach. Whether it was because of the wedding or the girl or the reporter, the macaroni sat like a lead brick in her belly. She rinsed her hands in the sink. 'Speaking of getting where we're going, anyone want to help me tackle some of those gifts after we clean up? They aren't going to send themselves back.'

Once the kitchen was spotless, Elizabeth walked slowly to the living room, the dread inside her welling. As with the other wedding planning details, it seemed like eons ago that she and Kevin had struggled to choose the gifts for their registry. The silver had been easy – Videen had wanted so badly for them to purchase the same ornate pattern that she'd had as a new bride, and her mother before her. 'That way, when your father and I go, you'll get ours too, and it will all match and you'll have something to remember us by.'

'Game, set, and match,' she'd said to Kevin. 'She's pulled the dead parent card.'

'But it will be my house too,' he'd argued, so she'd had to bow to his wishes to select a more masculine china pattern for the tablewear than the antique roses she liked. In this case, she'd actually loved his choice – a parade of jungle animals and palm trees around the rim of the plates – not that she'd given him the satisfaction of telling him so. She'd been too annoyed. A deep sigh escaped from somewhere low in her gut: all these small signs of an impending disaster, but she had failed to pay enough attention to add them up.

'Where do we even start?' she asked when her aunt and mother joined her.

'It doesn't really matter,' said Aunt Susan in a brisk voice. She sank into a white plush chair next to the hearth, in front of an empty space where Kevin's Christmas stocking had hung. 'It all has to be done so just pick a pretty package. And I've brought a nice bottle of wine because I bet we'll need it.' She twisted the top off a bottle of white, filled three glasses and passed them around.

'I've got the list here of all the names and addresses,' said Videen. 'If you write the notes, Susan and I can pack things up and we'll get done faster.' She picked up a yellow-lined pad from the glass-topped coffee table next to the couch.

'I find it spooky,' Elizabeth said, 'that the reporter followed me from New York and showed up here. No wonder Dad was so suspicious.'

'But it's more than human interest this time,' said Aunt Susan. 'I think the girl's in serious trouble.'

Elizabeth heaved a sigh. 'Her life makes my problems look pretty small. Even returning all these gifts.'

'Big projects always seem overwhelming at first,' said Aunt Susan. 'At the beginning, I always doubt I can fight my way out of the jungle. But good things happen if I take one loose end at a time, unravel and follow it. And that's what we'll do here too.

'And maybe we could come up with answers about Addy's case the way the reporter would have,' she added. 'We have an advantage because we are the ones who actually met her. You, twice.' She pointed at Elizabeth. 'For example, we can go back to that TV clip and see exactly who was on it. Maybe it was the politicians, though I think it more likely she was responding to your discussion about the baby. She must feel gut-punched by mixed feelings. And how would she ever meet a senator?'

'I can't imagine.' Elizabeth grabbed the gift right in front of her. It was a large rectangle wrapped in shiny white paper with polka-dotted blue ribbons meeting on the top in a burst of bows. The small card attached below was written in spidery silver calligraphy. *Congratulations Elizabeth and Kevin!* the outside message crowed. Inside, her great aunt had written: *We are thrilled beyond words that you two have found each other! With much love from Aunt May and Uncle John.*

Elizabeth groaned.

'That bad?' asked Aunt Susan.

Elizabeth tore the note off the box and handed it to her. 'Yes.' She pulled her hair back into a ponytail and let it go. 'May, my father's only living aunt,' she explained to Susan. 'She had me bring Kevin over for an inspection last year. And then she pulled me aside afterward and said I couldn't have chosen better. Let's face it, she'll be devastated.'

Videen smoothed her hands over her tweed slacks and grimaced. 'She wasn't the most gracious guest we phoned about the cancellation.'

Susan snickered. 'But not the worst either, you said. And besides, she's not the one who would have to spend a lifetime with that turkey. She chose her own gobbler.'

All the women laughed. Elizabeth selected the top sheet of white vellum notepaper engraved with her full name *Elizabeth Warren Brown*, and dashed off the note expressing her regret about the trouble over the wedding, and her thanks for the generous gift of the coffee maker that she was now returning. She slapped the note on the coffee table. 'One down, two hundred and forty-four to go. Next time it's me and the guy with a Justice of the Peace,' she said grimly. 'And we don't invite anyone. Should there be a next time.' She pulled another package onto her lap, this one enormous, and papered in silver. It was the juicer she'd been lusting after. 'Do you think I could keep this one? Maybe tell the Crooks that I need it to use on Kevin's fingers?'

Videen smiled and shook her head, then changed the subject. 'How do you imagine Olivia was able to get those other young girls to share so much information publicly?'

'Smart questions, asked as if the answers mattered,' Aunt

Susan suggested. 'How did they end up on the street? What were they running from? We'd probably be surprised at how openly they might talk if they felt someone truly cared. There'd be a variety of reasons.'

'An abusive family, of course,' said Elizabeth, looking up from penning her regrets about the juicer.

'Getting in trouble with the law for drugs,' said Videen.

'A pregnancy the girl didn't know how to handle,' added Aunt Susan. 'That seems to be part of Addy's story anyway.' She got up to fetch her computer, which lay open on the dining room table.

'Here it is, I think,' she said after a few moments, handing her laptop over to Elizabeth. It was a newsclip on the TV station's Twitter feed. 'I believe this was what was on TV when Addy asked to shower.'

Elizabeth nodded, peering at the screen, then gave the computer back to her aunt. 'Maybe we have to figure out if any of these men have connections with New York and Connecticut?'

'Troy Lester is the only local, a senator from Connecticut. I believe his chief of staff has family in Madison.' Susan tapped madly on the keyboard. 'Yup, he's visiting his folks for the holidays. And his Twitter feed says he'll be at Starbucks tomorrow.' She read aloud: *Blast into the New Year by meeting your senator at Madison Starbucks 9 a.m. (Or at least his chief of staff LOL.)* She tucked her feet under her bottom and swigged the last of her Chardonnay.

'I have a sudden craving for a cup of coffee.'

# FIFTEEN

Detective Meigs was so tired and the night was so slow that he nodded off at his desk. He woke with a stripe of drool running down his chin, startled by a clang in the front office. The blue-gray light of the fluorescents in the parking lot outside bled through the slats of his blinds. His neck and back felt crooked and aching from the awkward napping position, and his brain fuzzy with months of lousy sleep. Eight months into it, widowhood still felt like a trap clamped shut on his heart. With no way to gnaw it loose, he had dragged the clanking weight from spring into summer, and then into the shortening days of fall, and now into the frigid days of winter.

Mason, the desk sergeant, stopped in the hallway and peered into his office. 'Why don't you take a couple of hours off? Go home and see your daughter. Maybe grab a bite? Or take a nap, for pity's sake. You look like a ghoul. And you know there won't be any action here until after midnight, if there's anything at all.'

Even on New Year's Eve, small town Guilford wasn't crazy busy. Maybe they'd collect a DUI or two, followed by a couple of hours listening to drunks rant in their cells, but nothing catastrophic like a bigger city might get. The holidays in general were slow times for crime in this town – it was too cold outside for vandals, and his department's 'lights on and lock before you leave' campaign had caught on with the residents, so petty theft was down.

'Maybe I will take a dinner break,' Meigs said. 'I haven't seen much of Caroline lately, even with school out this week. It's almost as if she's on the night shift and I'm on days.' He forced a laugh. 'When I get back in, I'm going to look over everything I can find about this homeless girl with a new baby. Just in case the New York City cops missed something that wasn't obvious. And I'll call that policewoman – Ramsey, I think it said on her card.'

'Good idea,' Mason said. He started to walk away, but then turned back. 'It's not an easy time, Christmas,' he added, his expression sad. 'Even if you have a full house of family. I'll hold the fort and text you if something comes up.'

'Thanks. I'll be back by midnight at the latest,' Meigs said.

*Not an easy time* was the understatement of the century. The previous week, he'd insisted they attend the Christmas Eve candlelight service that Alice used to love, thinking the familiar carols would bring them both comfort. But all he could think of was his wife's memorial service – the last time he'd entered the church. And Caroline had wept through the entire hour, her shoulders shuddering silently but with violence. And then she'd refused to come down from her room at all on Christmas morning. The gifts he'd wrapped for her, some of them actually chosen by her mother before she died from Huntington's chorea, still lay on the dining room table, unopened.

On the one hand, he wanted to grab the girl by the shoulders and shake her. *Come on, we're in this together.*

On the other, she was acting out exactly what he felt inside. He missed Alice with a ferocity he'd never imagined. And poor Caroline was a teenager without the years of emotional defense that he'd built up so people on the outside couldn't see the ugly churning within.

He called Buffalina Pizza and ordered Caroline's favorite, the pie with cheese, simple red sauce, and basil only – no garlic, no onions, no meat. He would've chosen the meat lover's pizza packed with the goodness of nitrates that came in bacon and sausage and shredded beef pot roast. But he selected this as a peace offering, to show her he was thinking of her. That he took what she wanted seriously. That he wanted to start the new year off on a different and better foot.

Driving home after picking up the pizza, he felt nervous. Almost as if he was going on a date with someone he didn't know that well. Which was a stupid comparison – sick, if anyone heard it. 'Christ almighty, it's just a pizza,' he said out loud in a disgusted voice.

There were more cars than usual parked on their little street. From the looks of the lights blazing three houses up, the Davidsons were throwing the party. He hoped they had had the sense to identify designated drivers. For sure, Guilford patrol cars would be looking hard for any sloppy driving tonight. And usually the sight of his police vehicle kept misbehavior in this neighborhood to a minimum. He parked the SUV in the driveway and tromped through the packed snow on the narrow path to the side door leading to the kitchen. He sniffed the air, which felt heavy with moisture. A light dusting of snow had started and he was certain there'd be more coming. He'd make coffee first, he decided, and then go up to her room with the pizza.

In the kitchen, Caroline had left several cabinet doors open, and dirty dishes in the sink. The garbage was full, trash spilling out onto the linoleum. He swallowed his irritation. He'd told her she could have a friend over to study or watch TV during the day. She was a kid after all, a teenager in mourning. A desperate combination. He straightened up the mess while the coffee brewed. Alice had been meticulously neat and utterly organized. How was it possible that a daughter was so unlike her mother?

In the months before her death, Alice had talked him into couples' therapy. She needed him to be able to talk about her illness and she hoped to help him begin to grieve. In their last session, she told him that Caroline had asked if she could stay with him for a while instead of returning to her 'real' father in Santa Monica. She said Caroline wondered if he'd still be her stepfather, once Alice was gone.

He'd been touched. Grateful almost. Not that continuing to have Caroline living with him could ever replace Alice, but maybe they could muddle through together. And so he'd prom- ised his wife that his home was Caroline's, as long as she needed it. Forever, if she wanted. Maybe in spite of their differences, they could lean on each other, make a little family to replace the one they were both about to lose. They could watch TV, maybe even choose recipes from Alice's box of clippings and notes, and then cook meals together.

OK, so they'd order out.

But instead of a sweet domestic scene, he'd staggered into a war zone with an angry teenager intent on testing him, on trying every behavior that he found annoying and unfathom- able in other people's kids. Why had she asked to stay here if she hated him so much? He didn't get it. She hadn't been this challenging when Alice was alive. But then they'd always had Alice to moderate any tension. He had to remind himself of the therapist's warning, how adolescents often acted out their anger and their grief.

She'd been right. Any and all interactions lately had hard- ened into knockdown catfights; it didn't much matter the subject: what Caroline was wearing, whether or not she'd get to school on time – or at all. He'd almost threatened to send her back to California, to her father, but he held back, certain that would cost any warm feelings she might still have for him. And break his promise to Alice.

Or had he become one of those parents his coworkers were always complaining about, who had grown too soft, afraid to take their offspring on for fear they wouldn't be liked?

Coffee in one hand and the fragrant white box in the other, Meigs started down the hall toward the staircase leading to the second floor to invite her to share the pizza. Partway up the stairs, he began to hear the deep bass of some hideous rap music, and to smell patchouli incense, growing stronger as he got closer to what he'd started thinking of as Caroline's den. The incense was covering something – he wasn't the complete idiot she might think.

He felt his blood pressure soar and he rapped sharply on Caroline's door.

'Caroline,' he yelled over the music when she didn't answer. No response. He knocked again. 'Do you hear me?'

He waited for what he considered a decent interval – certainly shorter than Alice would have waited, but dammit, he couldn't measure up to Alice. She'd had the patience of a glacier; his was more like a forest fire, badly contained. Then he turned the knob and cracked the door, sickened by the stink of stale pot in the room. He shoved the door open past the salmon-colored towel Caroline had stuffed in the crack. It was oven-hot and there were kids sprawled everywhere. A new poster of a scruffy-looking rock band called My Chemical Romance was tacked on the far wall, covering the inspirational poster of a fuzzy ginger kitten hanging from a pole that Alice had given her daughter shortly before her death. *Hang in there, baby*, the poster read.

Clothing had been cast off on the rug in messy piles, and on the desk he saw a pack of cigarettes, an ashtray overflowing with butts, and his expensive bottle of rum drunk down to the last half inch. He looked again and spotted – worst of all – a hash pipe next to the cigarettes. Should he take it all on now, or just get these people out and try to talk to his stepdaughter later? The figure under the yellow flowered quilt on her bed stirred. No, it was two figures.

He put the coffee and the pizza on the floor outside her door. 'Caroline, get up this minute,' he said, his jaw clenched and fists balled.

'Go away,' she croaked.

Two quick steps across the room, and he yanked the yellow-flowered quilt from the bed, revealing a half-naked boy-man with messy brown hair pulled into a man-bun, droopy eyes, and an obvious hard-on.

'What the fuck, man,' the boy said, groping for cover.

Caroline sat up, the sheet clutched over her breasts, her dark hair tousled. 'Get out,' she said, pointing to the door. 'No one invited you in.' The other kids in the room began to gather their stuff, preparing to bolt.

The phone in his pocket buzzed.

Ignoring his stepdaughter and the phone, he lunged forward and grabbed the boy's left arm, his toughest cop gaze boring into the teenager's eyes. 'If you're not gone in three minutes, I swear I'll throw you out the window. If I don't shoot you first. And if you ever touch my daughter like that again . . .'

He let go of the boy's arm and strode from the room, trying not to picture the kid manhandling Alice's beautiful, screwed-up daughter, trying to calm himself down. She hadn't mentioned a word about a boyfriend. He should have told that kid to never come around again. He should have broken his fucking neck. On the other hand, he'd probably gone far enough, if not too far. He waited outside the door, hearing the soft murmur of voices and laughter and that stupid music, though someone had turned the volume down. Over all that he heard the boy stage-whispering to Caroline: 'You never said your father was a cop!'

'He's not my father,' Caroline said loudly.

His phone buzzed again. Elizabeth Brown. He'd call her later, after he'd dealt with this. His breathing was coming hard and his chest felt tight. Maybe he was having a heart attack.

Caroline and the other kids stumbled out of her room. She pulled on a pink fleece jacket and refused to look Meigs in the eyes. 'You are forbidden to leave—' he started, stopping himself before he grabbed her arm too.

She cut him off. 'Whatever. Good luck with that.' She glared through the tangled curtain of her hair and, without another word, stomped downstairs and out the front entrance with the boy and the other kids following, slamming the door behind her.

He wanted to call after her that she'd freeze to death without a real jacket and a hat. He wanted to sink to the top step and weep.

'Where are you going?' he whispered.

Wait, what was he thinking? Considering the empty bottle of rum and the smoky smell in the room, they were probably in no condition to drive. He vaulted down the stairs and burst outside as four carloads of Caroline's friends lurched away from the curb in front of the Davidsons' house. The new snow was falling already, covering their footprints in the yard. He memorized partials of two of the license plate markers and then retreated back inside to call Mason and ask the men on duty to watch for those plates.

# SIXTEEN

Gripping her plastic bag of belongings, Addy slid into the back seat next to Caroline and barely got the door shut before Randy threw the car into gear and screamed away from the curb. The car fishtailed on the snowy road, almost clipping a Subaru parked across the street. She hated this kid who was driving and couldn't understand why Caroline had coaxed him back into bed.

If Caroline's father was really a cop, they could be in serious trouble. On the other hand, could her new friend help her get Rafe's phone number from the police? Her eyes and nose felt moist as she remembered that Rafe could be dead by now. And Georgia was on her tail. She snuffled back the tears. A sudden wave of exhaustion overtook her anxiety and she sank back against the seat. She'd had so many impossible decisions to make in the last few days. And her body felt as beat up as her mind. Maybe more.

'Ride 'em cowboys! Where to next?' Randy asked the boy in the passenger seat, once the vehicle had recovered from the rear end slide.

'My brother's friend is having a major party in Madison. No chance of parental or police types showing up because he rents the place with two other guys. Not underage either, if you know what I mean.' The boy looked over his shoulder at the girls and winked. 'And he said we could come as long as the babes we bring are cute. We have that covered.'

Caroline giggled but Addy felt a reflexive shiver of worry. A major party probably meant alcohol and drugs would be super available – these kids had already had plenty to drink. She preferred to stay this side of sober.

Not that she didn't understand the pull of wanting to feel numb. She had a ton of ugly to forget. But staying alert aside, she hated to remind herself of her mother. Another beer or sometimes a shot had been her mother's answer to just about any problem in life. Which meant she stayed mired in the same sick rut, her wheels churning deeper and deeper into the mud.

But since Addy had no place else to be and no place to go, she kept her mouth shut. For a moment, she wondered if she should have stayed at Elizabeth's house. She could be sleeping, not headed toward more trouble with kids who seemed out of control.

Caroline reached over and took her hand for a moment, then leaned in to whisper, 'Don't worry, it won't be bad, only fun.' She fingered the gold bangle on her wrist. 'Thanks for sticking up for me with Randy. You know, back in my room? Sometimes he gets really excited and doesn't listen too well. I mean, I get excited too, but you know guys. They want you so much it's hard to say no. For me, anyway. It's kind of a compliment. Isn't it?' She flashed a heartbreaking smile and pecked Addy's cheek. 'Thanks.'

Addy did know guys. And she wished she could tell Caroline that in her experience they were out for their own pleasure. Paid or free. Young or old. Period, end of story. No, not a compliment. But how could she possibly explain how she knew? She squeezed Caroline's hand, soft in contrast to her rough skin, then let it go and leaned her head against the fabric of the seat.

'If you want,' Caroline added shyly, 'you're welcome to stay at my house tonight. Only if you want. You might have other plans?' Her sentence ended with a question mark in her voice, as though she couldn't bear to be pushy.

Addy's eyes flew open. 'But your father is a cop.'

'Don't worry about him,' Caroline said, grinning and holding up a pinkie finger. 'He's wrapped.'

'Thanks then. I'll let you know,' Addy said.

On the one hand, she didn't want a cop poking into her business. She could be arrested, right? Prostitution and child endangerment? On the other hand, she needed the phone number. And a friend . . . Maybe Caroline could get the number from her father's phone without asking or telling him anything. Rafe would get crazy mad if he thought she'd gotten the police involved. Tears crowded her eyes. She squeezed them tight and willed them away.

She was so tired. Felt like years since she'd last slept. The conversation in the car receded to a dull buzz and she dozed off. She was jolted awake some time later as the car took a sharp left into the driveway of a beat-up looking house across from the railroad tracks. It didn't look like the Guilford station where she'd arrived. But she didn't think they'd traveled long, so it couldn't be far.

This house was strung with flickering garlands of colored light bulbs alternating with empty beer cans – Budweiser and Pabst Blue Ribbon. A blowup Santa slumped in the yard, an empty bottle of Jim Beam duct-taped to one of his white mittens. A hand-lettered sign was stabbed into the snow beside the figure: *Your gifts will be late this year!* As they tumbled out of the car, a chorus of voices yelling 'Drink! Drink! Drink!' drifted from inside. Addy's insides clenched.

'Party time, girls,' said Randy, breaking into a big grin and reaching back to grab Caroline's hand. 'This is going to be the coolest New Year's Eve ever.'

When Elizabeth had had all she could stand of opening gifts and writing regrets, she said goodnight to her aunt and her mother and went upstairs. Eleven o'clock. They would have been married by now. The shrimp wrapped in maple-glazed bacon would be circulating and the champagne flowing. And she would be desperately trying to remember the steps to the dance they'd rehearsed and telling herself – and Kevin – that it didn't matter if she messed up. But he'd been annoyed that she hadn't had time to do the lessons justice – another piece of evidence that he was not her top priority. Had he been right? Had she not loved him enough? Or were the dance lessons another message from the universe saying that her plan to marry Kevin sucked?

She'd miss him terribly; she could feel tendrils of the loss under the anger and shame. Or at least miss the way they had been in college, before the reality of life in medical school and living apart had hit them. Back when they had planned meals to fix on his hotplate and spent nights studying or reading, cocooned in his room, or playing cards with friends. Back when the decisions weren't so hard and only involved the two of them.

She checked her phone again. Had she missed a text? She didn't actually expect an apology, or even an acknowledge-ment of regret. Though the Kevin she had known would be feeling sad, just as she was.

She tossed the phone onto her bed and went to her computer, open on the desk. She typed 'homeless girl's baby' into the search bar. The first page up included a story about a homeless family living in one room in a gnarly shelter. And then followed a story about how a random stranger had talked a young teenager with a newborn into calling home. This one had a happy ending, with mother and child in grateful tears over the resolution of their misunderstanding, and the girl on a bus, headed toward home with her baby. Elizabeth doubted that Addy's story could ever end so simply.

Nothing new from Olivia. And why would there be? She had spent the evening nosing around their house in Connecti-cut, not chasing down leads in the city. Elizabeth desperately hoped Olivia wouldn't try to make *her* life part of the story. Unfortunately, the Good Samaritan abandoned at the altar on New Year's Eve could make a sexy sidebar.

Next she tapped in 'drive-by shooting Bellevue South Park'. Nothing new there either.

So she sprawled out on her bed and put another call into Detective Meigs on his office phone. The call went to his voicemail and she left a message, describing how Addy had turned up at the Big Y grocery store, and how she'd brought her home for food and comfort, and how she'd run away again. She wasn't sure she was ready to call him on his cell again when he was likely to be out on a job. It wasn't an emergency – not yet, anyway.

'I'd love to talk to you about this when you get a chance. I realize the police are busy on New Year's Eve.' She tried to keep the irritation she was feeling out of her tone.

Finally, she made a list on the Notes app on her phone. Things to do tomorrow. Number one: retrieve Addy's clothing from the trash and go through it for clues. Number two: go to Starbucks with Aunt Susan to meet the senator.

She noodled over in her mind how to approach the man. They couldn't very well come right out and ask if he knew Addy, and how that might have come about. Could they? Maybe a better approach would be to chat with him as an interested constituent. But interested in what? She went back to the computer and Googled the senator's name, then began to read the material on his website. He claimed a special interest in the concerns of Connecticut women and children. He saw no reason why Republicans shouldn't co-operate with Democrats on this important issue. The question was how to get appropriate services to these women so they could return to the workforce and get their children into school, with appropriate clothing and necessary food in their bellies.

Who could disagree with that? It was obviously Public Relations 101. She typed his name and 'scandal' into the search bar. A page full of articles appeared, questioning his self-interest as he shaped health policy in the Senate. He also frequently traded health care stocks, raising questions about whether he used his position in Congress for personal profit. She skimmed a few. A *Washington Post* reporter called for an investigation of his influence as the chairman of the Senate

Health, Education, Labor, and Pensions Committee on acquisition of stock from a small company developing a treatment for Meniere's disease, notable for its debilitating bouts of vertigo. The point, she supposed, was that he was in a position to enrich himself with insider information. Again, this would have nothing to do with Addy.

Finally she searched on 'Senator Troy Lester + extramarital affairs + scandal'. The links that came up suggested he had been seen publicly at parties and dinners with women other than his wife. Maybe his wife was busy with other things, or hated political events, or disliked him? Though one woman had actually sued him for sexual harassment. The case had been settled out of court. Would she talk about her experience? Probably not if she'd settled the claim. These days no one in the limelight made a move without a nondisclosure agreement.

Elizabeth Googled the senator's wife. She volunteered for a number of local charities and was often seen at galas and events supporting them. In the only photo she found of both the senator and his wife, they were attending a dinner and auction for the Save Our Connecticut Children organization. And that name sounded very familiar. Hadn't her father's secretary, Wilma, served on the board for years?

Elizabeth jotted more notes into her phone, and then set up a Google alert for the senator with the search terms she'd used. Then she turned off her phone and computer. She didn't want to be tempted into random Googling or kept awake by flashes of light on the screen signaling the arrival of emails or texts.

Tomorrow was the beginning of a new year. And yes, she was going to do some things differently. Like lay things out to Kevin in a neutral and reasonable way about the tattered finances of the wedding. Why should she and her family be the ones to deal with the aftermath? Tomorrow, she would call him. She wouldn't allow him to hang up until he'd agreed to a plan about handling their disaster. Paying bills, returning presents, canceling joint accounts – he could and should help with all this. And if that went well – ha! – she might tell him that she'd miss him.

And then she'd look through Addy's things. And go for coffee with her aunt. And call or visit Wilma to inquire about the children's organization and her experience with Mr Lester's wife. She wasn't going to sit at home and wait for things to happen.

# SEVENTEEN

Addy floated around the fringes of the party, feeling edgy as she watched the others get staggeringly wasted, and keeping an eye on Caroline. She would like to get her new friend out of here, but how? And go where? Her father had been so angry that she couldn't imagine going back there. Caroline was almost comatose by the time a couple of the older guys who lived in the house suggested playing strip poker. Hard to choose which of them looked more ridiculous, the guy with the greasy hair down to his chin, dyed purple on the ends? Or the fat dude wearing a Statue of Liberty headpiece who kept shouting 'Rock and Roll!' every time a new song began to play?

Randy was blotto, and therefore eager to play cards with these guys and a few of their girlfriends. He probably thought he'd get to see some naked boobs, but he was too soused to notice that the game was rigged. Within fifteen minutes, he had been stripped down to his embarrassing underwear that should never have been seen in public, a pair of boxers decorated with spaceships blasting off.

'You don't have much left there, Captain Underpants,' said the purple hair guy. 'Nor do we really want to see the rest of it.'

'What else you got left to play with? Money?' asked the fat dude.

Randy gulped audibly, his skin color fading white. 'Five bucks?' He tried to laugh.

The purple-tipped guy sneered. 'You got here somehow, how about your car?'

Randy snuffled, his shoulders hunching forward like a hermit crab, pulling in. 'I can't do that. It belongs to my mom. I'd be grounded for the rest of my life.'

'Oh no, Mommy's going to ground him!' shrieked the fat dude, slapping his hands to either side of his face.

The two guys swapped narrow-eyed glances that roiled Addy's stomach. 'That leaves your girlfriend, doesn't it, Captain?'

They turned to look at Caroline, who was splayed on a futon in the far corner of the room. Her eyes were closed, and her beautiful hair was spread out on the dirty blue denim like the dark aura of a floating mermaid.

Randy's face faded even more. Suddenly, he bolted from the circle, jogging to the bathroom. Behind the door, Addy heard the sound of violent retching.

'I don't think she'd mind a bit,' said the purple-haired guy, cocking his head at Caroline.

'For one thing, she won't remember. For another, knowing you, it'll be quick and painless.'

'Take it outside, asshats,' said a brunette with a low-cut top that showed off a lacy black bra. She lit the cigarette dangling from her lips. 'Go roll in the snow and cool your ridiculous selves off.'

But they ignored her and headed toward Caroline, one of them grabbing her arms and the other her feet, lifting her dead weight to drag her toward one of the bedrooms. Caroline stirred, complaining that her wrist hurt in a soft and woozy voice that stabbed Addy right to the heart.

'Outside, asshats,' said the brunette again. 'Leave the girl alone.'

The boys ignored her.

Addy wondered if she could fight them off. Even if the brunette helped her – a big if – there were too many of them. And they were stupid drunk, so there'd be no appealing to reason. She could think of only one way to save her friend. The thought made her absolutely ill. But she'd done it before and she could do it again.

'That girl has no idea what she's doing,' Addy said in a hard street voice. 'It would be like screwing a sandbag. Take me instead. Let's step outside.'

# EIGHTEEN

Back at the station, Detective Meigs told Mason about the kids driving off, half-loaded. 'The cars were too far down the street to see the markers clearly. Here's what I got.' He handed him the notes. 'I'm thinking I should drive around—' His voice cracked with emotion.

'Better yet,' said Mason, clapping him on the shoulder, 'I'll alert the patrols and you stay here and head out when we find them. Which we will.'

So Meigs retreated to his office. He remembered he'd missed a call from Elizabeth Brown during the melee with the teenagers, and a voicemail message from her was waiting for him when he reached his desk. It was late to return her call, but he felt relieved to focus back on the missing girl and the shooting. With any new case, he liked to start at the beginning, try to sketch out a timeline and place important events on a paper map. There'd been a crazy in-service training in his department about ten years ago, something about understanding your psychological profile as a cop. Most of it he and the other guys had laughed off as silly psychobabble. But he'd always remembered the instructor telling him he was a visual learner, because that made sense to him. If he could see it, he began to see patterns that opened up solutions to a case.

He brought up a New York city and tri-state areas map on his computer, and located the subway stop where the girl had given birth. But why there? What was she running from and where was she going? If she'd known she was close to her due date, why hadn't she stayed put or gone to a hospital? She must have been scared to death of someone in order to run.

Next, he dropped a locator pin on the coffee shop where Elizabeth had brought the baby, and then the little park where the man had been shot. And then Elizabeth had returned home to Guilford, so he marked that too. He wondered how it was that Elizabeth was such a cool customer after all these unsettling events. He printed out his map.

With that in front of him, he played back Elizabeth's message.

Good God, the girl had followed her to Connecticut. They'd had her in their home but she'd fled again. How did she get here and what did she want from Elizabeth really? He sent out a message to the cops on duty, BOLO for a teenage girl who had recently given birth and might be in danger. And he instructed the officers on patrol to include Elizabeth's home in their sweeps of the town. He dropped those two location pins on his map. Then he uploaded a search for missing teens in the New York area with the little information he had, adding Connecticut because she'd come here. Though he didn't know her last name, Addison was not common, so maybe he'd have some luck. Tomorrow he would call the New York police officer as he'd promised to see what they might have turned up, including information about the man who'd been shot. And he'd try to track down the reporter who'd shown up at the Brown house.

Next, to kill some time while waiting to hear for news of Caroline, he tackled his staff annual reviews. He found these difficult, but absorbing once he plunged in. The kind of thing that could distract him from his worries. The trick was to go through each officer's file to remind himself of their strengths and problem areas, and then figure out how to say enough of the good that they could also hear the criticism and, God willing, grow into better cops.

Some time later, and completely immersed in his work, Meigs's cell phone buzzed across the desk and he snatched it up. 'Yeah?'

It was one of the night-shift patrol officers, a friend of the desk sergeant, Mason.

'Detective, I don't know how to say this so I'll just spit it out. The Madison cops picked up some kids at a house party that had gotten way out of control. Your daughter was one of them.' He cleared his throat before continuing. 'They were going to charge her, until your name came up. They're holding her at the Madison station. They called it in to us and I said I'd fill you in.'

For a moment, Meigs felt confused, so deep in his work that he didn't even remember he had a daughter.

Caroline.

Shit.

'Don't bother coming back,' Mason hollered after him as he sprinted out the back door to the parking lot. 'Take care of your girl.'

As Meigs drove onto the highway, he listened to the scanner, rehearsing what he'd say to Caroline when he got to the station. She had to live by his rules, dammit, end of story, if she was going to live with him at all. And his rules did not – no way – include wild parties. Or drugs and boys in her bedroom. Or his booze. Even smoking was out. How did young people these days not understand the dangers all around them? And did she not remember that he was a cop when she brought illegal substances into his house? Of course she did. Had she done this before? Oh God, he hoped not. Was she trying in some twisted way to get his attention? If so, she had it now. And he was very sorry if she'd felt she had to pull a stunt like this to raise a flag.

He activated the flashing lights of his vehicle and drove faster. Although the time to do something useful would have been earlier tonight, not now, when she was in the Madison police drunk tank.

Christ, he should have insisted she stay home after he'd stumbled into that party in her room. He should have demanded the keys from all those kids, and then called their parents. Just how drunk was she? At least drunk was better than dead. He felt chilled, with a pain in his stomach, a familiar wrench that surfaced every time he felt he was failing Alice by failing her daughter.

Finally he pulled off at Exit 62, and reached the Madison town campus where the police department was located, set back in a stand of oaks, bare-limbed and snow-covered. He sprang out of the car and jogged to the main entrance, breathing heavily, his breath puffs of silver in the darkness. 'I'm Detective

Meigs, Guilford PD,' he said to the dispatcher as he flashed his badge. 'You're holding my daughter?'

'Come on back,' she said, and buzzed him into the squad room. 'Have a seat and I'll call the officers involved.'

Have a seat? Not on your friggin' life. Meigs paced the hallway, studying the most-wanted flyers that papered the wall. You never knew when it would pay to have memorized a face. Two years ago he'd spotted one of those hoodlums in the grocery store line ahead of him and made an instant collar. Besides, it kept his mind off why he'd come. As if that were possible, especially with another set of distressed parents huddling in a corner of the room. The woman was weeping, the husband reduced to awkward pats on her thighs and back.

'Jack Meigs,' said a deep voice behind him.

Meigs whirled around. Frank Martin, the Madison chief, reached out to pump his hand and clapped him on the back with the other. 'How're you hangin'?'

'Straight,' said Meigs, feeling a surge of irritation. How the hell were you supposed to answer a question that dumb? 'You're keeping busy. I caught your interview in the local rag. You went from zero to sixty since you took over this dump.'

Martin bent one wrist and then the other, cartilage crackling. 'Once the wife left, there wasn't much to go home for. Might as well work.' His lips stretched into what passed for a grin. 'What are you doing here, anyway?' he asked, looking around at the empty room.

'Sharing data,' Meigs lied. Badly.

Martin must not have been informed that Caroline was his stepdaughter. He'd find out sooner rather than later, but Meigs couldn't stand the idea of hashing it out before he'd gotten all the information about what had actually happened so he could take some control of the situation. He didn't want the sympathy, accompanied by a half-cocked eyebrow that questioned how in the hell he could have let something like this happen. They'd had too many conversations back in their rookie days about how stupid people can be – how they close their eyes and turn their backs – even when their kids were headed straight for trouble. Maybe especially then.

'Good to see you, man,' said Martin. 'Let me know if you need anything. And let's have a beer sometime, as long as we're both single.' He punched Meigs in the shoulder and shambled toward the back of the station.

Two uniformed men emerged from what Meigs assumed was the break room. 'Detective Meigs? Sorry to keep you waiting,' said a burly guy with a massive, shaved head, McNally on his nameplate. 'We were finishing up another interview.'

Meigs stared at the two patrolmen. At two in the morning? 'Where's Caroline?'

'Down the hall,' said McNally. 'We had to take care of this young lady first.' He pointed back at the room they'd come from. A young woman, girl really, sashayed out and headed toward the waiting area, her elbow clasped by a lady cop. Her T-shirt stopped three inches shy of her jeans in spite of the damn cold weather. She had long brown hair and frosted bangs that she blew out of her eyes as she passed the men, flashing the ring in her eyebrow and meeting Meigs's gaze with well-developed disdain.

Meigs shook his head. 'And why exactly was my daughter brought in?' he asked, teeth gritted, barely breathing.

'She was at a party and a neighbor called it in,' said McNally.

'Meaning what? Don't pussyfoot around, dammit. Just tell me.'

'A group of kids imbibed way too much, both alcohol and drugs,' McNally continued. He took a drink from a Styrofoam cup, made a face, and fired the cup into the trash. Coffee splashed out of the cup, against the wall, and trickled down the green paint. 'Some of these kids, like your girl, were underage.' His face reddened and he ran a finger inside his collar, which appeared to be pressing into his neck. He looked at the other cop for help.

'It wasn't pretty,' said the second cop, snapping a wad of pink gum. 'Some of the party had moved outside. Too blasted to notice the cold.' He blew a bubble and sucked it back in, but both men kept their faces bland, eyes on Meigs.

Meigs felt lightheaded, like he'd been punched in the gut hard, and he was staggering but hadn't yet fallen.

'So anyway, that young lady' – McNally continued, jerking

a thumb at the girl with the bare belly – 'was puking in the front yard. And then we caught one of the dickwads who lives there leaning against the garage with another girl on her knees in front of him. Apparently she'd lost big in a poker game and the winners were willing to accept blow jobs in exchange for letting her off the hook moneywise. The other guys were circled around watching him struggle to get his zipper down. Maybe waiting their turns?' McNally pointed to the waiting room again, where the girl with the bare belly had gone to meet her parents. 'You know what that young lady said when we asked why one of her friends would do something like that?'

'You won't believe this,' said the gum-smacker. 'Barely sixteen years old and she says, haven't you heard there's a recession? Just like that, in the snippiest voice you can imagine.'

Meigs was speechless for a minute, staring at those men like they were talking Chinese, pushing that image away from his mind as hard as it tried to push back in. No matter how many times Meigs had told himself to stay calm on the ride over, he could feel his anger shifting from simmer to boil. You've got hair-trigger hackles, Jack, Alice used to tell him. He suddenly wanted to rip the throat out of the Bazooka-chewing cop.

He took a step forward, his hands fisted.

'If we'd known Caroline was your—'

'Then what?' Meigs said through clenched teeth. 'You'd have left her with those scumbags in the middle of nowhere? What exactly was she doing?'

'Easy there,' the second cop muttered.

'She was with the crowd that was watching,' said McNally.

Meigs felt a small surge of relief. 'She's not charged with anything?'

'Actually, she was barfing in the bushes, too.' McNally shook his head. 'Like I said, we moved in and broke it up before it could get any uglier.'

Meigs forced air into his lungs and attempted a smile. 'Did you grab a boy too, maybe five foot ten inches, dark hair in a girly ponytail, stupid-looking? He was lurking around my house earlier.'

The Madison cops laughed. 'Most of the guys ran off – except for the one shaggy purple-haired dude who was handicapped by the trousers that fell around his ankles as soon as we showed up. He couldn't move fast enough. He's in the holding tank. But your daughter's not talking.'

Meigs sucked in another deep breath and wiggled his fingers, which he'd clenched tightly as a winched rope. At least they hadn't found Caroline crouched in front of some troglodyte. Or not that they were saying. 'Appreciate your calling me in,' he said. 'I appreciate what you did. Where is she?'

'We're holding her in one of the interview rooms. You're free to take her. Maybe you'll get more from her once she's out of here. She was pretty frightened,' said the gum-smacker.

'And sick,' added McNally. 'One more thing we should say, there's another girl with her. And your daughter is refusing to be separated from her friend.' He rolled his eyes, signaling that Meigs could sort this out by himself.

They led him down to the end of the hall and pushed open a gray steel door. Caroline was slumped in one of the metal chairs, her head resting on the table, cushioned by her bunched-up pink fleece. She appeared to be sleeping. The other girl, a small brunette with huge sad eyes that did not match the belligerent set of her mouth, leaped to her feet and moved closer to Caroline. The knees of her gray sweatpants were wet.

Addy was on her feet instantly when the three cops came into the room. She recognized the rust-haired guy who charged in first as her friend's stepfather.

'Caroline, let's go home.' His voice came out hard and loud.

Caroline picked her head up and her eyes got wide, and then narrowed. Her lips pressed into an angry line, and her face turned the color of oatmeal, with eye make-up smeared everywhere. 'I'm not leaving unless my friend can come too.'

'Who the hell is . . .' Caroline's father glanced at Addy again, taking in everything about her, his gaze lingering on the wet knees of her sweatpants. She flushed with shame. 'Your friend should go home with her own parents,' he said.

'If we could have a moment?' Officer McNally grabbed

him by the elbow and pulled him a couple of steps away, as though he assumed they were deaf, or too hungover to listen. 'As we said, we couldn't get much out of either of them. The girl claims her name is Barbara and she's eighteen so refuses to have us contact her parents. No ID on her.'

Caroline's father blew out a whistling breath. 'Knowing my daughter, we could be here all night arguing about "Barbara".'

Officer McNally nodded. 'Or you could take them both home and sort it out in the morning.'

'Come on then, both of you,' said Caroline's father.

Caroline grabbed Addy's wrist and stalked past the two officers without looking at them. The woman at the front desk handed them their belongings – a phone for Caroline, the plastic bag for Addy. Caroline loped ahead of her father, clasping Addy's hand, darting toward the front door and out to the parking lot, all without speaking.

'Good luck,' McNally called after them.

Caroline's father waved a hand over his shoulder.

Outside, he squeezed his remote and the lights inside his vehicle – a Guilford police department SUV – blinked on with a cheerful chirp. Caroline climbed into the back seat after Addy, slammed the door and hunched down, head pressed against the passenger-side window. Were her teeth chattering? Addy felt that cold – and frightened – too.

'Caroline,' her father said, opening the driver-side door and poking his head in. 'What the hell was that all about? What were you thinking?'

She said nothing. He slid into the car and started the engine, pushing the heater fan to high. Caroline closed her eyes and leaned her head on Addy's shoulder. Black eyeliner was smudged on her lids and cheeks.

Her father banged a fist on the steering wheel, causing them both to flinch. 'Caroline, what were you doing with those people?'

She pulled the hood of her jacket over her face and sunk down lower into the refuge of pink fleece. He shifted into drive and hurtled out of the lot.

'Are you high now?'

Dead silence.

'Don't you understand that you could have died of alcohol poisoning? You could have been gang-raped and ruined for the rest of your life.'

Addy felt sick to her stomach. She felt as though she was truly one of the ruined, and neither Caroline nor this man had any idea.

'Who are these people?' he asked. 'Where did you meet them?'

Again, Caroline didn't answer.

'Barbara,' he said, swiveling his head to look at her. 'Who is your family? I need to let them know that you're OK.'

Addy stayed silent. She didn't have people who would be waiting to hear whether she was OK. Except for her grand-mother, who'd probably given up months ago.

He twisted the radio on – Christmas music tinkled. He turned it back off and they drove the remaining few miles in silence.

'I saw what you did,' Caroline whispered to Addy, gripping her hand so tightly that it almost hurt. 'Thank you.'

As soon as the SUV rolled to a stop in their driveway, Caroline bolted from the car with Addy in tow, ran to the front door and rattled the knob. Locked. She stepped aside, waited for her father to unlock it, and then pulled Addy into the house. By the time he'd snapped the deadbolt behind them, she had sprinted upstairs to her room, Addy right behind her, and slammed the door with an eardrum-clanging clash.

# NINETEEN

Elizabeth watched her alarm clock blink the minutes all the way from 4:59 to 6 a.m., and finally gave up trying to get back to sleep. In the dark swirl of dreams about the wedding and Addy, her fears and disappointments had loomed large, and she felt herself slide into useless rumina-tions. What had really made Kevin decide she wasn't worth marrying? In the light of morning, she didn't buy his *too perfect* explanation. Would she ever find a guy who might suit her better? Her own parents, though devoted to each other in their own peculiar way, did not provide the model of deep romantic love that she craved for herself. In the beginning, she and Kevin had had that. But lately, maybe they'd fallen into a repetition of her parents' pattern – two people yoked together by mutual agreement but with separate lives. They hadn't even figured out where they'd live after they got married, for heaven's sake!

She couldn't help wondering if her failed marriage might also be connected to the shadowy feelings that came with being adopted: she hadn't been wanted by her flesh and blood mother. A bad start to anyone's life. Had this uneasiness set her up for a lifetime of disappointments?

She shook her head. Her own life had been a jamboree compared to what Addy's baby would face. And that thought brought another rush of questions to mind about Addy. She'd worked so hard to follow Elizabeth deep into the Connecticut suburbs, looking for her friend's phone number. And yet she'd fled when she learned that Elizabeth no longer had it. Was there another way they could have helped her?

If all these thoughts weren't enough to ruin any chance of sleep, snow-whipped winds had howled outside for the last few hours. A storm always felt worse near the water. Elizabeth had been up on and off throughout the night, imagining that she heard car engines or gunshots or cries for help, her pulse racing in response to each.

She closed her eyes and brought up the mantra her yoga teacher chanted at the end of a class: 'May we be happy, may we be healthy, may we ride the waves of our lives wherever they take us.' The last bit was the hardest. Some days, like the past few, it felt impossible.

Coffee might help. And doing something semi-useful.

Outside she heard the clunk and scrape of a plow, clearing the snow in their driveway. She pulled an old pink terry bath-robe over her pajamas and slid her feet into bunny slippers that dated back to high school days. Downstairs, coffee was already made – someone else couldn't sleep either. She grabbed the biggest mug in the cabinet, poured it full of the steaming brew, and added a dollop of cream and some sugar. The first sip tasted like heaven. Then she slipped into the garage to retrieve Addy's clothing, which her mother had placed in a brown paper bag and tucked into the trash. Her father's car was already gone. A record early start on New Year's Day, even for him, certified maniacal workaholic.

She began to sort through the contents of the bag. Addy's white athletic socks were gray with dirt and age, the heels and toes perforated by quarter-sized holes. Ditto the fleece-lined booties – grubby and worn. The plaid flannel pants were faded and worn; they might have been soft, but surely not warm. And the gray sweatshirt with its barely visible gold logo was shapeless, thin, and spotted with bloodstains and grease.

She reached into the pockets of the oversized car coat, which smelled different from the other clothing, not fresh, but not stale either. She found the remnants of an old Kleenex, one hand-knitted green mitten, and a book of matches from a bar in Poughkeepsie. She grabbed her phone and Googled the bar, which looked like a working person's hangout, nothing fancy, but not a horrible dive. Had Addy waitressed there at one time? Honestly, she didn't look old enough to work in a bar, despite her insistence that she was nineteen. As Elizabeth finished the last of her coffee, she flipped the coat open to check the lining one last time. The name *Judith* and a phone number had been written in faded blue ink on the back of the label. Now Elizabeth wondered if Addy had stolen the coat – maybe even on the train to Connecticut? It certainly wasn't her size.

Thinking about what had happened with the last mysterious phone call she'd made, Elizabeth blocked her number from being displayed, and dialed. A bleary female voice answered.

'So sorry to bother you on a holiday this early. I'm Elizabeth Brown, and I'm calling about the young woman – a girl, really – who was wearing your coat. It's a tan canvas car coat with brown corduroy collar and cuffs. Is this Judith? Your phone number was on the label.'

After a few moments of silence, the woman asked: 'Who did you say you are?'

'My name is Elizabeth. I'm a friend of Addy's.'

'A friend?' the woman asked. 'How did you get this coat?'

'I gave her a ride to Connecticut,' Elizabeth ad-libbed, talking faster than she could think. 'I'm hoping you might be able to help me track her down so I can return it to her. She left it in my car.' She groaned to herself. This sounded unlikely, with the weather this bad.

'She told us she was looking for her sister. A medical student . . .' The woman sounded entirely unconvinced.

'I am a medical student, but not her sister. In fact, I don't even know that she has a sister, but she was looking for me, I can assure you of that. And I'm now looking for her, as I'm worried she's in some kind of serious danger.'

The woman said nothing but at least she didn't hang up.

Her words tumbled out as she tried to explain their connection in a more compelling way. 'The truth is she followed me from New York to Connecticut and now we seem to have scared her off. We wondered – that's my mother and my aunt and me – whether you have any idea where she might have gone. Or even where she came from. I'm worried sick about her.' She was babbling – what if this person was a threat to Addy, too?

'If she didn't leave my coat in your car, how did you get it?' the woman asked.

'I'm a little embarrassed to say this, but after we fed her a snack to tide her over to dinner yesterday, she took a shower. When she didn't come out of the bathroom, I went in and discovered she'd gone out the window.' Elizabeth's voice broke with emotion. 'This time she had no coat at all. And it snowed all night. We're in suburban Connecticut – there are no shelters for kids in trouble anywhere within miles. I was hoping you could help me find her.' She got up to grab a paper towel from the rack beside the sink and blow her nose.

'I don't think I can help much. When we saw her yesterday, the only thing she had with her was a plastic bag. Poor kid,' said Judith, and then explained how Addy had approached them and asked for a ride with a story about getting left behind. 'We didn't believe it for a minute, and we felt awful leaving her in the city, but what was the alternative? We couldn't very well take her to the cops, could we?'

Elizabeth didn't answer that question. Maybe turning her over to the authorities would have been the best thing to do. Though she suspected Addy would have found a way to bolt. 'Did she give you any hint about where she was headed? Other than the sister thing, I mean,' Elizabeth asked.

'There was something strange. She asked us to charge her phone. She was supposed to be on some kind of church youth trip, but she claimed the bus left without her at the rest stop.'

'Who would leave a teenage girl behind? It doesn't make sense,' said Elizabeth. 'Unless the bus was part of her imaginary story.'

'Yes,' said the woman, Judith. 'I couldn't help noticing a series of text messages that came up on the screen while it was charging. We didn't mean to be nosy, really, but in our rig, when you plug in a phone, the Bluetooth brings the latest messages up on the screen. This did not look like a young girl's phone.'

'Because . . .?' Elizabeth nudged.

'This was a BlackBerry, and it seems like all the kids these days have to have the latest iPhone, right? Although I suppose it could have been a hand-me-down, because she sure didn't seem to have a lot of money. Or was it stolen? We didn't know.

'The texts themselves were about insurance companies, or maybe it was medical stock tips? We thought this was all odd, but it wasn't our business either.' She sighed. 'You'll let me know if you learn something more? Or if there's any way we can help? I feel really terrible now.'

'I think you did help, by being kind and giving her the ride,' Elizabeth said. After signing off, she got up and poured a second cup of coffee. What in the world had Addy been doing in New Jersey? Had she stolen the phone? Was this related to the baby or the shooting? She sighed. What did she really know about the girl, period?

Rainbow, the yellow tiger cat, sauntered into the kitchen and came over for an ear scratch and a few extra kibbles. Her mother had adopted him the year Elizabeth started college – the first sign that her parents might survive her absence. Her mother had dreamed of a slew of children – she came from a warm, expansive family – but after the discovery of her severe endometriosis and the hysterectomy that followed, no babies had been possible. Her parents had been waiting for several years to adopt a child when Elizabeth made her appearance.

Rainbow hopped onto a kitchen chair and, from there, onto the table. 'Does your mother allow this?' Elizabeth asked him. The cat sprawled across the list of chores that needed to be accomplished to undo the wedding cancellation damage, and then began to preen his stripes in the patch of sun. As she moved him off the table, she saw the papers underneath the wedding list. The Connecticut Department of Children and Families was pleased to inform her parents that they had been approved as foster parents. The results of their home study had been positive. Since they had completed the required paperwork and classes, a DCF worker would be in touch after the holidays about prospective placements.

Videen bustled into the kitchen. 'Rainbow!' she scolded, smiling fondly at the cat who had hopped back onto the kitchen table. She picked him up and plopped him onto the floor. 'Who were you talking to, sweetie?'

When Elizabeth didn't answer right away, Videen's gaze moved from her daughter's face to the papers on the table. She looked instantly guilty. 'Oh dear, I didn't mean for you to find out this way. I didn't mention it because I was worried about burdening you with more than you already had on your plate, with school and the wedding and all. And then when Kevin pulled his stunt—'

'It's fine, it's great, you'll be amazing. I'm just surprised,' Elizabeth broke in. 'Does Dad know about this?'

'Of course!' Videen laughed. 'He knows that I've wanted to do it forever. It was now or never. We're not getting any younger. I had to do some pretty fast talking, but in the end he agreed that I've spent most of our married life supporting him and now it's his turn to support me.' She sat down at the table and took Elizabeth's hand. 'It will change our lives, having a child living with us. A child who could have a lot of problems. I didn't think it would affect you that much because you've got a big career ahead of you. You're launched – we are both so proud. And we thought you'd be married.' Her face fell.

At that moment, someone knocked on the door to the laundry room. Elizabeth got up and peered out the window. Kevin's old red BMW sat in the driveway. 'Oh, Lord,' she said. 'Speak of the devil.'

'Shall I leave you? Do you want me to talk to him?' her mother asked.

'No, no. I don't think so.' The offer was tempting, with her heart doing somersaults and her stomach churning. On the one hand, allowing her mother to take over would feel so easy. On the other, it was her life, her canceled marriage, her college boyfriend, her mess. She'd have to face him sometime. It might as well be now.

'I'll be fine. I'll holler if I need you.'

Her mother scooped up the tiger cat who now hung from her arms like a ragdoll, pecked Elizabeth on the forehead, and hurried out of the kitchen. Elizabeth took a deep breath and opened the door.

'It's cold out here,' Kevin said with a lopsided grin, the one she had noticed that first day in the college dining hall. He was wearing his favorite faded jeans with the hole in the thigh, and a ski jacket with lift tickets stapled onto the pocket. Elizabeth could have named the resorts on those tags – Sugarbush, Mount Snow, Killington, and his favorite, Mad River Glen.

'I would've called first but I thought you would tell me to stay away. Can I come in for a minute?'

Elizabeth stayed silent, afraid she would cry if she said anything. And she didn't want to appear weak. Finally she stepped back and waved him in.

'And besides, I wanted to tell you I'm sorry in person,' Kevin said. 'I think us not getting married is the right thing to do. But the timing sucked, I know that. And I know my parents haven't been very gracious.'

'Understatement,' Elizabeth muttered. 'Maybe I misheard, but it seems like you told me you'd be covering the wedding expenses that aren't reimbursed. Which is not what your mother told mine.' She sounded awful to her own ears – shrewish and sharp – but the shaky whimpering that hovered just below her tough words would feel far worse. 'Not to mention humiliating me and my family in front of everyone we know and care about.'

'And plenty of people you don't,' he said.

'What's that supposed to mean?' A flash of white-hot anger pushed her sadness aside.

Kevin exhaled noisily. 'You don't really want to know.'

'Go ahead.'

'Listen, Lizzie, I don't want to fight. I mean this only in the nicest way. And yes, I'll pay for anything you can't get reimbursed. But the point is you need to figure out what you really want, then stand up for yourself.'

'I don't know what you're talking about.' She crossed her arms over her chest and frowned, wishing she wasn't in her pajamas. It was hard to be taken seriously while wearing bunny slippers.

'Our wedding,' he said, 'was your mother's idea of a celebration. And honestly? I was the cardboard groom. Any man could have filled that spot, as long as you were getting married. You can't ever disagree with your mother – you're afraid she'll melt or fray at the seams and fall into pieces.'

'I don't think that's fair,' Elizabeth said. 'Or true. If she cared a lot about something and I didn't, why fight her on it?' She noticed him look longingly at the coffee pot, but she wasn't ready for a friendly chat at the kitchen table. 'I'm her only daughter and she was thrilled when it seemed I'd met my life's love. And she loved you, too.'

He winced, then ran his fingers through his dark curls. 'I don't mean to dump all the blame on you and Videen. I got swept away in the family stuff just as much as you did. My mother pressured me about us planning to live together without getting married. And I felt pressure from your side to move things along too. I should never have proposed when I did. I think we panicked at the idea of growing apart. Maybe if we'd had more time to get to know each other as independent people, we'd have ended up in the same place.'

'I certainly hope not,' Elizabeth said. 'This has been pretty much the worst few days of my life.'

'I'm really sorry,' he said, looking forlorn. 'I feel awful about the wedding. I feel awful about everything. And I missed you. It would've been one hell of a party, whether we'd had the dance steps down or not.'

She nodded. 'It would.'

'I'll come by with my brother later this morning to pick up the gifts and bills you want me to handle. Sometime around ten, OK?' Kevin asked.

'OK. And for what it's worth, I'd been practicing. We would have been fine.' She made herself look at him again, to remember the boy she'd once promised to marry.

Once he was gone, she sank back down at the table, feeling simultaneously better and worse. Then her cell phone buzzed, announcing the arrival of an email.

It was a Google alert on Senator Lester. She skimmed the contents, feeling her stomach churn again.

# TWENTY

Meigs was up before the sun on New Year's Day. He waited in the kitchen, mainlining coffee, determined not to approach Caroline until he heard signs of life from her room. He wrestled with how to talk with her about the incident the night before.

Ms Hart's advice from couples' therapy, dispensed as his wife was passing through the last hideous stages of Huntington's chorea, circled through his tired brain. Alice had been bedridden by then, unable to attend the session.

'Remember to watch for the ways that Caroline might act out her sadness. She's a good kid in a lot of pain,' Ms Hart had said. 'And like you, she's very private. But worse than being a tough-guy cop, she's a teenager.'

She had smiled gently. He remembered dropping his head to his hands and moaning. When he'd straightened up, Ms Hart had leaned over and laid a calming hand on his balled fist.

'This should be a time when she's launching out into the seas of the big world,' she'd continued. 'But she's losing her touchstone, the safe haven that would have allowed her to try things out, and then return home for a reset from time to time if they didn't work. She'll wear her pain outside like a spiky suit of armor. It'll take all of your patience not to lash out.'

She'd been absolutely dead on about his stepdaughter's prickliness. Caroline had refused to talk about her mother with her girlfriends or her teachers or, as far as he knew, her dreadful boyfriend. Half the school had shown up for the funeral and the morning had stretched on almost unbearably as they greeted the mourners. She'd finally fled with a friend, and he couldn't blame her. How could she speak about a loss that deep with kids whose most tragic life event might have been a failure to make the cheerleading squad, or a lacrosse game lost in the state semi-finals? Of course there would have been others who had suffered their own great anguish, who might have helped her grieve, if she had been able to open up.

Though he had experienced the agony of Alice's death alongside Caroline, what he'd lost couldn't touch the pain of losing a mother when you most needed her. And the longer they went without acknowledging their shared grief, the more impenetrable the wall building between them felt.

Through the darkest hours last night, he'd heard footsteps padding in the hallway and then the sound of retching in the bathroom upstairs that they shared. Caroline would be feeling like crap after the night she'd had, maybe even still be a little drunk. On the one hand, he felt sorry for her. On the other, this could be the best time to make a serious impression. He'd be kind, but firm.

When he finally heard the murmur of voices and the beat of some unrecognizable music seeping through the ceiling, he took the stairs two at a time and waited for a moment, gathering his calm.

He knocked.

'Go away,' she said.

He knocked again.

'Get lost,' she said, but he opened her door. The room still stunk of booze and stale smoke from yesterday's party.

Caroline froze when she saw him, her face a ghoulish blue in the reflection of her computer screen. She launched away from the desk and threw herself across the bed, burrowing under the covers next to her friend. Barbara buried deeper under the quilt, too, so nothing was visible except for a tangle of two heads of hair.

'Get out of my room,' Caroline said, her voice muffled by the bedcovers.

All his good intentions evaporated in an instant. 'Right this moment we need to call Barbara's family. Now. Where do they live?'

'Clinton,' Caroline said. The town east of Madison along the shoreline. 'She's already called. They're coming to get her at noon. And I'm going to her house.'

'You're not going anywhere. Your behavior is not acceptable,' he said, peeling the sheet away from her face.

She put her fingers in her ears and began to hum, a move so heartbreakingly childish and yet so provocative, he couldn't not react.

'Purchasing and using illegal substances, sleeping with boys, disappearing with other delinquents . . .' He felt himself winding up. 'Do you have any idea what kind of a woman exchanges sex for money?'

He winced at his own words, stopping himself before he said something harsher. Something that would humiliate her new friend. But he had to make her understand the risks her so-called friends were taking, how scared he was for her safety, how out of control it all felt. Only months into this new living arrangement and he was up to his neck in teenage quicksand and sinking fast.

'If you can't live by my rules and behave like a decent human being, this plan isn't going to work. And that begins with talking about what happened last night.' He jabbed his finger at her to emphasize his points.

She pulled a pillow over her head.

Meigs grasped the carved pineapple knob of her bed's headboard and squeezed it until he was breathing evenly again. 'You have another choice,' he said. 'I can call your father and you can move back home.'

Caroline rolled over, removed the pillow, and stared right at him, her face streaked with tears and snot and eyeliner.

'That's what you want, isn't it? To get rid of me? You'll do what you want, won't you?' she said. 'You always do.'

'What's that supposed to mean?' Honestly, he couldn't think of one family decision over the past year that had been what he wanted. And that had felt OK, not great, but OK, because Alice and Caroline needed to come first.

She buried her face in her arms and began to sob loudly. 'You never wanted a kid. You're happy I screwed up. Go ahead and call.'

Feeling a surge of anger and sadness and helplessness, he yanked her door open, pulling so hard the knob came off in his hand. He stared at it blankly – he'd backed himself into a corner, hadn't he? Dropping the doorknob on her nightstand, he retrieved the phone from his pocket, found her father's name in his directory, and dialed. After two rings, the voicemail picked up.

'This is Jack Meigs,' he said, when instructed to 'tell it like it is, dude', by a man who sounded stoned. 'Alice's husband,' he said, then added: 'Former husband. Caroline's stepfather.'

He cleared his throat, feeling furious and awkward. He'd never met the guy in person. Paul hadn't even shown up for Alice's funeral. Not that a guy should be expected to cry over his ex-wife, but Christ almighty, his daughter needed his support. The one telephone conversation they'd had had spiraled into a shouting match. That was about Caroline, too. Paul had allowed her to cancel her plane trip from California to Connecticut, where they'd arranged for her to spend a month of her summer vacation with her mother before returning to boarding school.

Alice had been dying. She'd understood that Caroline couldn't handle that reality. It became clear enough when Caroline chose boarding school over living with either parent. Still, Alice had cried for hours about the change in plans until Meigs couldn't take her sadness. He'd called Paul and given him hell about knuckling under to Caroline. Since when does a grown man let himself get jacked around by a teenage girl, he remembered yelling at him.

Since now, he thought grimly. Now he understood how hard this parenting business really was.

'We need to talk about Caroline. Call when you get a moment.'
He rattled off his cell number and hung up. 'You are grounded,'
he said to Caroline.

'For how long?' Caroline croaked.

'For two months. Maybe more. I'll let you know.' He saw
Barbara's eyes flash wide before she disappeared again into
the burrow of bedding.

Then he wheeled around and left the room, knowing he'd
been too harsh. This was the trouble with taking responsibility
for a teenager mid-stream. From where he sat as a cop,
parenting was easy: set limits, and set them firmly. Know that
underneath their protests, the kids want these boundaries.
And need them.

But in the flesh, it wasn't so easy.

'Nobody could live by your rules,' Caroline shrieked at
his retreating back. 'You're a stupid cop! I might as well live
in prison!'

His cell phone rang as he reached the top step. 'Meigs.'

'This is Officer Ramsey, NYPD. I'm calling about the
teenage girl who abandoned her baby. The woman who
accepted the infant lives in your town?'

'Yes, go on,' Meigs said, freezing in place at the note of
panic he thought he heard in her voice.

'This is a courtesy call,' she said. 'Not that I expect anything
to show up on your end.'

Meigs waited. Then why had she called him? 'Something's
changed in the abandoned baby case?'

'Yes. The Department of Children and Families worker
went to the hospital to take custody of the baby this morning
and turn her over to the foster parents. On the way to their
home, the worker was held up and the baby was stolen. The
woman was shot in the head. She's alive, but barely.'

Meigs whistled. 'Whoever took the baby didn't want a
witness,' he said. 'Was the infant injured? Any leads on the
shooter?'

'We don't know about the child. Two witnesses swear
it was a woman. Another was sure it was a slender man. The
car stopped at a red light, the shooter opened the back door
and plugged the driver in the back of the head. Cool as a

cucumber. Then they undid the car seat restraint and walked away with the baby. No one was close enough to give a good description or even take the license plate number down.'

'Sounds like a professional hit,' Meigs said. 'You don't shoot someone in the back of the head unless you mean to. Anything we can do from here, let us know.'

'If the runaway mother shows up, we need to talk with her,' said Ramsey.

Feeling bad that he hadn't managed to call her first, Meigs explained that the mother had turned up at the Browns' house, but then quickly disappeared. 'Our patrol officers are watching for her. We had a busy night here, but of course we'll help in any way we can,' Meigs said. 'Happy freaking new year.'

# TWENTY-ONE

E lizabeth parked her mother's car in the lot in front of the CVS at the corner of Route 79 and Madison's main drag. The street was mostly quiet, not surprising for early New Year's Day after a storm. A thin quilt of snow covered the pavement, although the humps along the sidewalks suggested the plows had already been busy. The lights from the Starbucks shone brightly, blurring the condensation that covered the front glass and obscuring the scene inside. Coffee drinkers streamed in empty-handed and others exited with steaming cups, and bags of what Elizabeth imagined to be cake and scones.

On the way to the coffee shop, she had filled her aunt in on Kevin's visit. And as they'd driven into Madison, she'd remembered the Google alert she'd received last night, linking the senator to a woman in New York, who'd faced and then evaded charges of running a prostitution ring. The senator's office had not returned the anonymous reporter's call.

'I meant to dig around a little more, but I got distracted by Kevin. And' – she turned to look at her aunt – 'discovering the paperwork approving my parents as foster parents. Did you know about this?'

Aunt Susan scrunched her face in apology. 'I did. Videen asked me not to say anything to anyone else, so I promised I wouldn't. She wanted to tell you herself. I bet she was sorry you found out like that. *I'm* sorry that you found out like that, you've had one hell of a week.'

Elizabeth blew out a breath of air and tried to let go of the tension in her shoulders and neck, which felt as though it was inching upward from her stomach through her chest, slowly strangling her. 'She felt bad, but I'm honestly happy for her. And it's none of my business really. But it feels like all the pieces of my life are shifting. And that steadiness at home – the sense that nothing would ever change – was my touchstone. You know?'

Susan leaned over to hug her. 'I know. We'll talk more about this later, OK?' she said as she got out of the car, snugging her coat's collar under her chin and ducking her head low against the blast of Arctic air. They hurried through the biting wind and pushed open the heavy glass door into the coffee shop. Elizabeth unwrapped the plaid scarf that she'd wound around her ears and mouth, and wiped the wind tears from her eyes. As they stomped the snow from their boots onto the gray rug inside the door, Elizabeth inhaled the scent of freshly ground coffee and peered around the shop in search of the senator's staffer.

'Oh good Lord,' said Aunt Susan. 'That nosy reporter has already beaten us to him.'

Sure enough, in the far corner nearest the front window, where a group of brown leather chairs had been settled around an empty space as if there was a fire pit, the young man they'd seen on the senator's Meet the Staff webpage was seated. He had papers spread on the small table next to him along with an open laptop and two phones. And in the chair directly across from him sat Olivia Lovett.

'What now?' Elizabeth muttered.

'We get our coffee and we butt in. Unless you'd rather leave him to her?'

'Absolutely not! We aren't convinced that she has Addy's

needs and interests at heart,' said Elizabeth. 'She conned me
into believing that at first, but now? I think she wants to sniff
around until she finds a big splash of a story. And this could
surely be one. What if she's the reporter who tracked the
senator's contact with the alleged prostitution ring? We are
not going to roll over so she can see a front-page byline and
trash Addy's life worse than it's already been trashed,' she
added, feeling a surge of anger.

'I'm with you, girl,' said Aunt Susan.

As they stood in line waiting for their lattes, Elizabeth's
mind whirled back to the scene in the subway. How in the
world had a teenage girl ended up alone, giving birth in
the most dreadful circumstances imaginable? And could
that trauma have anything at all to do with the senator?
Honestly, it seemed unlikely. But on the other hand, Olivia
was here, and she was an expert investigative reporter. So
maybe there was a connection. But Olivia was not the only
dogged woman interested in this case. Elizabeth would not
give up until she found answers. And got Addy the help she
needed, or at least whatever help she could accept. But first
they'd have to find her.

Coffee in hand, she wove through the maze of coffee-
drinkers and mustered up a big, phony smile. 'Olivia, so nice
to see you again.' She nodded at the reporter and then thrust
her hand out to the staffer. 'I'm Elizabeth Brown, one of your
Connecticut constituents.' Not exactly true anymore, as she
lived in New York City. But he wouldn't know that. 'And this
is Susan Warren. My aunt is a ferocious political activist—'

'Don't let her scare you,' Aunt Susan said with a chuckle.
'I love politics and I'm impossibly intrigued by politicians.
When I saw your note on Twitter, I couldn't resist the chance
to meet you and our senator. You said he'll be along too?'

'My pleasure,' said the staffer, shaking each of their hands
in turn. He had a firm grip and intense eye contact so that
Elizabeth suspected she'd never forget his face, or he hers.
'Ron Christenberry. As for Senator Lester, he promised to
come but he tends to overschedule himself and run late.
Please join us,' he added, waving at the two remaining chairs
in their fire pit circle.

'Good morning,' Olivia said, appearing much less enthused about the new arrivals than Ron, Elizabeth thought.

'Your accommodations were satisfactory?' Susan asked Olivia. 'We apologize for my brother-in-law's brush-off last night. He treasures his family time, especially around the holidays.' Her eyes twinkled with mischief.

Ignoring that, Olivia said, 'Ron and I were talking about the senator's commitment to supporting women and families and children. In these times, when so many support services have been eradicated or cut back, it's crucial that our lawmakers speak up for the powerless.'

'And I,' said Ron, crossing one long black-jeans-clad leg over the other to settle deeper into his chair, 'was in the process of assuring Ms Lovett that this is one of the senator's most important priorities.'

'I find it confusing,' Olivia said, leaning forward as he leaned away, 'that while the senator claims to stand for policies that will help women and children, his voting record shows that he has not come out in favor of universal healthcare, or Medicaid expansion, or even Head Start – hardly a controversial program.'

Ron uncrossed his legs. 'People don't understand that politics is not always straightforward. Sometimes you need to give in or appear to give in on issues while you make your entry through the back door. There's a lot of horse-trading,' he added. 'And how can I put this . . . Senator Lester is known for refining his positions over time.'

His tone was not condescending, and yet Elizabeth felt something off about his fast answer. Too polished? Too pat? All that, but maybe also a hint that Ron considered himself responsible for this 'refining'. The man behind the man.

'If I might butt in for a moment,' said Aunt Susan. 'To be honest, from where I sit it appears that your boss has taken stands that look more promising for your team's future electability, rather than for the actual benefit of women and children.'

'Ooh, ouch. That was a stinger,' said Ron, keeping a cheerful smile on his face and winking at Elizabeth.

She frowned, wanting to make sure he understood she was

on Susan's team, not his. 'Maybe it would help us understand if you explained a bit more about the benefits of your health-care proposal. As a medical student, this issue is important to me.'

'Of course,' said Ron, ignoring Aunt Susan and beaming at her from across the small open space. 'And congratulations on your career path. I never had much patience for school, so I salute you. As for healthcare, obviously the previous iteration was not working. Insurance companies were fleeing the system, premiums were rising – we are working hard with other senators and representatives to craft a proposal that will thrive in the marketplace. Because what's good for the marketplace is good for the American people. And this is where Senator Lester's excellent business background is a major asset.'

Now he was beginning to sound like a canned stump speech, a candidate on the road before an election, giving the same talk he'd given a thousand times. And full of himself besides. Elizabeth couldn't help arguing.

'But in the meantime, the poorest folk will slip through the cracks,' she said. 'Showing up at the emergency room when you feel ill because you can't afford insurance and you don't have a primary care doctor so this is the only place that will treat you is an absurd treatment model. It couldn't be less cost-effective.'

'Maybe it would help if we use a concrete example,' said Olivia. 'Perhaps you read about the subway baby who was given away by her teenage mother earlier this week. She passed the infant to this young woman, who in turn called the police.'

She pointed to Elizabeth. Ron's attention swung to her, the small lines around his lips and eyes tightening, and she immediately wished that Olivia hadn't identified her.

'I'm well aware that this happened in New York, not Connecticut,' Olivia continued, having to raise her voice over the cacophony of grinding beans and frothing milk. 'But let's assume it could also occur in your state. What kinds of support services would you recommend providing to prevent this kind of tragedy?' All of the machines behind the counter cut off at the same time so her last sentence became a shout in the silence. 'I'm talking about teenage pregnancy, homelessness, and girls who feel so much pressure that they risk the well-being of their own children.'

The people at the tables nearby turned to gawk.

'I'll get to that, but excuse me for a quick moment.' Ron stood up to shake hands with a tall, dark-haired man who had approached their group in a blast of cold air. He looked even more handsome in person than he had on TV.

'Good morning, boss,' Ron said cheerfully. 'Good to see you up and about in this new year. You have some fans waiting to meet you. Please meet Olivia Lovett, who is with the *New York Post*, Susan Warren, and Elizabeth Brown. Elizabeth was the woman who received the newborn in the subway and turned her over to the police.' Ron laid his hand on Elizabeth's shoulder and then flashed a toothy smile at all three of them. 'You're in luck,' he said. 'The man you really wanted to meet is here in the flesh.'

Elizabeth didn't believe that he meant this, though he might have been relieved for the respite from Olivia's grilling. In the conversation so far, she'd gotten hints that he considered his boss to be a buffoon who needed to be spoon-fed opinions on the issues by a staff more competent than he would ever be. Was he the one who knew Addy, rather than the senator himself?

'Such a pleasure, thank you for coming out. Please call me Les. Everyone does. Brrrr, it's a cold start to the year, isn't it?' Without waiting for an answer, he sat in the chair that Ron had dragged over and added: 'Are you all with the press?'

'My niece and I are just normal constituents,' said Aunt Susan, 'with an interest in the inside scoop. A hankering to see how the sausage is made.' She finished with a sly wink.

Senator Lester winked back at her and smoothed his wavy hair. He took a sip of his coffee and produced another warm smile. 'I could hold forth on politics in America for hours, but no one wants that. Any particular questions I can answer?'

'We were just talking about the baby born in the New York subway and the healthcare issues that incident raises,' said Ron, blinking at his boss. Either he'd gotten something stuck in his contact lens or he was signaling a furious Morse code of . . . something.

'I believe we read about that in the *Times*,' said the senator. 'Apologies that it wasn't the *Post*,' he added, looking at Olivia. Though he didn't sound the least bit sorry. 'I simply don't have time to read all the papers out there. There was an issue of safe haven in this story, if I remember correctly?' He glanced at his staffer for confirmation.

'Safe haven, yes,' said Ron. 'Our state is slightly more restrictive than New York, as the child would need to be brought to an emergency room in order to meet the letter of the law.'

'In New York,' Olivia said, 'you can leave your baby, up to thirty days old, with any responsible person at a suitable location in New York. Sometimes it takes a little doing to determine the meaning of *suitable location*. If a prosecutor wanted to split hairs, he might question whether turning an infant over to a stranger in a subway would be considered *suitable*.' She frowned and tapped her pen on the table. 'But the point is, what services could the state provide that would help a young mother to avoid this painful choice in the first place?'

'The healthcare proposal that the senator supports would answer many of these concerns,' said Ron. 'This is a terribly sad story and we can see why you would be interested in the case.' He gazed across the table at Elizabeth and then nodded to his boss.

'Heartbreaking,' said Senator Lester. 'And you were right on the scene. What was the young woman like?'

'I hardly had the chance to find out,' Elizabeth said. She didn't feel right telling these men that Addy had come to her house. 'She looked exhausted and desperate, as one would after giving birth alone.' She felt a swell of sadness. 'The baby was perfect though, with a full head of dark hair already. Perfect little pink lips.'

'I wonder if there's anything we can do concretely for the child?' Senator Lester asked, glancing over at his staffer. 'Like help find her a caring home. I could phone one of my New York colleagues and offer assistance.'

'They might welcome your help,' said Olivia. 'Although I suspect the incident is becoming a bit of a hot potato, politically speaking. There's already a lot of pressure to identify the mother and find out her story. Lots of people calling the police and local politicians. I suspect that's mostly so the powers that be can assign proper blame.'

'A cynical outlook there,' said Ron, grinning at Olivia. 'You don't think much of your elected officials.'

'I know it's popular for women to advocate for choice,' said the senator, 'but I'm of the opinion that the unwanted babies themselves are most in need of support. My wife agrees – she sits on the board of Save Our Connecticut Children.'

'Good for her.' Elizabeth glanced at her watch. 'This has all been so fascinating – a fresh slant on what goes on behind the scenes. Before we go, I wonder, Senator, if you have any comment on the story I read in the news this morning linking you to a prostitution ring?' Everyone at the table stared at her.

'I have no comment on that ludicrous allegation,' said the senator, his face reddening. 'It's absolute bullshit.' His expression hardened, turning his boyish good looks into something fierce and mean.

Elizabeth broke her eye contact with him and got to her feet. 'Thanks for meeting with us this morning. And for your service,' she added as an afterthought.

Susan stood up and nodded, then took Elizabeth by the elbow and began to steer her toward the door.

'I'll walk you out,' said Ron. When the three of them reached the door, Ron looked at Elizabeth with a warm smile. 'You are one feisty lady. I expected a question like that from the reporter, but not you.' He took a small bow. 'I couldn't help noticing that you don't have a ring on your finger. I'd love to get your number. Maybe we could go out for another coffee, or even dinner.'

'She may not be ready for that yet,' said Aunt Susan, 'as she's recovering from escaping a nasty close call with a turd of a fiancé. But she will be at some point . . .' And to Elizabeth's shock and horror, she read off her niece's phone number to Ron, who tapped it into his phone.

'Why don't you give us your contact info, too?' Aunt Susan asked, and then took the two business cards that Ron handed over.

Elizabeth waited until they were outside to yelp: 'Why in the world did you do that? I'm certainly not ready to date anyone, and if I was, it wouldn't be that smug piece of work.'

'For Addy's sake,' Aunt Susan said. 'If he calls to ask you out, and then he brings up the topic of her and her baby, we might get some confirmation that she and the senator were somehow involved. Or at least knew her. You sure knocked the senator cold with your question.'

They huddled against the knifing wind and hurried to the car. Elizabeth pulled off her hat and shook out her curls. 'That question just burst out of me.' She grinned and started the car. 'As for Ron, he seems like an affable, smart guy, so why didn't I like him? I didn't like either of them.'

'It's not just the politician thing, he's a little too slick,' said Aunt Susan. 'Even the senator should keep an eye out for that guy. I think he's got big ambitions.'

'Then there was the senator's rant about saving unwanted children – it felt hollow,' said Elizabeth. 'Even though his wife sits on the board of Save Our Connecticut Children.' Her voice trailed off. It could be interesting to speak with the senator's wife. Not to hear about the organization, but to get her sense of him. Assuming she'd say anything – he would be a frightening enemy if crossed or exposed, she suspected. And there could likely be nondisclosure agreements preventing her from speaking as well.

Aunt Susan looked at her, then squinted. 'You've got something up your sleeve.'

'I was thinking about going to New Haven to chat with my father's secretary.' She tapped her chin with a gloved finger.

'A sudden interest in emergency room procedures? I thought you were thinking of specializing in pediatrics?'

'Wilma sits on the board with Lester's wife. She's passionate about finding solutions for unwanted kids so they don't end up in the foster care system.'

'But surely she's not working today?'

'She stays home on Christmas Day and Sundays because my father insists, but other than that, she's always at work. Though I hate to leave Mom dealing with Kevin and his brother. He's coming by to pick up some gifts and bills.'

'Oh my, I would love to take a crack at Kevin,' said Aunt Susan, grinning. 'And I wouldn't worry about your mother. Your father treats her like she's one of those French wine glasses that cost a fortune, and if you pour a heavy red wine into them, they shatter. Videen may have gotten a little more delicate over the years, but I think that's because he shelters her.'

'OK, that's a plan,' said Elizabeth, nodding. 'You won't hurt Kevin, will you?'

'There won't be any visible bruises or blood,' said Aunt Susan, holding crossed fingers up in the air.

# TWENTY-TWO

By the time Caroline's father had finished his phone conversation out on the landing, left a message on someone else's phone and stumped downstairs, Addy had disintegrated into weeping. She hated, absolutely despised, feeling this out of control. But she couldn't help it. She'd heard enough from his side of the conversation to know that someone had shot the social services worker who'd picked up the baby at the hospital. Killed them off. It had to be Georgia. Heather had suffered a similar fate, after all. If anyone got in her way, blocked the path to what she wanted, she simply destroyed them. She'd killed this woman in order to steal Addy's baby – there was no other explanation. But Georgia wasn't done yet. Addy knew she wouldn't stop until she had the phone . . . and had made sure Addy and Rafe couldn't breathe a word about it to anyone.

'Don't worry about all that,' said Caroline, waving in the direction of her father, her forehead furrowed with concern. 'He always starts out acting like a hard ass. Even if my stupid father calls him back, chances of him wanting me to live in California with him are slim to none.'

Addy didn't know what Caroline was talking about. Before he'd left the message, he'd been talking to a cop about another shooting. She sobbed harder, and dug deeper into Caroline's bedding. How could she possibly explain the truth?

'Even if I do go,' Caroline continued, sounding desperate to comfort her, 'I'll take you with me. My real dad owes me more than one plane ticket. He never paid child support in his life. If I ask for a ticket for you, I bet he'll come through. Now he lives in Venice, right near the beach. It's way cool if you don't mind the homeless people.' She stopped speaking, looking horrified at the idea she might have insulted Addy.

'Don't worry about not having a normal family,' Caroline said, patting Addy's back. 'My mom died last spring, and trust me, I'll never be normal again.'

Addy poked her head out from the nest of pillows. 'What happened to her?'

'Huntington's chorea. Stupid disease. Nobody survives it. There's no treatment. All you can do is watch them die. And of course my mom being my mom, I was supposed to talk about it. Fat chance.' She wiped away the tears that seeped from her eyes and tried to smile. 'Everyone's got something awful in their life. Yours isn't any worse than mine. It couldn't be.'

But that only started Addy weeping again. And no matter how Caroline tried to comfort her, she could not stop. Hers was worse. It was. Because she was to blame.

'Is it about last night?' Caroline finally asked, her lips quivering as though she was on the verge of bawling herself. 'I'm so sorry about what happened. It was my fault. I've never had a friend who would do what you did for me.'

Addy tried to smile, but she couldn't stop thinking of Heather and how badly she'd let her down. No matter what she did for new friends, or even old, nothing would make up for leaving Heather behind to die. And then leaving the baby for Georgia to find. Her stomach cramped with a terrible pain and she began to cry harder, big gulping sobs that left her feeling as though she could not breathe. Smothered by her own stupid mistakes.

'Addy, you're scaring me,' said Caroline. 'Nothing can be this bad.'

Addy wiped her face with the corner of Caroline's flowered sheet. Either she had to tell her or she had to leave this minute.

But go where? 'The baby that your father was talking about in the hall?'

Caroline nodded.

'That was my baby. And Georgia's going to track me down and make sure I never say a word about it. She'll kill me too.'

'That can't be your baby,' Caroline said. Her mouth fell into a puzzled 'O'. 'You can't have a baby, you're just a girl. Anyway, why would you give away your own baby? And who's Georgia?'

Addy stared at her, snuffling and wheezing. She knew what would happen now: Caroline would tell her father that she was a bad kid, rotten through the pulp to the seeds, as her mother used to say. And then he'd make her leave, or take her to jail. Because it was a crime to abandon a baby in a subway, she knew that. It had been her job to protect that pitiful little thing, in a way that she had never been protected. And she had failed.

'I'm a hooker,' Addy finally said. There was no point in trying to keep this a secret. It would only come out later, when Caroline had become more important to her and it would be harder to lose her kindness. Better to cut the ties now and move on.

'I don't understand,' Caroline said. 'You're not a hooker. I know girls who do it with more than one guy—'

'It's easy,' said Addy, in her hard street voice. 'I ran away because my mother was a bitch. And her boyfriend wanted to screw me. Then Georgia found me in New York City. I didn't know all the girls at her house were earning money by getting sent out to hotels to have sex with strangers. It doesn't matter now anyway. It's too late to change what happened.' She threw back the covers and began to search for her clothes, which she'd dropped everywhere before falling into bed the night before.

Caroline leapt out of bed and grabbed both of her wrists. 'You can't leave. I won't let you. It doesn't matter what happened before. You're my best friend now, and if you're in trouble, I want to help.' She flung her arms around Addy's neck and squeezed and squeezed until the iron in Addy's spine began to soften and then melt and she finally hugged her back.

'I'm so sorry about your mother,' she whispered.

'Thanks,' Caroline whispered back. They clung together for a few more moments.

'What if we tell my father about the baby?' Caroline asked. 'He's mad at me now, but I know he would help.'

'Your stepfather?' Addy pointed at the stairs and Caroline nodded.

She couldn't believe that any cop would be willing to help her, even if he was distantly related to Caroline. And considering what had gone on last night and this morning, she doubted he would help her now – or ever. And the truth was she didn't know Caroline well enough to trust her completely either. She shook her head. 'No cops.'

'Then what can we do?' Caroline asked. 'Who can we ask?'

Addy's mind went dark, because there was no one. She was certain that her grandmother loved her. But Gram was in no condition to face this kind of messed-up evil.

'What did you do with the baby?' Caroline asked.

'There was a woman in the subway. She was pretty and she looked nice. That sounds so ridiculous . . .'

'But she took the baby?'

Addy nodded.

'Did she adopt her or something?'

'No, she turned her over to some cops and they took her to the hospital. And now Georgia's stolen her away.' She could feel herself winding up into another meltdown.

'Are you sure it's the same baby? Let me see what comes up if we Google.' She crossed the room to her desk and tapped a few words into her computer. The police report Addy had seen in the newspaper at the rest stop came up, followed by a brief story about the shooting and the baby's kidnapping.

'That's her,' said Addy, feeling heavy and dead inside. 'That's me.'

Caroline stared at her for a few minutes.

This was it, the moment when she'd tell her to leave.

'What about this woman in the subway?' her friend finally asked. 'Do you think she would help us?'

A little crack of light forced its way into the darkness that filled Addy's heart. Elizabeth had gotten involved when she didn't have to. She'd tried to help. And now Caroline wanted to help her too. And she knew the worst.

'She might,' Addy said. 'They were kind to me before I freaked out and ran away. Is there someone besides your stepfather who can give us a ride? I know where she lives. It's over by the marsh, just out of town.'

Caroline wrinkled her forehead. 'She lives here in Guilford?'

Addy explained how she'd followed her out on the train. She blew her nose and looked at her new friend. 'But you're grounded. You shouldn't come.'

'Course I'm coming,' said Caroline, as she punched some numbers into her phone. 'That bastard Randy, he owes me a lot. He could give me rides for the rest of his life and we still wouldn't be even.'

# TWENTY-THREE

On the drive into the hospital, Elizabeth thought more about what Susan had said about her mother, about how things were not always as they seemed. Kevin had accused her of folding in the face of her mother's dreams about their wedding, turning the celebration into her vision of perfection, not theirs. This criticism rankled. And if Kevin had been sitting in the car with her, she would have denied it. But in her heart, it struck a true note. She had a way of puzzling out what others wanted from her and setting off down that path, without a word ever spoken. In her mother's case, the path turned out to be the fancy wedding with hordes of guests and the perfect gown. For her father, it was attending medical school.

But where was she in all this? She forced herself to stick with the question, not skim over it, as she had done many times in the past. Somewhere around the first East Haven exit off I-95, the answer came: she tended to get so busy pleasing the people in her life that she had no idea what she really wanted. And deeper still, she caught a glimmer of why. Her parents had chosen to adopt her because they couldn't have a child of their own. To her mother in particular, Elizabeth meant everything. And in exchange for their love, Elizabeth yearned to do and be what they wanted her to be. In trying to fulfill their hopes and dreams, she may have lost sight of her own. Kevin, of all people, had seen some of that. And he'd also seen that their relationship was based on a college kids' fantasy. He had been able to recognize that if they went ahead with the wedding, their marriage would be teetering on a base of paper-mache.

She paid to park on the recently plowed street nearest the emergency room and clambered over the piles of snow left alongside the road, sinking to her knees in the loose drift. Once she reached the hospital building, she stopped outside her father's office to shake the snow out of her boots. Inside, she wasn't surprised to see her dad's secretary, Wilma, at her desk. A tall woman with wide hips and natural curls that escaped from her bun no matter how she tried to contain them, she must've been a beauty as a young woman. These days, she still looked pretty, if a little faded. And she was always on duty whenever Elizabeth called, fiercely protective of her boss's time and energy. Elizabeth suspected that she didn't have a big life outside the office. Exhibit one: at work on New Year's Day.

'I'm so terribly sorry about the wedding,' Wilma said, as Elizabeth hung her coat on the rack next to the door. She looked stricken, as though she was somehow responsible for the event's failure. She was like that, a quivering blob of emotions that she absorbed from the people around her – a human mood ring. Elizabeth had always felt sad for her lack of family, and had insisted they invite her to the wedding, even though some of her father's colleagues had been struck from the guest list in favor of a few more aunts and uncles on Kevin's side.

'She won't know anyone,' Elizabeth's father had protested. 'She'd have to sit with a table of strangers. Won't that make her feel awkward?' But Elizabeth and her mother had prevailed, and Wilma had been thrilled with the invitation.

Elizabeth flashed her a weak smile. 'Thank you,' she said, approaching her desk. 'And thank you for your generous gift.' Wilma had sent one of the most expensive items on their registry, a fancy food processor that Elizabeth had felt guilty even listing. She'd been certain no one would buy it. 'Bailing out was probably the right move, but we have a snarl of plans to unravel.'

'First of all, I want you to keep that gift for yourself. You deserve it, married or not married.'

Elizabeth started to protest, but Wilma wouldn't allow it, and continued to talk. 'I once made a decision that was the hardest thing I've ever done. I still think it was right, but I was heartbroken for a long, long time.' She lifted her shoulders into a shrug.

Elizabeth looked at her, intrigued. 'What happened?'

'Someday I'll tell you. Are you feeling OK about not getting married?'

A lump of sadness choked Elizabeth's throat and she fought to shove it down. 'I know I'll be all right eventually. But this is so hard on my parents. They hate to see me down. And Mom enjoyed every bit of the planning, except for the arguments with Kevin's family. I know she's disappointed. And Dad can't stand for either of us to be upset so he's ready to kill Kevin.' She began to sniffle. 'Honestly, I think I am going to miss him – a little. And it was going to be a magical night. With Kevin dumping me, well . . . it's hard not to feel as though something's wrong with me.' She was horrified to find herself blubbering.

Wilma hurried around the desk with a handful of Kleenex and clasped her in a firm hug. 'You're perfect exactly as you are,' she said, rocking her like a baby.

'I'm pathetic, aren't I?' Elizabeth pulled away from the hug to blow her nose and dab at her eyes. She looked at the mascara that had bled into her tissue. 'I was thinking of shadowing Dad for a couple of hours, but I can't go out there like this. The people coming into the hospital today are in a lot worse shape than I am.'

'For heaven's sake, take the day off. I'll make you a cup of tea and we can have a nice chat. I've got cookies too, lots of them. Gifts from my friends in the department. No one knows what else to get an old spinster, married to her work.' She grinned and bustled off to fill her electric kettle and get out mugs and tea bags. 'Caffeine or herbal?'

'Definitely caffeine.'

Once the kettle whistled, Wilma came over to the couch where Elizabeth was sitting and unloaded a tray with steaming mugs and a plate of homemade goodies. 'My favorite is the chocolate lace.'

Elizabeth picked up one of the cookies, nibbled, and nodded. 'Addictive.'

Wilma set her mug on the table and reached for Elizabeth's hand. 'This isn't really my place to say, but since I'm outside of the situation, maybe I could help with some perspective. I know it feels awful now, but isn't it possible that Kevin's cutting you loose could be an opportunity to look at all the big questions in your life? To ask what it is that you really want, not what others want for you?'

'I was thinking that on the way in,' Elizabeth said. 'Maybe after I've gotten over feeling so sad. And pissed.' She grinned, took a sip of tea, and patted her lips with a pink napkin. 'I have a question for you on another topic. My aunt and I met Senator Lester at the Madison Starbucks this morning. I saw an article online mentioning that his wife sits on the board of Save Our Connecticut Children. I remembered that you do too.'

Wilma nodded.

'It rang hollow, what the senator was saying about how much he cares about women's and children's issues, and I wondered what you've heard about him?'

'Believe me, I've heard plenty,' Wilma said. She tweaked a few curls that had escaped from her twist. 'I think he's a lot of talk and very little action. Between us – and saddest of all – I don't think his wife even likes him. Now there's a marriage that probably never should have happened.'

'But is he capable of something truly evil, like frequenting underage prostitutes?'

'I couldn't say he wasn't,' Wilma said slowly.

# TWENTY-FOUR

Detective Meigs was paging through the *Guilford Courier* in the kitchen with a third cup of coffee when his phone buzzed again. The Madison police department came up on the screen. 'Meigs,' he answered gruffly, hoping for – what? At least no more bad news.

It was McNally, one of the officers who'd fielded the fallout of the party Caroline had attended. 'When you took your daughter home last night, we neglected to give you a sweater that belongs to either her or her friend Barbara. We could have a patrol car swing by later this afternoon. Or the chief suggested I tell you that I'm going out to interview one of the girls who was at the party. We plan to prosecute the dickwads who own the house and provided all the alcohol to the teens. Hopefully she'll be a good witness. He thought you might want to ride along. Unofficially, of course. If so, can you meet me at the Starbucks in ten?'

Meigs hesitated, wondering if Caroline would stay put if he went out for half an hour. No, bad move to leave her here alone. Could he ask the neighbor next door if she'd keep an eye on things? He wanted badly to see those thugs punished.

'I can be there in fifteen,' he told McNally. He hung up and called the neighbor to explain that his daughter was grounded and he needed to run out for a short while. 'We're having a bit of a rough patch and I'm not sure she'll stay put.'

'Of course,' she said. 'I'll watch like a hawk. And I'll text you if I see anything off.'

Maybe this girl they were interviewing would know something about Barbara. He didn't believe she was nineteen. No way. Even if she was, it felt wrong not to inform her parents about the party. And he doubted she lived in the next town over. He needed to find out what the hell she was doing in the middle of the night in the middle of nowhere

– a girl he'd never seen before, when he'd known most of the kids in this town and some of the surrounding towns for their whole lives. Just as his own cop father had known their parents.

He could not get the image of the girl's sweatpants out of his mind – the knees wet from her kneeling in the snow. It made him sick to his stomach. And even sicker about what could have happened to Caroline. He was relieved to hear that the Madison cops were following up on what had gone on at the party – he knew he wouldn't get the truth from the girls. He trudged upstairs.

'I'm going out for half an hour,' he said, standing outside Caroline's closed door.

No answer.

'Mrs Preston will be watching the house while I'm out. Remember, you're grounded.'

He considered asking what she wanted for supper, but doubted she'd reply to that either. The pizza he'd brought last evening as a peace offering was stashed in the fridge. They could eat that if cereal or frozen TV dinners didn't appeal.

'I'll be back well before noon. I want to meet Barbara's parents when they get here,' he added, and tromped downstairs. He didn't actually expect to see Caroline and her friend emerge from her room any time soon – she'd be too angry about his setting limits and calling her father. And maybe she was justified in the latter – he didn't feel too good about dragging that loser into his family business either.

He drove like a banshee on the way to Madison, reviewing the events of the night before. All the participants would be feeling dreadful this morning, not only Caroline. Maybe with a hangover, and after a night under the influence of her parents, this girl would be ready to talk.

McNally's cruiser was idling in the coffee shop parking lot. Meigs parked his SUV and slid into the passenger seat.

'Happy New Year,' McNally said, his face shaded with sympathy. 'It could have turned out a lot worse last night. A couple of kids in Meriden died early this morning – alcohol poisoning.'

Meigs nodded, at a loss for words.

McNally drove them north to Wildcat Road, then hooked a quick right onto 79 and then onto Randi Drive. The homes in this neighborhood were enormous and dressed elegantly for the holidays. The street had been plowed and a few early birds were out shoveling their driveways. They parked along the curb, trudged up the front walk, and rang the doorbell of a huge brick home with white shutters and a silver wreath on the door. The woman he'd seen in the waiting area at the station last night opened the door, just wide enough to see them. She looked drained and ten years older than she had the night before.

'Yes?'

'I'm Officer McNally from the Madison police.'

The woman's body stiffened and her face turned the color of powdered sugar.

'This is Detective Meigs. I am hoping to talk to your daughter, to get more information about the party last night. We're planning to prosecute the men who hosted it, so any details she can add will be helpful.'

She still hesitated.

'If we don't learn the truth, it will happen again. Only maybe worse next time – kids could die. It could be my daughter, or yours,' Meigs added, though he'd promised to keep quiet on the way over. His voice cracked and he could see her soften in response.

She opened the door and waved them in. 'I'll wake her up. You can wait in there.' She pointed to the living room off to the left, where everything was white and gold, including the ornaments and lights on a massive Christmas tree. 'And you can leave your boots right here.' She pointed to an Oriental carpet by the door that looked nicer than anything Meigs had in his home.

They shucked their boots off, then paced into the room. The fireplace was filled with white candles. One photo sat above the ornate crown molding on the mantel – a large family portrait taken before the girl had bleached her hair. Aside from the kid in the center, the photo included the mother he'd just spoken with, only with her hair done and lots of make-up, the serious-looking dad, and a big black Labrador with his pink tongue hanging out that made him feel sad. They'd lost their dog Barney the year before Alice died and it had nearly killed her. Dogs shouldn't go before their owners – the pain was too hard.

The mother and daughter came into the living room and sat on the couch across from the two men. She did not resemble the spitfire he'd seen leaving the police department the night before. Wearing teddy bear pajamas, with her hair in pigtails, she looked exhausted and very young. But he could see her pulling on her attitude like a well-worn suit.

'This is my daughter, Bethany,' said the mom. She swiveled to face the girl. 'The policemen have some questions for you.'

McNally asked about the party hosts, whether and how alcohol and other drugs had been provided, and whether she'd felt threatened or intimidated at any point during the evening. Bethany's answers were rude and mostly not of much use, Meigs thought.

He leaned forward, his elbows on his knees. 'About last night, my daughter Caroline Miller was there. Do you know her?'

Bethany made a face. 'I know who she is. But I don't hang out with the stoner crowd.'

'Bethany!' her mother scolded.

'Don't worry about it,' said Meigs, though his blood had started a slow boil. She'd obviously had a lot of practice at getting under adults' skins. Caroline wasn't a stoner – he would have noticed. Or would he? He certainly hadn't anticipated the party at his house. 'She was with another girl at the party. Barbara. Do you know where she met this friend? Or anything about where she lives or her family?'

'No idea,' said the teddy bear girl, and then she yawned and stretched. 'But she wasn't dressed like one of us. Those boots she had on were prehistoric.' The girl's mother grimaced but Bethany continued to talk. 'She kept Caroline from getting raped, I can tell you that much for sure.'

Meigs jerked back, feeling like she'd hacked him in the windpipe.

'Bethany!' her mother yelped again.

The girl rolled her eyes. 'He said he wanted answers. I'm just trying to help.'

'Go on,' said Meigs.

'Her stupid boyfriend lost everything in a poker game almost as soon as they arrived. The older guys were scamming him but he was too freaking drunk to even realize it. He sat there in his underwear sniveling about how he couldn't give them his mother's car cause she'd kill him.' She heaved a dramatic sigh and pulled one pigtail out of its rubber band, and then the other. She slipped the sparkly pink bands over her wrist and snapped them.

'Obviously, his girlfriend was the only thing he had left to trade, only she was passed out on the futon in the corner of the room. Two of the guys were going to carry her into the bedroom when her pal stood up for her. She told them it would be like having sex with a sack of potatoes. Or was it flour? Doesn't matter.' She gathered her loose hair up and wrapped it around her hand as if this was normal conversation. 'So then her friend went outside with them, and well . . . I'm certain you heard the rest from the other cops. It was so cold outside, the kid who supposed to go first couldn't perform. He couldn't even get his pants unzipped.' She snickered. 'He'll never live that down!'

Bethany's mother held up a hand to cut her off, looking shell-shocked. 'Where did you learn to talk this way?'

Meigs's own hands were shaking, though he worked to keep a bland expression on his face. She might know more, but he wasn't at all sure he could stand to hear it.

'Tell us about the guys who were hosting the party,' he said. 'Had you been to this house before? Did you know them?'

'Nah,' she said. 'They've been out of school forever. This was a *special occasion*.' She grinned, but her lips quivered a bit and the gray hue of her skin belied the boasting words.

He and McNally took down the names of all the other kids she could remember attending the party. 'We may need to talk to you again,' he told the girl. He glanced over at McNally, who nodded, and they both stood up.

'Thank you for speaking with us,' McNally said.

Meigs followed the younger cop out of the room, stuffed his feet back into his boots, and started to the door. The mother's voice followed them out.

'Young lady, you get up to your room right now. When your father gets home with the bagels we will talk about your punishment.'

'Whatever,' the girl answered.

Meigs thought about Bethany's words as they wound their way out of the neighborhood. Even if she was only halfway right in what she'd reported, the implications for his step-daughter were sickening. How did she even know these people? And who was this girl who had offered to take Caroline's place? He felt like a coward, not quite able to face them, sick and angry about what Caroline had gotten herself into. And stunned by Barbara's sacrifice. Another disaster had skirted so close to his little family – he could never have forgiven himself for allowing that to happen. And he didn't see how they could have withstood a second blow. Caroline had lost so much already.

McNally retraced the route to downtown Madison and dropped Meigs back at the CVS lot. 'Don't worry, we'll get them,' he said, as Meigs got out.

Since he was here, he dashed into the drugstore to grab aspirin, shaving cream, and Tide with bleach. He hadn't done a load of laundry for either himself or Caroline in a week and a half; the last time he'd been out of detergent and the whites had come out gray. His stomach rumbled, reminding him that he'd not eaten breakfast this morning. He chose a packet of peanut butter crackers and a soda drink, and started toward the registers, nearly mowing down a slender woman with a long braid down her back.

'Jack Meigs,' she said. 'Happy New Year.'

'Annabelle Hart,' she reminded him when he didn't answer right away.

The couples' therapist he'd seen with Alice. He mumbled New Year's greetings back.

'I hope things are going well for you and Caroline,' she said.

'It's hard,' he admitted. No point in trying to hide that from her – she had already seen him at rock damn bottom.

She nodded in sympathy. 'Anything in particular?'

He surprised himself by spilling out the story. 'There was

a gathering last night, with underaged teens and some stupid, cretinoid older guys. The drinking got out of hand and the neighbors called the cops because of the noise. They found a girl on her knees in front of one boy with a bunch of other kids circling around to watch . . .' His voice seemed to catch and he cleared his throat so he could choke out the words. 'Apparently, the girl did this to protect Caroline, who'd had too much to drink to protect herself. I'm trying to understand the girl's point of view, why she was willing to make this sacrifice.' He threw her a pleading look. 'You know teenagers better than I do.'

Ms Hart bit her lip, then gave a quick nod. 'Of course, I would have no way of knowing without talking with the girl,' she said. 'But in general, the attachments teenage girls make to their friends feel very powerful. The loyalty between these two girls sounds familiar in that way. Although Caroline's friend apparently took that to an extreme. Not many girls would have done it.'

'And so why would she?' Meigs was genuinely puzzled. Grateful, but puzzled.

'I can only guess of course, but it makes me wonder whether she'd been involved in an emotionally abusive relationship, in which the man wielded psychological control. In other words, she'd grown to experience this kind of thing as the norm in her life. Maybe learned that this was part of what she had to do to survive.'

'Good God,' he said.

The therapist shook her head – yes, she'd seen it all. 'In other words, she could have been unconsciously acting out – repeating – a destructive event that occurred in her past.'

There was a silence that he knew better than to disturb.

'Please don't tell me this friend was Caroline.'

'Thank God, no,' he said quickly. 'It's a new friend of hers. Appeared out of nowhere. I'm worried, of course.'

'Of course.'

He glanced at his watch. Almost an hour had passed since he'd left the house and he'd told Caroline thirty minutes.

'Is there anything particular about teens,' he asked, 'that would explain their actions differently? This bothers me a lot

– why would this group of kids go along? The kids watching
. . . I don't get it,' he added, his voice pained.

Ms Hart sounded sad, too. 'Only that kids these days have
somehow gotten the idea that oral sex isn't a sexual act at all.
It's very disturbing. The girls don't understand how damaging
their actions can be to their subconscious feelings about
themselves and their bodies. Lord only knows what the boys
are thinking.'

'Not much thinking going on there at all,' said Meigs. He
felt queasy, as though the subject of his inquiry had shifted
underneath him without his intention. He had the urge
to steady himself on a nearby shelf containing half-price
Christmas decorations, but took a deep breath instead. How
could he possibly deal with this kind of problem in his own
family? He didn't have the patience or the subtlety. There were
rules. If you didn't follow them, there were consequences.
And those rules were supposed to keep bad things from
happening. Honestly, the whole story broke his heart.

Ms Hart coughed and asked gently, 'Is there something I
can help *you* with?'

'Not unless you specialize in impossible stepdaughters,'
he said, wishing he could take it back as soon as he'd said it.
'And hapless stepfathers.'

'I've seen one or two of those,' she said, smiling warmly.
'Please feel free to call for an appointment. With or without
Caroline. As you already know, our discussions would remain
confidential.'

He climbed back into his car with the container of detergent
and the sack from CVS. He dug around until he found the
crackers, pulled them out and twisted the cap off the soda.
Anything was better than Starbucks coffee and crumpets. He
thought about what Rebecca Butterman, a psychologist
friend whom he deeply admired, had told him the Christmas
before this one – how holidays highlight broken spaces in the
psyche, usually hacked open during some family crisis.

He inhaled a couple of crackers and washed them down
with soda, watching the cars going by, their tires clacking in
the snow. Maybe these were people who felt as he did, that
holidays were a trap, a rotted track pocked with landmines for

families who weren't normal and happy, the way Christmas jingles said they should be. How many of those 'normal' families could there really be? Didn't all of them have some kind of problems? Surely he could manage one rebellious teenager. It was strictly a matter of keeping his cool and laying down the law. And doing a better job of letting her know that he loved her and understood that she was suffering, Alice would have told him that.

As he turned his engine on, he spotted a woman who reminded him of Elizabeth Brown pulling out of the Starbucks parking lot with another lady. Had she heard from the girl who'd given birth in the subway after she'd shown up then suddenly disappeared yesterday? What a shock that night must have been. He'd call her as soon as he checked in with home and then the station.

All the bits of the past few days floated through his mind – the newborn, the shooting, the party at his home, the party where the possibly damaged girl had sacrificed herself for his daughter. He felt sick with a sudden jolt of recognition. Could Barbara be the girl who'd given birth in the subway? How in the world had she gotten hooked up with Caroline? He recalled the therapist's words. 'Emotionally abusive relationship . . . what she had to do to survive . . . a destructive event in her past . . .' Good grief. It was staring him in the face.

He stuffed his trash into the white plastic CVS bag, roared out of the parking lot, and charged across town toward home. He needed to find out who Caroline's new friend really was and get her the help she needed to be safe before he turned his attention back to his stepdaughter.

# TWENTY-FIVE

R afe followed the directions on his GPS, finally turning onto a narrow road that wound through a snowy swamp. It had been easier than he'd thought to track down Elizabeth Brown, even without Mitch's expertise. People should realize that a simple Internet search would turn up almost everything they thought was private. Between White Pages and a lack of privacy settings on Elizabeth's Facebook profile, finding her family home in Guilford had been a snap.

He despised the suburbs – too much open space, nowhere to disappear the way you could in the city. And with Georgia hot on his heels, he was going to need to disappear fast. If she found Addy first, she'd grab the phone and shoot the girl. And he'd be next for sure.

The address he'd punched in brought him to a two-story old-fashioned white shingled home with candles in every window and lights on the fir tree near the driveway. Damn. If Addy had wiggled her way into this family, she was a better con man than even he. And it might be damn difficult to cut her back out of this pack.

In his mind, he pulled up the image of the beach town and the bungalow near the water that he'd told her about for the last six months, the house that he'd seen in a magazine. He pictured the whitewashed Adirondack chairs on the porch from which they'd be able to watch the waves roll in, the string of fairy lights around the windows, the driveway made of oyster shells that would crunch when they drove up to their home. All fictional, of course. He'd go mad with boredom living in a place like that. But he might need to call on those memories to lure her away from here.

He parked at the far end of the driveway, face out, so he could make a quick escape, and brushed the crumbs off his chest. He hadn't had time to stop and eat, just filled his gas tank at a highway rest stop and grabbed a burger and fries to go. Then he'd washed a tab of speed down with a Red Bull, as he was starting to feel sluggish and slow. That wouldn't do now, with his search for Addy coming to a head.

He ran his fingers through his hair, got out of the car, and headed for the front door with its gold pineapple knocker centered in the fancy wreath. At that moment a woman with a cap of curls and a red coat came outside with a snow shovel. He felt a surge of adrenalin. He could charm the gown and crown off the Statue of Liberty. One suburban grandma didn't stand a chance. He grinned at her and waved. She took a step back, unsmiling, holding the shovel with both hands as if to fend him off. What was she thinking? He could have ripped that away in an instant. He stomped his feet on the sidewalk and pretended to shiver, a prelude, he hoped, to being invited in.

'I'm Rafe Lawrence.' Not his real name, of course, but this didn't look like a neighborhood that would welcome Hispanics, or anyone who wasn't snow white. In fact, he couldn't believe that Addy had anything to do with these people.

'I'm looking for a girl named Addison.'

The woman appeared more alarmed and uncertain – a dead giveaway that Addy had been here. Or was here right now.

'I'm sorry, I don't know anyone with that name.' She pursed her lips and shook her head.

'You may have read about this in the papers. She delivered an infant all by herself in a New York subway station. I'm the fiancé.'

The woman took another step back, reaching for the door handle. He had to work fast.

'Can you imagine anything more terrible?' Rafe sighed with feigned compassion. 'Anyway, I'm the father.' He tapped his heart with his fist. 'And I feel absolutely sick that I wasn't with her. Her parents had threatened to take the baby away if she ever saw me again. And she panicked and ran. Anyway, now I'd like to do the right thing for her. And for our child.' He pressed a hand to his eyes as if he was blinking back tears.

'Terrible,' she said. 'But I can't help.'

Another shake of her head and he could feel his anger beginning to mount. 'According to the reports I read, it was your daughter who took the child from her.'

The woman bristled. 'My daughter didn't take her, the girl thrust the baby into her arms. She had no choice. And then when Addy showed up, we tried to help . . .' She pressed a gloved hand to her lips.

'Addy was here?' he asked. 'Is she here now?'

'I've nothing more to say.'

Rafe heaved another big sigh, trying not to let his irritation seep through the veneer of sensitivity he was attempting to construct. 'Do you have any idea where she might have gone? Did she mention her parents?'

The woman shook her head. 'No family members that we are aware of.'

'Maybe a friend?'

'I have nothing else to say. Bad enough my daughter was nearly killed yesterday. I don't know who you really are, but I'm going to go inside and call the police if you don't clear out right now.'

That imbecile Mitch. How had he managed to get himself shot in such a public and damning way? Not only was he now of no use, he could very well have ruined his chances of finding Addy and the kid. His prospective adoptive parents would be outraged, and demand the money they'd paid be returned – or something worse. Never mind the bigger payday they could have scored if Addy had met him with the kid and the senator's phone, as they'd planned. He had to get that phone before Georgia did.

'I hadn't heard that about your daughter, but it sounds terrifying,' he said. 'This whole thing has been awful for me, but I can only imagine how much worse it is for my Addy. May I give you a phone number in case she gets in contact with you? She's in grave danger and I want nothing more than to help her.'

She disappeared inside, then came back with a pad and pencil and spoke through the cracked open door she'd secured with a slender chain. 'I'm ready for your number,' she said.

He read it off to her. These people were ridiculous. As if that chain could keep her safe from anyone.

'Please, please tell her I love her and I will take care of her and our baby forever.' He held his hands out, pleading. 'I don't know how else to say it. I love her.'

Rafe backed down the stairs, jogged to his car, and roared out of the driveway, furious at the ignorance of this suburban woman. How could she have let Addy slip away? She must have been able to see the girl was in trouble. And now he was left with nothing to go on. But she was here in this little hick town – he was sure of it. It would only be a matter of circling through every street until he found her.

# TWENTY-SIX

Randy texted back to say he was grounded and couldn't help, so the two girls slogged through the snow along the shoulder, dropping through the crunchy cover with each step. They'd gotten a laugh out of evading the next-door neighbor, Mrs Preston, by ducking out through the screened-in porch and climbing over the back fence. But now the wind had picked up across the marsh, whistling over the water and through the reeds, knifing through the castaway coat and fleece hat and scarf that Addy had borrowed from Caroline, and chilling her to the bone. She didn't remember Elizabeth's house being this far away, but last time she'd been desperate, on a mission to find Rafe.

A white sedan, dirty from road slush and with windshield wipers flapping, passed them, spraying them with gray sleet. Then the driver jammed on the brakes, fishtailing on the icy road. Addy grabbed Caroline's hand, ready to dive into the brush and drag her friend along if they needed to. The car backed up slowly and the passenger side window rolled down.

'Addy, sweetheart, is that you? I've been looking all over for you.'

Rafe. The welcome sight of his face and voice brought a jolt of relief and joy so fierce her knees buckled. He was alive!

He shifted the gear into park, leaped out of the car and enveloped her into a tight hug. 'Come on, come on,' he said, opening the back door. 'It's freezing out here girls, get in. My chariot awaits.'

Addy slid in but the other kid did not. 'Who is this?' she muttered to Addy.

'I'm her boyfriend,' Rafe said, and then laughed. 'Her baby daddy. The love of her life.'

Addy laughed in response, gone from glum to giddy in an

instant. She leaned outside, grabbed her friend's hand and pulled her into the car. 'We were looking for you, believe it or not. This is like a Christmas miracle. This is my friend Caroline. She's been so nice to me.'

Rafe slammed the door shut, circled back around the car, and got into the driver's seat. 'Addy, honey, I can't believe you had the kid by yourself. I wanted to be there. I wish you would have called me like we said.' He gritted his teeth, and Addy could sense his annoyance underneath the words.

'I lost your number,' said Addy, trying not to whimper. 'It was in the pocket of the coat I gave away with the baby.'

'Why the hell did you give the baby away?' he asked.

She started to cry, all the sorrow and hardship of the last few days, and even the last year welling up inside and spilling out. Caroline drew her closer and wrapped both arms around her.

'Why do you care?' Caroline asked in the snottiest voice imaginable. 'I don't believe you're the baby's father – my stepfather would never talk that mean. You don't act like any father I know.'

'Not that it's any of your business,' he snapped, and turned to Addy. 'I found her a wonderful home. Someone I know who desperately wants a child and has the money to raise her decently. How could you not understand that the baby was our future?'

Addy shrugged and struggled not to cry again.

'What did the cops say about where they were taking her? We need to get her back.'

'Is that all you want from Addy?' Caroline asked. 'Supposing she can't get the baby back? Or what if she decides she wants to keep it after all? She is the mother.'

Addy could see Rafe's temperature rising, see the hot red blood creeping up his collar, washing over his chin and staining his cheeks. And she could imagine quite clearly what he was thinking: *Who is this little bitch?*

'It doesn't matter,' Addy said in a soft voice, as she smiled timidly at her friend. 'The main thing is he's going to take care of me. Both of us.'

'He isn't going to take care of anyone but himself, Addy,

don't you see?' Caroline said. 'Someone's paid him for the baby, that's what I think.'

'Who the hell are you anyway?' Rafe asked. He pulled over to the side of the road and glared into the back seat so he wouldn't swerve into the slushy reeds.

'My father is a detective right here in town. And he taught me to trust my instincts. And my instincts tell me you're a loser. So don't even think about pulling any stunts. He's probably tracking us this very instant.'

It was like goading a bull. Addy watched Rafe grind his teeth, trying to keep his cool. 'I am her boyfriend.' His gaze bored into Addy. 'I am not like your pimp who was going to use you to extort God knows how much money from that twerp senator you were screwing.'

Addy felt a sharp stab of fear and her eyes went wide. He'd never said anything so harsh before. To plenty of other people, but not to her.

'What senator?' Caroline asked.

Rafe ignored her and focused on Addy. 'You've got the phone, right?' he asked.

Addy rustled in her plastic bag, found the phone and handed it over.

'Now where's the fucking baby?'

'Georgia stole her.' Addy began crying so hard that she was blowing bubbles of snot and having trouble breathing. 'She killed the government worker – shot her in the head. And ran away with her. She'll kill us too – you know she will.'

# TWENTY-SEVEN

After saying a quick hello to her father, Elizabeth headed home from the hospital, thinking about how lucky she was to have Wilma in her life. She pulled the car into the garage and shucked off her coat and boots in the laundry room.

'I'm home,' she called out.

Her mother bustled from the living room into the kitchen. 'That was quick. Not much going on in the ER?'

'Did you learn anything about the senator?' Aunt Susan asked, coming up behind her sister, placing her hands on Videen's shoulders.

Elizabeth reported her discussion about the senator's wife and how Wilma seemed to think he'd be capable of getting involved in something unsavory. 'He's not a nice man. And Wilma couldn't have been more supportive about the unwedding either,' she said, adding a deep sigh. 'She helped me put into words what I've been starting to realize. This change gives me a new start, the chance to think about what I really want – in my life, in a marriage, in a man.'

'Absolutely,' said Aunt Susan. 'And better now than after you tied the knot.'

'For sure.' Elizabeth frowned, then noticed that her mother's face had grown pale.

'What happened with Kevin?' she asked. 'I hope he didn't give you any trouble.'

'Up against the two Warren sisters, he didn't stand a chance,' said Aunt Susan. 'He took a whole carload of gifts, and we made him sign in blood that he'd write the thank yous and regrets this week. There's absolutely no excuse for his relations thinking that our side is rude.' Aunt Susan slung an arm around her sister. 'You do look a little peaked,' she said.

Videen had slumped into a kitchen chair, both hands gripping the polished maple table. 'We had another unpleasant visitor this morning,' she said. 'Addy's Rafe came looking for her. He said all the right things, like he loved her and he wanted to take care of them both, but he gave me the creeps.'

'You should have called me,' said Elizabeth.

'It all happened so quickly, I didn't have time to do anything – even let you know he was here,' she said, looking helplessly at Aunt Susan.

'I hope you didn't allow him into the house,' Aunt Susan said, rubbing her sister's back.

Elizabeth's cell phone rang and she pulled it out of the pocket of her jeans. The screen read *Ron Christenberry* – the senator's staffer. She held up a finger to her mother and aunt, mouthing his name, and retreated to the living room to answer in private. 'Hello.'

'This is too fast, I know. But hear me out,' said Ron with a chuckle. 'I should have played it cool and waited a couple of weeks so you didn't get the impression I was a stalker or an overeager beaver, desperate for a date. But the thing is the Senate is back in session in Washington after tomorrow, so it's now or never. In spite of that awkward preamble, could I possibly persuade you to have dinner with me tonight?'

Elizabeth laughed. She pushed a few packages aside and settled into the couch, tucking her feet under her butt. 'I appreciate the invitation, but it's way too early for me to have dinner or even coffee. I hope you understand, it's not about you – I need time to sort out what happened with my ex and to lick my wounds a bit.' She pushed out another fake laugh.

'Maybe I could call you in a couple of weeks then?' he asked. 'We often visit Connecticut to stay in touch with our base. And New York's really not that far away.'

'Sure,' she said, though part of her doubted she'd ever say yes to this guy, no matter how patient he was. Or how much she wanted to know what he and his boss knew.

'One other thing,' he said, 'and I feel a little clumsy about asking. You and the other ladies were talking about the subway girl and her baby this morning. You said she stayed at your house.'

Elizabeth tried to remember the conversation exactly. Had she said this? She didn't think so.

'I'm wondering if she had any belongings with her that didn't look as though they were hers,' Ron continued.

'Like what?'

'Such as a BlackBerry phone. This is embarrassing to admit,' he said, 'but someone stole the senator's personal phone. I was able to track it to New Haven, but it seems to have run out of juice.'

Elizabeth made a face to herself, but let the silence sit as she thought about how to reply. Because how in the world would Addy, a poor, pregnant young woman – girl, really – get close enough to an important senator to lift his phone? But this was a second connection between those two, the first being Addy's strong reaction to seeing the man on television.

She remembered reading that the senator had an appetite for affairs. And Wilma had agreed that it was possible Les would have gotten together with someone underage. Could he be the father of Addy's baby?

Ron had made a huge gaffe bringing this up – both of them knew it, she suspected. Because there was no logical reason, not even a half-baked reason, for these two people to have met. Yet Addy had the senator's phone. She must have. They'd tracked it to New Haven, and then to her parents' house.

Finally, Elizabeth said, 'Addy left her old clothes behind when she fled, along with a borrowed car coat. But I certainly didn't see a phone.'

'Oh well,' he said, 'it was a long shot. Someone somewhere lifted that phone and we're asking everyone to keep an eye out for it. No matter how unlikely. So many people come in and out of our offices, both in Hartford and DC. And he's known for misplacing things. I spend half my working life tracking down his possessions. In this case, the phone died or maybe the thief turned it off. We saw that it was located in New York City, went dead, came alive in New Haven, but then it went dead again.'

She could almost hear him scrambling to back away from his question. Because not one thing about it made sense. Addy didn't come from Connecticut or Washington, she came from New York.

'I'll look forward to chatting with you in a couple of weeks,' she said. 'And Happy New Year. I hope the politicians can pull together this time around. We need all the help we can get in this country.'

She hung up, thinking madly. She dashed back into the kitchen. She was horrified and sickened by the thought that the senator had got Addy pregnant. It confirmed she was in danger. And Elizabeth right along with her. Because now they knew that she knew.

'I'm going to the police department,' she said. 'I'm positive Senator Lester is somehow involved with Addy. And not in a good way. I think he's the father of her baby.' She didn't have to spell out anything more – the shock on her mother and Susan's faces said it all.

# TWENTY-EIGHT

Detective Meigs parked on the street, then slogged around the side of his house to the kitchen, ducking his head against the sleet. The air seemed to feel colder every time he stepped outside, and the patches of black ice in the driveway proved him right. Leaving his boots by the door, he took a slug of the cold coffee from the mug he'd left in the sink earlier and rushed down the hall to the stairs.

He stood outside Caroline's door, listening. No music, no talking, nothing. They must be sleeping, and no wonder, with the night they'd had. Slowly, quietly, he eased the doorknob to the right and peeked into the room.

The girls were gone.

He searched all the rooms on the second floor and even looked into the attic, hoping they were hiding. He called Mrs Preston. 'Caroline's gone,' he said. 'Did you happen to see her leave?'

'Oh my goodness,' she said. 'I'm so sorry. Are you sure? I swear, not one car came by your house. I watched like a hawk. If I'd seen her, I would have run out and tackled her.'

He thanked her and abruptly hung up, bowled over by a wave of panic. All he could think to do was get to the office, get help. He had to find her, get to the bottom of her connection with this girl. And he had to do a better job as a father. He yanked the phone out of his pocket and dialed Caroline's number, but got no answer. All thumbs, he poked in a text message.

*DINNER 6 pm*, he typed in caps. *COME HOME AND WE'LL TALK ABOUT EVERYTHING.*

Which of course she would ignore, wherever she was. He scrolled through his older messages, remembering that Caroline had told him the name and address of the boy she liked, back when they weren't engaged in this family civil war. Randy was his name, and he lived further north near the Guilford

High School. He punched the address into his phone and went back out to his vehicle. Maybe Randy knew something, and he'd be more likely to tell in person.

The kid lived in a small ranch house surrounded by a fence. Two yapping mutts came springing through the snow in the yard, announcing his arrival as he strode up the driveway to the front door. A heavy-set woman with gray roots showing through her blonde hair answered his knock.

'I'm Detective Jack Meigs. I'd like to speak with your son, Randy,' he said. 'He's been dating my daughter and there was some trouble last night at a party. Serious trouble. And now my girl is missing.'

'Randy would have nothing to do with that,' she said, although she seemed unsurprised to hear this news. 'He's been in the house all morning.'

Meigs stared at her, wondering how he could possibly break through. 'I need to talk to your son. Please. My daughter has disappeared and he may have some knowledge about that.'

She looked at him. 'I can't imagine he knows anything.'

'Perhaps you weren't aware that he was at the party,' Meigs tried, angling for her pride of parenthood. As he'd expected, she bristled.

'We know about the party because we had to pick him up in the middle of the night. And he's grounded with no computer and certainly no car, so I can assure you he wasn't involved in her disappearance. He's been stripped of his driving privileges for the foreseeable future.'

'If he was at the party, it's imperative that I speak with him. She may have told him her plans or he may have noticed something that could help me find her. She could be in danger.'

The woman sighed. 'He's probably sleeping, I'll go wake him up.' She disappeared up the worn, blue-carpeted steps and reappeared minutes later with her son in tow.

The kid was dressed in sloppy gray sweats. He had a few pathetic whiskers on his chin and his ridiculous little ponytail looked greasier that it had the night before. What in the world did Caroline see in this miserable wretch?

'Caroline is missing,' he said without any preamble. 'Did she say anything to you about where she was going?'

The kid scuffed a slipper at the wood floor. He did not meet Meigs's eyes, and why would he, when the last time they'd crossed paths he'd been in bed with Caroline? He would have to push back the revulsion he was feeling in order to get anything out of this moron.

'Tell him whatever you know,' his mother said in a stern voice. 'Unless you want to be grounded until graduation.'

'She texted me about an hour ago, something about her friend being in trouble and they needed a ride. She was pretty torqued when I told her I couldn't get the car. Which is really unbelievably not fair,' he said to his mother. 'It's not like I left the scene of an accident or something.'

'Never mind the car – you are not leaving this house until you've shown you've learned a lesson,' his mother said.

'Good,' Meigs said. He knew he needed to dial his anger back to get anything else from this kid. And not get thrown out by the mother. 'Did Caroline say where she wanted you to take her?'

'No. Just that she needed a ride. And it had to do with her friend.'

'Barbara,' Meigs said.

Randy looked perplexed. 'Not Barbara, Addy.'

Meigs felt instantly queasy. Addy was definitely the name of the homeless girl who'd delivered a baby two days ago. 'Tell me what you know about Addy,' he said. 'Absolutely everything.'

'I don't know a lot,' said Randy. 'We met her yesterday at the Big Y when she asked us how to make some quick cash. We helped her figure out where to stand to beg and what kind of sign to make to tug at heartstrings.' He laughed, but no one joined him. 'I think she was from New York. We didn't really take a family history. Then Caroline invited her over to a party at your house, because she said there would be no parents around.'

'You let them have a party without supervision?' Randy's mother asked.

'Of course I didn't,' Meigs snapped. 'I was working last night, and her instructions were to stay inside. She could invite a friend to study or watch TV. A girlfriend. There was no way she could interpret that as permission to throw a party.' He ran a finger inside his collar. This house was overheated, and so, by God, was he. He turned to the boy again. 'As far as my daughter is concerned, you are permanently persona non-grata.'

He stormed out of the house, feeling helpless and distraught. Caroline would be furious to hear she was banned from seeing this kid. If he ever found her.

# TWENTY-NINE

'Hable ow do you know Georgia has her? Where the hell did you hear that?' Rafe demanded.

'Caroline's father,' Addy said. 'We heard him talking.'

'Why would Caroline's father know anything about Georgia?'

'The cop from New York called to tell him that someone stole the baby. We overheard it.' Her voice quivered and Caroline took her hand and squeezed, then Addy began to weep again. She knew Rafe hated this, but the last few days seemed to have drained every bit of strength she had left right out of her body. 'And then we looked it up on Caroline's computer. As soon as I read that the worker had been shot, I knew it was Georgia. You have to stop her. We have to get her back.'

'Shit!' Rafe stomped on the gas pedal and the car shimmied from the shoulder to the road. 'We're going to have to get out of this hellhole, fast,' he said, more to himself than to them.

Caroline dropped Addy's hand and leaned forward. 'Can you let me off on the green?' She turned back to Addy and lowered her voice. 'You should come with me. You'll be a lot safer with my father than this jerk.'

Addy could see Rafe's eyes in the rearview mirror. And they scared her, boring in on Caroline. He looked as angry as Georgia got sometimes, just barely in control. Angrier than she'd ever seen him. Nothing like the man who'd sweet-talked her into running away with him.

'Let me out now,' Caroline said, louder this time.

Rafe slammed on the brakes, shifted into park, and heaved himself half over the seat. He slapped Caroline across the face. Her neck snapped back against the back seat and tears sprang to her eyes. A red stripe bloomed across her cheek and blood trickled from her lip. From her reaction, Addy guessed this might be the first time anyone had hit her. And the total shock of it might have hurt just as much as the contact.

Caroline took her cell phone from her pocket and started to dial.

'Give that to me.' Rafe held out his hand.

Caroline jiggled the door handle but it wouldn't open. He'd pressed the childproof lock button.

'Now.'

Caroline put her iPhone in his palm.

Once he turned back around and began to drive again, Addy whispered: 'Try to stay calm. Don't piss him off any worse.'

'We need cash. We need food. We need another car,' Rafe muttered to himself. He glanced back at Caroline. 'Where do kids in this town go to hang out when they don't want to be found?'

Caroline snuffled.

'Answer him,' Addy whispered. She watched the fight drain out of her friend.

'There's an abandoned house off the highway in Madison,' said Caroline. 'They keep the electricity on because it's been for sale forever. But there's no heat or water or anything. We'd never go there in winter.'

# THIRTY

Meigs rushed back to the police department, searching his whirling mind for the next move. He parked in the back lot, checked his gun into his locker, and hurried through the sally port and past the holding cells that were almost always empty in this town. He nearly bowled Mason over as he turned the corner into his office.

He grunted a quick 'sorry'.

'What's wrong?' Mason asked. 'You look worried.'

He let out a big sigh. 'Caroline's gone missing. She was grounded, but . . .' He shrugged. 'Obviously she didn't listen. It's probably nothing, but remember I told you about the homeless girl and her subway baby?'

Mason nodded, already looking concerned.

'I think the girl Caroline's been palling around with is her.' He rubbed the stubble on his chin. 'I can't fathom what they'd have in common, though.'

'What's that girl doing in this town?' Mason asked.

Meigs explained how she'd followed Elizabeth from the city, looking for the phone number she'd lost. 'I visited Caroline's ridiculous boyfriend to see if he knows anything.'

'How did that go?'

'It went like shit,' Meigs grunted.

Mason grinned. 'I've never met a teenage boy who passes muster with the dad of the girl he's dating.' His expression turned serious. 'Sorry to hear about your daughter's trouble last night.'

Meigs looked up, surprised and embarrassed, but a little bit touched too. Even without formal charges against Caroline, the whole department would have heard about her trip to the Madison station. News traveled between the shoreline departments like wildfires in a bone-dry season. Suddenly he dreaded the rest of the day. He wasn't in the habit of hashing through his feelings with colleagues – they weren't social friends. Let's face it, he wouldn't have talked about how he was feeling even if they were. This had been one of Alice's gentle complaints – he was happy staying home with his family when he wasn't at work. He didn't need cocktail parties or dinners out where the food was worse than what Alice cooked at home. The truth was he cared about his family. He cared about his work. He didn't care that much about food. Or friends.

But maybe he needed one now. 'To make things worse, the girl's baby was snatched this morning and the children's services worker was shot.'

Mason dropped into the chair in front of Meigs's desk and

started to type. 'Most kids share more about themselves than they should on social media. And certainly more than they tell their parents. Do you follow Caroline on Snapchat or Instagram?'

Meigs shrugged helplessly.

'Have you looked at her Facebook page?' Mason asked.

'I hate the whole idea of Facebook.'

'Did your wife stay in touch that way?'

Meigs remembered a blowout fight Alice had had with Caroline. The upshot had been that if she wanted to stay involved with Facebook, she had to let Alice befriend her. After trying a few combinations of names and birthdays, he was able to come up with his wife's password.

Mason navigated to Alice's Facebook page, and from there, to Caroline's. Meigs hung behind him, peering over his shoulder.

'She hasn't posted anything this morning,' Mason said.

'Not surprising. What would she write? What a way to start the New Year – drank so much I puked in the bushes?'

Mason said nothing to that, but what could he, really? Meigs watched him browse quickly through the latest news from Caroline's friends. Most of it had to do with too much homework, unfair teachers, and what to wear to an upcoming dance. And how boring it was to have a whole week at home, stuck with their families.

Mason scrolled down further and Meigs saw that twenty of her friends had commented on 'Pass a Drink', which involved sharing recipes for cocktails. He groaned, covered his eyes with his hands, then forced himself back to the screen.

Caroline had contributed a recipe for a 'red-headed slut', promising that the ingredients would be available in any parent's liquor closet. She was showing off, he thought. He couldn't imagine she'd steal his booze. But then he remembered his empty bottle of rum, and from there his mind hurtled back to the kid in her bed. Maybe he'd been the culprit. A slob like that who had the gall to mess around with someone's daughter, right under her father's nose, would not hesitate to steal alcohol.

He could feel the veins in his forehead throbbing. He would

stop at the hardware store on the way home and buy a padlock for the liquor cabinet. And he'd lock his beer in his trunk. He didn't care – if he had to, he'd drink it warm, over ice, or give it up. He continued to read as Mason scrolled back up. 'Stop there!' he said.

In one of Caroline's earlier profile photos, she had her arms draped around two willowy girls, long-haired and smiling, no trace of her recent angst in her expression. Mason clicked on the first of three photo albums that his stepdaughter had posted. He'd make a good father, Mason would – just the right combination of strictness and kindness. Not like Meigs, careening from one end of the spectrum to the other, never sure exactly what was the right amount of discipline. Being a cop felt a hundred times easier.

He couldn't help tearing up at the last picture: Caroline and Alice, a photo he'd taken last summer on the deck at the back of their house. He blew his nose as Mason moved on to 'New Year's Eve'.

First there were pictures of the gathering in Caroline's bedroom, before he'd arrived and broken it up. Then a selfie of four kids in front of a shabby house – Caroline and Randy, with another kid he vaguely recognized from the Guilford football games. And a second girl who could have been Addy or 'Barbara' – she'd covered most of her face with her hand as the photo was snapped. The photos of the party inside this house made his skin crawl. Many of the girls had stripped off their coats and were wearing party clothes – low-cut tank tops and short skirts. Mason skimmed the other photos: kids dancing, sweaty, hands in the air, breasts heaving. In the background of a few shots, Addy hovered, clutching her plastic bag.

He drooped back against his bookshelf, wondering where in the world Caroline could have gone with this girl. And who might be in pursuit – if in fact that was what was happening.

Meigs's phone rang and the name *Miller* came up. He punched *accept*, thinking of Caroline as he did so. He was ready to stand firm against whatever crappy arguments she dished out about the punishment she no doubt felt was way too harsh for the crime of having a little fun. And when he saw her, he'd hug her tightly and rock her like a baby.

'Paul Miller here,' said a deep voice. 'Caroline's father. You rang?'

'Hours ago,' Meigs growled.

Mason stood up and began to edge out of the room.

'Caroline has gone wild. I had to pick her up at the Madison police station in the middle of the night because she'd been involved in a party that got way out of control. Drinking, drugs, sex for money or drugs. And now she's disappeared, even though I clearly grounded her.'

It sounded like Paul had his own party going on in the background.

'Are you coming?' asked a velvety voiced woman on Paul's end of the phone.

'You're a cop, aren't you?' Paul asked. 'What do you want me to do?'

'She is your daughter,' Meigs snapped. 'I thought you might be interested.'

Paul heaved a sigh. 'I'm at a sales conference in Hartford. I'll try to get there as soon as I can. I never thought her living with you was going to work, but Alice insisted. Caroline would have been a lot better off staying in the private school. And then she could have easily come home on holidays. I'll put in a call and see if she can transfer mid-semester.'

Meigs hung up without answering.

'She's moving back to California?' Mason asked, eyes wide like a scolded basset hound.

Meigs wiped his eyes with his sleeve. 'She won't live by my rules. It's too dangerous,' he added, then wished he hadn't put it like that.

'Well,' said Mason, 'if she has a better relationship with her father, if he can help her . . .'

'I don't know if she has a better damn relationship,' Meigs said. He shouldn't take it out on Mason; he was a nice guy, just trying to help. 'Daughters are not so damn easy.'

Mason broke into an enormous grin, groped for his wallet and extracted a photo of two adorable smiling girls with dark curly hair and big brown eyes. 'I forgot to show you my Christmas picture. They're four and six,' he said proudly.

'They are gorgeous. Hang on tightly,' Meigs added as he left the room. 'I'm going out to drive around.'

# THIRTY-ONE

Elizabeth hurried into the front vestibule of the police department and rapped on the window to get the attention of the woman typing behind the glass. 'I need to see Detective Meigs,' she said. 'It's rather urgent.'

'He's stepped out and I'm not sure when he'll be back,' she said. 'I can leave him a message, tell him that you stopped by.'

'But I've been trying to get hold of him. And it can't wait,' said Elizabeth, wondering why they didn't understand the concept of *urgent* in this department. Probably everyone thought their problem was important and should be addressed ASAP, the same way people did in the hospital emergency room. 'Is there someone else I can speak with?'

'Sergeant Mason is the officer in charge today, I'll see if he's available.'

A handsome man whose uniform fit him rather better than most of the officers she'd met in the past week came to the door and ushered her in to the room where she and her parents had been interviewed. She summed up her experience with Addy following her from New York to Guilford. 'Maybe Detective Meigs told you about this?'

She wished he'd give her more than a quick 'yes', but of course he wouldn't tell a citizen more than what was publicly known.

'The thing is her boyfriend – or so he said – came by our house looking for Addy. I think he scared my mother half to death.' Now she had his attention. Should she also tell him about the senator? No. She'd rather tell Detective Meigs himself about that.

'When?'

She glanced at her watch. 'Maybe an hour, hour and a half? He claimed he wanted to find Addy to take care of her and her baby, but my mother found the story unbelievable and the man himself creepy.'

'In what way?'

'Pushy and angry, I'd say.'

'Did he threaten her?'

'Not in so many words. It was more the underlying feeling.'

'Does she know where he was going next or what he was driving?'

Elizabeth felt her shoulders slump. 'The only thing we have to go on is a phone number. He asked her to call him if Addy turned up.' She handed him a slip of paper with the number written in her mother's neat hand. 'And now it seems that Addy's baby may have fathered by Senator Troy Lester.' She couldn't blame him for looking both appalled and disbelieving.

'Detective Meigs has stepped out, but I'll pass this on to him immediately. You should return home and lock your doors. We'll handle this, OK?' He waited until she nodded, and then showed her out.

Elizabeth returned to the parking lot, got in the car and ramped up the heat and the seat warmer. Then she checked her phone. She'd missed two text messages from Olivia Lovett, whom she'd hoped had packed her bags and returned to the city. She opened the first one: *Think a man has Addy. He's got two girls in the back. One matches her description. Both look like teenagers and are terrified. Following.*

And then the second: *Sorry. Driving and texting. Bad me. Exit 62. Will call police.*

And then she saw a voicemail that had come in a little earlier, also from Olivia.

'I know we've had a rocky start, but please believe me. This is no publicity stunt. Addy is going to need you when all hell breaks loose. I've called the cops but meet me—'

The voicemail was cut off as quickly as it had begun.

Elizabeth's first thought was that this was a trap. But why would Olivia do something like that? She might have ulterior motives related to her career, but it seemed unlikely that she wanted to hurt anyone. Addy was in danger. And that danger was near. She certainly wasn't returning home now with all this going on, but she texted her mother and Aunt Susan, telling them to double lock the doors and ask her father to come home. Then she headed toward Exit 62, looking for Olivia's rental car.

As she drove toward downtown Madison on Route 1, she caught sight of a dirty white car with gold New York plates several cars ahead. Olivia's rental, she thought. She would follow her to Exit 62. And call in the cops.

# THIRTY-TWO

Meigs retraced his path to Randy the boyfriend's home near the high school. He parked in the driveway and hurtled up to the front door, pounding, causing the dogs to yap frantically. The kid's mother cracked the door open.

'There's been a new development about my daughter. I need to speak to your son again.'

She opened her mouth to protest.

'Now. It's absolutely critical. Her life could be in danger.'

Her lips pressed into an unhappy line but she didn't question him, just shouted to the second floor. 'Randy! The police are here again. Come in,' she told Meigs, reluctantly.

Within minutes, the kid shambled down the stairs.

'Have you heard from her?' asked Meigs.

Randy shook his head, looking scared. 'No. Is she—'

'If Caroline went somewhere with this Addy, where would they go?'

'I have no clue.'

Meigs took three quick steps forward, almost grabbed the kid by the shoulders, then reined himself in. 'Think, man. This is my daughter.' He knew he was pressing the kid too hard, but if he'd held something back before, it could mean the difference between Caroline living and . . . 'Think!'

The boy cowered.

Meigs cleared his throat and stepped away. 'I'm sorry. I'm sick with worry.' He ran his fingers through his hair and tried to speak in a normal voice. 'Where would kids from this town, or even Madison, go if they wanted to drink or smoke dope or whatever, without supervision?'

Randy looked down at his feet, the color in his cheeks rising again. 'Sometimes we hang out behind Walmart, if it's warm enough. Or in Westwoods, but not a day like today. An empty house maybe?' He narrowed his eyes and met Meigs's gaze. 'Honestly, it's easy enough to figure out whose parents aren't home and just meet up there.'

'How about right now? Is there a party going on?'

'Pretty much everyone I know is grounded.' He couldn't help smirking.

'If a person wasn't grounded,' Meigs said, ignoring the smirk to stay focused, 'and they wanted to hide out for a bit, where would they go?'

'Maybe that place over on New Road? It's been for sale forever, but no one ever looks at it. There's no heat, so maybe not. Don't worry about me and your daughter,' the kid added. 'Everything was too much drama with her anyway.'

Meigs wanted to strangle him, but he spun around and jogged back to his car, more worried by the minute. He drove to his house, but Caroline wasn't there, nor was there any sign that she had been.

Back at the station, he found Mason in the IT room, flipping through case files.

'I think we'd better file a missing person report. It's early but—'

'Good,' said Mason. 'We've got to find her. That's what's important. And that Elizabeth Brown came by – she says her mother met Addy's boyfriend, who'd come looking for her. She's very worried about her being in danger. We'll put a BOLO out right now, get some patrol cars looking for him and intensify our search for Addy.' He sounded almost as frantic as Meigs felt. 'That Elizabeth Brown just called dispatch and said something about following a car with two girls in the back toward Exit 62.'

'I'll ride shotgun. But before we go, a guy named Paul Miller's in your office,' Mason added. 'First you might want to take care of monsieur?' He tipped his head in the direction of the office.

Meigs strode down the hall and jerked his door open, dreading this moment. A slim man with chestnut hair curling over the back of his blue Oxford shirt was sitting in his chair. Behind his desk.

'You couldn't have driven the speed limit,' Meigs said, frowning so hard his cheeks hurt. On a good day, with no traffic, it took a solid hour to drive from Hartford.

'We're talking about my daughter,' Miller said. 'I didn't figure a damn speeding ticket would matter. What's our plan?'

# THIRTY-THREE

Elizabeth followed the white car, careful to hang back enough that she wouldn't be spotted. But the car had disappeared by the time she pulled onto the Hammonasset Connector.

Then she drove north, all the way to the intersection of Horse Pond Road, but the white car had vanished. She pulled off the side of the road and texted Olivia again.

Part of your message missing. Where are you headed? Call me?

When no response came, she drove south and took a right onto New Road, which circled back toward Madison. She noticed a set of fresh tire tracks on the driveway leading to what looked like an abandoned house. She could hear the whoosh of cars rushing by on the interstate, a stone's throw away, but this house appeared deserted. The structure was barely visible through the brush that had grown up along the drive, but she noticed peeling paint and the screen door hanging off its hinges, banging with each puff of wind.

She dialed Aunt Susan's number. Her parents would only freak out. And she didn't have time to convince a different

police dispatcher that this was an emergency. She'd ask Aunt
Susan to call a second time. She would do a better job of
insisting that she needed help. 'Pick up pick up pick up,' she
whispered. But instead the answering message kicked in.

'I'm walking up to the abandoned house on New Road,
following Olivia,' Elizabeth said after the beep. 'I'm going to
peek in the windows because she thinks Addy's in trouble, and
I do too. I won't go in, promise. But call the cops again, OK?'

She crept up the driveway, careful to keep in the shadows
of the bushes, though the deep snow made this difficult. After
she'd sunk into the snow to her knees once too many times,
she moved to the path made by what she felt sure would be
Olivia's car. She felt something poke her back, hard. Adrenalin
pumping, Elizabeth whirled around, clapping her hand to her
racing heart.

'Put your hands on your head and keep moving,' said a
man holding a gun. He wore a dirty black jacket, a knit cap,
and an expression full of rage.

She raised her hands to her head and slogged up the hill.
'Who are you?'

'Get inside,' he said, when she paused as they reached the
rickety front steps.

With one hand on a flimsy wood railing, she stumbled
up the stairs. At the top, she froze, hearing a muffled cry. He
jabbed her again. Three steps further and they were in the
kitchen, old-fashioned but not in a charming way – all torn
linoleum and tired avocado appliances. The air felt icy,
colder even than outside, and it smelled as though no one
had lived here in a long time. Except for mice, some of them
long deceased.

'Who are you and why are you here?' he asked.

'I'm looking for Addy,' she said.

'Over there, go!' he said, pointing at a door across the room,
yawning open to the basement. She swallowed hard but did
as he told her. She had to hope Aunt Susan would get her
message and call the cops. Or that Olivia was watching . . .

She felt her way down the steep, narrow staircase, barely
lit by the man's flashlight and one bare bulb. As her eyes grew
accustomed to the dim light at the bottom, she could see that

another door across the room was ajar. The mewling sound she'd heard when they came into the kitchen erupted from the recesses of the basement. A human cry. She bolted across the last few feet, and then saw them.

Addy was crouched on the cold concrete floor in her underwear, back-to-back with another teenager. They had duct tape slashed over their mouths, and their hands were bound together behind them with more tape. Both faces were pale, streaked with tears and dirt, eyes black with fear. They stunk of sweat and they shivered with cold.

'My God,' she said. 'You poor things.'

The cellar door banged shut.

'Get away from them now. And throw your cell phone over here,' said the man from the shadows at the bottom of the stairs.

Addy's friend began to cry; a stream of mucus dripped from her nose and coated the duct tape. Elizabeth couldn't bear to watch them suffer.

'I'm going to take a closer look at these girls,' she told the man, shifting from fear to anger now.

She knelt to their level, put a palm to each face, noticing a nasty discoloration on the brunette's right cheek. Tears dripped over the bruise, leaving streaks of mascara. The girl struggled to breathe past the tape covering one nostril.

'Look, she can't get any air,' said Elizabeth fiercely, standing to face the man, her hands on her hips. 'Where are their clothes? I don't know who you are or what this is all about, but you have to stop this right now.'

Before she had time to react he hurtled across the room and slapped her face. She staggered back, slamming her head against the wall, and sank to the floor. Her head and neck throbbed with pain and she felt frozen with fear.

'Don't do that again,' said the man. 'Or I will shoot you right here. And the girls too. I will leave all of you in that closet. It will be weeks before someone notices the smell. Because you and I both know no one's coming into this house until spring. And the cold weather will slow down the rot.'

He took a seat in a rickety wooden chair by the washer, then leaned back on two legs. He pulled a phone from his pocket, clicked through several screens and swore. Was this the phone for which he'd given her mother the number? Had Susan passed this information on to the police?

'Goddammit,' he said, tapping furiously with both thumbs.

Or could this be the senator's missing phone? Elizabeth's mind was racing. Surely someone would be tracing it if Rafe had charged it enough to get online again? That oily Ron Christenberry would be all over it. Not that it would be at all helpful to have him show up. The girls had begun shivering hard enough that she could hear their teeth rattling. Cold or terror? Elizabeth herself was freezing – and she was completely dressed. How would they get away from this man? At least she could try to reassure the kids.

'Excuse me, sir,' she said in a soft voice. 'Would it be all right if I shared my sweater and my coat?'

'Fine,' he said. 'What the fuck do I care? We're not staying anyway. As soon as it gets dark, we're gone. Some of us.'

Elizabeth approached the teenagers and draped one with her sweater, the other with her puffy coat. She peeled the tape back from the nostril of the dark-haired girl, cooing softly. 'You'll be OK,' she said. 'Don't be scared.' Why had he brought them here?

'How much money do you have on you?'

'Maybe five bucks?' she said with a squeak. 'I could run to the ATM.'

He just laughed.

'Here's the plan,' the man said several minutes later, as the chair clattered back to the floor. 'You have a debit card, right?'

Elizabeth nodded.

'We're going shopping. I need money and a few other things. Something to eat. I'll make you a list.' He pulled a scrap of paper from his wallet and a pen from his pocket and began to write.

'Not to make trouble,' said Elizabeth, 'but wouldn't it be easier if you went to the bank and the store by yourself?'

'Haven't you ever heard of cameras at ATMs? I don't have to explain myself to you. Stupid bitch,' he muttered to himself. 'And don't get the idea you'll make a break for it, because there's no way out. Got it?'

The girls keened, their eyes wild. He punched a number into his phone and spoke brusquely. 'I'm going to get food and money and then we split. You know the drill – forty-five minutes or you get rid of the evidence.' He hung up. 'Let's move it.'

Elizabeth's teeth were beginning to chatter, too, both with fear and cold. She had no idea why they were here or who he was calling. She glanced over at the girls, their faces stricken with terror. The man opened the door to a crawlspace hidden away at the back of the cellar, forced the girls inside, then closed the hatch.

'Could we let them have their clothes?' she asked.

'Fuck no!' he snapped. 'This way they remember who's in control. Let's move it.'

'We'll be back soon,' she whispered through the hatch. 'Have faith.'

She clomped up the stairs ahead of the man, and he switched off the light. She could hardly bear thinking about the girls left alone in the dark.

# THIRTY-FOUR

As instructed, Elizabeth aimed her mother's Mercedes into a parking spot near the cart return and pulled through so the car was facing the exit. She turned off the headlights and handed the keys to the man. On the short drive over to the supermarket, she'd remembered a horrific story about a home invasion several years earlier not far from this town. A captured woman had been taken to the bank with instructions to keep quiet unless she wanted her daughters to die. So the mother said nothing and withdrew her money in silence. They all died anyway in the end. Later, a teller reported noticing how tired and tense and maybe even frightened she'd looked as she asked for her cash. When the entire story had been pieced together, the teller admitted to feeling desolate about not informing the police.

But in the real world, people didn't like to pry into other people's business. Who would believe her if she took off and started screaming for help? Elizabeth thought about the girls in the cellar and how their lives hinged on what she did. Or didn't do. Her throat closed but she swallowed away the fear.

'Let's review,' the man said as they approached the entrance. 'You go in, pick up a small basket, shop, check out, and withdraw the maximum cash with your debit card.'

She nodded, rubbing her arms with her hands to increase the circulation under the thin cotton of her shirt. 'I think it's two hundred.'

'And you'll pick up . . .?'

'A six-pack of Red Bull, submarine sandwich, ice cream, condoms, beer,' she repeated. 'Macaroni and cheese – the kind you don't have to cook. And plastic spoons.'

'And if you say one word to anyone?' He peeled back his jacket to show her the gun.

'You'll be watching. Your partner is with the girls. We all die,' Elizabeth said flatly.

'Make it quick,' said the man. 'Let's get this over with. I'll be staying close enough to see you every step of the way.'

Elizabeth trotted into the store, feeling his presence behind her. She picked up a red plastic basket and started toward the deli aisle, stopping to select a foot-long sub sandwich that looked like it had been sitting in the case for a couple of days. New Year's Day – chances of the staff making something fresh were slim. But what difference did it make? She added two more to the basket. The girls would need to eat. Then she veered in the direction of the canned goods and drinks, grabbing chips and microwavable macaroni and cheese as she went.

She added Red Bull and Budweiser to the basket, which now banged against her hip under its awkward weight. After tucking a box of ribbed condoms in with the other goods, she hurried to the frozen food aisle, nearly slamming into Teresa Hopper, her mother's best friend, as she turned the corner.

'Elizabeth!' Teresa said, a surprised look on her face. 'I'm so sorry. Are you OK?' Her expression quickly morphed into sadness. 'And awfully sorry about the wedding. I wanted to call over to your house, but I figured you needed some time to process without outsiders butting in.' She leaned in to give Elizabeth a hug.

'You're hardly an outsider.' Elizabeth tried to smile.

Teresa dropped two gallons of Rocky Road into her basket. 'With the three boys home, we're out of just about everything in my house.' She looked at Elizabeth's basket, her gaze taking in the condoms, the Red Bull, the fake mac and cheese, the subs, the beer. She glanced at Elizabeth's face and back to the basket again.

Elizabeth could sense her captor, just paces away.

'We have to treat ourselves sometimes when the urge strikes, don't you think?' she said inanely. She opened the freezer door and perused the ice cream shelves. To her, her voice sounded tinny and false. But the man was definitely close enough to hear her prattling. 'Something about the cold weather just calls out for chocolate. Or so Mom always says, and you know how she loves it. Have a good night,' she said, as she snatched a container of store-brand chocolate and let the freezer door bang shut. 'I'll see you soon, I hope.'

She wanted so badly to fling herself at Teresa and beg her to call the cops. Instead, she scurried past her mother's friend, blinking furiously. The man followed and moved into the self-check line behind her.

'You damn well better not have said anything to her,' he hissed.

'You were right there,' she whispered. 'You heard what I said. She's my mother's best friend. I had to talk to her or she would have gotten suspicious.'

She scanned each item and then went to the end of the checkout to load the food into plastic bags. Her mother loathed wasting resources; she'd hate Elizabeth using plastic when her own cloth bags were secure in the trunk – ridiculous to have such a thought right now. When she was finished, she inserted her debit card into the machine and requested two hundred in cash. A giant red X came up on the screen, indicating that she had asked to withdraw more money than was in the account.

'Damn him,' she said, despair washing through her.

'What's the problem?' he hissed.

'My ex-fiancé must have drained the account. We started sharing it because we were going to get married.' She felt panicky tears burning the back of her eyes, but she knew he'd go crazy if she showed any emotion publicly. She found a tissue in her pocket and blew her nose. 'There're only forty-seven dollars left.'

'Christ,' he muttered. 'Get what you can and let's go.'

She punched in forty and left him to collect the money that dropped into the lower slot. If sharp-eyed Teresa hadn't noticed anything awry other than a junk food splurge, they were lost. She picked up the plastic sacks and started to the car, the man steps behind her. For a moment, she considered dropping the bags and running. She could duck behind the blue Volvo, roll under the nearby Eclipse, scream bloody murder.

But she believed him when he said the girls would die if she tried to bolt. And most likely she would too, even if it involved a shootout in the parking lot of the grocery store. He could not afford to leave a witness. Whoever he was. She would have guessed Rafe, if he hadn't treated Addy so badly. And who the heck was the other girl? She stashed the groceries in the back and slid into the driver's seat. Darkness had closed in while they were in the store, and the cheery holiday lights of the shops across from the grocery store had flickered to life.

On the return drive, the man's phone buzzed. He fumbled in his shirt pocket, yanked the device out, pressed a button, and then began to surf through a series of screens. Elizabeth kept her eyes on the road, now covered with a fresh layer of icy slush, pushing herself to think of possible escapes. Part of her felt so shocked, so numb with disbelief about the events of the last hour that she had trouble thinking at all. She slowed down as she drove toward Main Street, waiting for a car to back out in front of them.

'Christ!' he yelled. 'Fucking Georgia! Don't just sit here – pull around. I've got to get the fuck out of here.'

She gunned the engine and sped through the light at the corner by the library as it turned from yellow to red.

'Where did you learn to drive, lady? A school for the blind?

When we get to the house, pull around the back and park face out.'

They drove the rest of the way in strained silence. She bumped up the driveway, pitch dark now except for the beams of her headlights, and parked where he'd instructed. He jogged around to her side of the car and snatched the keys from her fingers.

'Now move it,' he said, poking her in the ribs with his gun. 'Leave the goddamn groceries where they are.'

She stumbled back into the house and he jabbed her with the gun again, forcing her across the kitchen toward the cellar. At the bottom of the stairs, he yelled: 'Get them up and let's get out of here.'

Elizabeth darted across the room, opened the hatch to the crawl space, and helped the teenagers to their feet. They stumbled out of the dark, blinking in the light of the bare bulb overhead, and trembling.

'Can we cut the tape around their wrists?' Elizabeth asked.

'Absolutely not,' he roared. 'Upstairs. Now!'

When they reached the steps, she helped the girls jockey their positions until the brunette was in the lead, Addy following backwards. The brunette was crying now, strangled moans coming from her taped mouth, her nostrils caked with mucus and blood. Elizabeth felt sick about their helpless nakedness, not even their hands free to cover themselves. She tried to keep her sweater and her coat draped over their shoulders. As frightened as she felt, she imagined their terror must be much worse.

'Shut up,' said the man to the sobbing girl, 'or I shoot all of you right now.'

Elizabeth touched the girl's shoulder and smiled. 'I'll help you,' she mouthed as she herded them up the steps. 'We'll get help.' But from where and from whom – and what did he have in mind? Where was he taking them? At least here in this town there'd be a chance that someone would find them. She'd told the police. And Aunt Susan would make sure they came.

The girls shivered in the frigid air as they shuffled across the kitchen and emerged onto the stoop. He pressed the clicker on her mother's keys, and the car gave its usual cheerful chirp as the trunk popped open.

'Everybody in,' he said, pointing.

'You can't mean to force us all in there,' Elizabeth said. For God's sake, where was Olivia? Hadn't she called the cops? And what about Aunt Susan? She was usually all over her messages. 'It's not big enough. Besides, it's not fair to make them get in with their hands ta—' He smacked her face hard with the back of his hand. Elizabeth grunted and blinked away tears of pain. The girls' eyes widened.

'Let's go,' she said, and pushed them toward the car. She could not let herself think about what it would feel like to be jammed in that small space with two other people. Or what might happen to them after that. At least he hadn't shot them in the cellar. 'Sit on the edge and then you can drop over and wiggle back in,' she said to the girls. 'I'll be right here with you,' she whispered.

The girls folded themselves into the trunk, Addy first, and then the other girl. Elizabeth climbed in, wedging herself into the remaining corner. The man slammed the trunk shut and she gasped, battling a moment of sheer blind panic, the urge to scream and pound on the lid.

Had she heard another car door slam?

# THIRTY-FIVE

Addy felt a flicker of hope flare in the darkness as another car crunched up the icy driveway. She pushed back her feelings of shock that Rafe had treated them like animals. Why should it come as a surprise? No one was really on her side except for herself. And her grandmother, who was too old and weak to help. And maybe Elizabeth, and probably Caroline. Though that thought made her sick with guilt: it was her fault that poor Caroline was in this trouble to begin with.

A car door slammed and then she went rigid, hearing

Georgia's voice, harsh and angry. 'Nice to see you again, Rafe.'

Rafe would be scared now too; he knew Georgia was ruthless when it came to people who'd crossed her.

But then another voice spoke. 'I saw you put the women in the trunk. Everyone's alive right now and that's good for you. It can only go downhill from here. We know too much about you both and the police are on the way—'

Then came the reedy cries of a baby. Addy couldn't help it – she began to sob. Then she couldn't breathe and she was gasping for air and her mind went completely black.

Elizabeth heard a loud thunk, followed by a groan, and then no more hopeful chatter from Olivia. Either she was dead or unconscious. Either way, no help for them.

'You're finished, Rafe,' said the woman with the harsh voice. 'You've double-crossed me one time too many. Give me Lester's phone or I shoot you dead right here. Exactly like your dumb friend Mitch.'

'This is none of your business anymore,' Rafe shouted. 'I've got the phone and I've got the girl. Give me the baby and clear out. Go home to the hole you crawled out of. I have nothing to lose here.'

Elizabeth heard the sounds of scuffling, and then gunshots and someone screaming in pain. One car door opened and was slammed shut, and then another, and the motor of her mother's Mercedes roared to life. The car lurched back down the bumpy lane, banging Elizabeth and the girls against each other in the dark. She could hear the raspy cries of a newborn. How far could Rafe get if he'd been shot? If it was Rafe driving . . .

She took a few deep breaths, closing her eyes and trying to pretend she was somewhere else. The girls needed her to stay calm. She could not allow herself to be swept away in the hysteria she felt pushing to the surface. She fumbled above her head and put her hands on the space blanket her mother always carried in case of emergency. She inched it down and tried to tuck it around the girls. Touching the face nearest to her, the one she could reach, she began to work the duct tape loose from the girl's mouth.

'I'm going to pull this off,' she said in a low voice, once she had loosened the edges from the tender skin around her upper lip. 'It'll sting, but you'll be able to breathe. Promise me you won't yell once you're free?'

She could feel the girl nodding her assent, so she counted to three and ripped off the tape. Sucking in big gulps of air, the girl began to weep. 'I'm so scared. And so thirsty.'

'Shhh,' said Elizabeth softly, stroking her hair. 'I know. I'm going to help. Who are you?'

'Caroline Miller,' came the answer. 'And my friend—'

'I know Addy,' said Elizabeth. 'She's a very brave girl. And so are you. How did this happen? How did you meet up with this man?'

The car braked hard, throwing her against Caroline, then away as they pulled out of the driveway and onto New Road. Left turn, west, Elizabeth thought to herself. Maybe she'd feel a little less helpless if she could keep track of where they were headed.

'We were on our way to your house looking for you to help us,' Caroline snuffled. 'And then this man drove up and had us get in the car. He said he loved Addy so much, and he wanted to take care of her and the baby, like a real family.' She began to cry harder, deep sobs that Elizabeth was afraid could be heard by whomever was driving the car.

'Shhh, we have to stay quiet.' Elizabeth smoothed the hair away from Caroline's face. She found the same Kleenex she'd used in the Stop and Shop in her coat pocket and wiped the girl's eyes and nose.

'He's a horrible man. Addy thought he was going to save her and the baby. But he isn't. Now he says we're going to Las Vegas, we can make a thousand dollars a week as hostesses. After he tries us out and teaches us a few things.

'I just want to go home.' She was sobbing now, big, noisy, wet hiccups of terror.

'Shhhh, shhhh, I know you do,' said Elizabeth, patting her gently. 'I'll help you with that. Who are your parents?'

'My stepdad is Jack Meigs. He's a policeman,' she added.

Elizabeth gulped, hope leaking away like air in a punctured tire. Would Rafe know this? Was he smart enough to have found this out? Even the worst criminal wouldn't expect to accidentally kidnap a cop's daughter without terrible consequences. If he knew who Caroline was, he would leave only scorched earth behind him. He wasn't an amateur without the courage or know-how to use the gun he'd been flashing. He'd shot one woman already, possibly two. She wondered how badly he was injured. And how much time did they have before he realized the only things he really needed were Lester's phone and the baby. He might have thought he needed Addy in order to somehow collect the infant, but if he now had the baby, she and Caroline were toxic assets.

My God, she had to think fast. She was the adult. She had to come up with a plan. Suddenly, she remembered the trunk release. Five years ago, her mother had walked out on a local Mercedes salesman when he'd referred to it as a 'Soprano button'. She'd thought it was insulting to Italians everywhere, including her own ancestors. Her father had been furious, wondering what difference this could possibly make in the grand scheme of things. It would be so much more convenient if both of their cars came from the same dealer. But she'd stuck to her position and they'd bought the car up near Hartford instead.

'So what if I have to drive further for service?' her mother had said. 'That salesman offended my grandmother's people.'

When the car slowed for a moment, Elizabeth groped for the handle and yanked. The trunk sprang open.

# THIRTY-SIX

M ason drove the squad car, with Meigs barking out directions to the abandoned house that Randy had mentioned. If the girls weren't there, he'd think of something else.

'What if we don't find them?' asked Paul, leaning forward from the back seat, his fingers pressed against the Plexiglas divider.

Meigs ignored him, wishing the divider was soundproof.

'What's the plan? Are we randomly driving around?'

'First of all, shut up,' said Meigs. His radio crackled before he could say more to Paul. Like, if he'd been a decent husband and father in the first place, none of this would be happening, which felt a little too close to home.

'Dispatch, do you read me?'

'Yeah,' said Meigs. 'What is it?'

'We have a hysterical woman on the phone who believes she saw a hostage in the Stop and Shop. Want me to patch her through?' The dispatcher's voice was flat, as if suggesting this was probably a citizen fruitcake. There had never been a hostage taken in the local grocery store – it didn't happen in this town. But with an officer's daughter missing, now would not be the time for jokes.

'Go ahead, ma'am, we're listening,' Meigs said. 'State your name and your business.'

'I'm Teresa Hopper. I was picking a few things up in the Stop and Shop and I happened to see my best friend's daughter, Elizabeth Brown. I knew right away that something was wrong because of what was in her basket. And she wasn't wearing a coat or even a sweater.'

Mason looked over at Meigs and lifted his eyebrows.

'Go on,' Meigs said.

'First of all, Elizabeth's fiancé left her at the altar. I don't know if it was a matter of infertility – I mean infidelity, or what.' She burst into hysterical giggles.

Paul snorted in the back seat and Meigs waved him quiet.

'That's a doozy of a Freudian slip! I'm sorry, I'm just so upset,' said the woman. 'What I'm trying to say is that she had no reason at all to buy contraceptives. She and her fiancé had just broken up, hours before their wedding. And yet there was a box of condoms, larger than life, right in the middle of all her groceries. The kind with ribs.' Another peal of hysterical, high-pitched laughter. 'Second, Red Bull? Elizabeth only takes her caffeine the normal way, in coffee. Preferably in the form of a skim-milk latte. She's a medical student and very aware of what poisons she puts in her body. The ice cream was the final straw.'

'The ice cream?' Meigs repeated.

'She's very careful about what she eats, exactly like her mother. She's incredibly disciplined; you'd have to be to get into medical school. There's no way she's out buying ice cream. And if she did break down and buy it, store brand chocolate? Get real! Elizabeth would never waste calories on that. And then she said it was her mother's idea – and that was her favorite flavor. Her mother is deathly allergic to chocolate.'

'Yes, ma'am,' said Meigs. He could check this out later.

'Anyway, I noticed all this, and I thought to myself, she seems kind of nervous. But maybe it was just a bad day, you know, like everybody has? Because cancelling a wedding is a big deal. It's got to have been a terrible week. And she's probably embarrassed as heck about everything. So I finished shopping and paid for my groceries, and left the store to get into my car.'

She paused and Meigs said impatiently: 'And then?'

'There was Elizabeth driving off in her mother's car with a man in the passenger seat. Big guy, kind of scruffy looking. That's not her fiancé, no way. He's Irish, all pale cream skin and dark hair. And besides, why wasn't she wearing a coat? Maybe it's nothing, Teresa, I said to myself. But how will you feel if your best friend's daughter was abducted and murdered and you never said a word to the police?'

'Supposing it was a new boyfriend,' said Meigs, 'what if that's why the wedding was called off? Wouldn't that explain the contraceptives and the other items?'

'But not the ice cream. Or the coat. Why would you go out without a coat in this weather?' said Teresa, whispering now. 'At first, I wasn't going to call, but I got so worried. I'm not supposed to know this, but her heart was absolutely broken. Her mother told me so. I'm telling you right now, Elizabeth Brown was not on a love tryst. She was afraid.'

Meigs twirled his finger and pointed down the road to indicate that Mason should step on it. 'Go through it all one more time, ma'am,' he said. 'Tell me every detail you can remember.'

She reviewed the condoms, the Red Bull, the ice cream. Chocolate, she was certain Elizabeth had selected. And several foot-long submarine sandwiches, something Teresa had never, ever seen Elizabeth eat – and this was a girl she'd known for her entire lifetime.

'Tell me again what she said to you?' Meigs asked.

'Something about the cool weather being just right for chocolate, and how her mother loved it, which makes no sense at all,' Teresa said.

'What car was Elizabeth driving?'

'Her mother's black Mercedes.'

'Thanks for calling,' Meigs said, and clicked her off. He called the dispatcher back and asked her to alert all officers to be on the lookout for the black vehicle with a possible hostage situation.

Meigs's phone buzzed. This time the caller was Susan, Elizabeth's aunt. 'My niece left me a message,' she said breathlessly, 'about going to an abandoned home on New Road.'

'We're on it,' Meigs said, as Mason lurched into a U-turn, headed to the highway, the fastest route to Madison.

'Does this have something to do with Caroline?' Paul demanded, his breath frosting the Plexiglas.

'Black Mercedes pulling out just ahead,' said Mason, stomping on the gas and flipping the switch for lights and siren. 'The trunk's flapping open. See if you can read the plate.'

# THIRTY-SEVEN

E lizabeth felt the sharp acceleration of her mother's car. Now that the trunk lid was banging like crazy, she regretted pulling the release. What were they supposed to do, throw themselves out on the asphalt, the girls bare-limbed with hands taped behind their backs? The asphalt frozen, and snow and ice everywhere else? The car made two turns and she heard the tires clicking as they did at higher speeds on the highway, and then finally, mercifully, the whooping sound of a siren somewhere behind them. The car sped faster, wind whistling through the open lid of the trunk. She stopped trying to talk with the girls, just clasped Caroline's shoulder and prayed.

Suddenly the car slid off the road and bounced onto a rough surface, jouncing the girls and Elizabeth in a tangle of bodies. Caroline had started to cry again and Addy was moaning through the tape covering her mouth. Moments later, the car screeched to a stop.

Rafe flung the trunk lid fully open, his face angry and sweating. He looked demented and dangerous, and now she could see his coat was soaked with blood around the right shoulder.

'Get out, let's go.' He jerked Elizabeth's arm and dragged her from the trunk to the pavement, then shut the lid again. It was sleeting again, cold, wet needles pelting them in the darkness.

'Move it. Run! Now!'

Meigs called the station for backup as Mason banged the cruiser off the highway behind the Mercedes. He drove too fast past the McDonald's parking lot and pitched to a halt at the distant reach of the rest stop. A man walking a Golden Retriever looked up in alarm as the cruiser's doors burst open.

'He's running into the woods! With a woman!' Mason shouted.

They bounded out of the car and began to sprint through the sleet, leaving Paul locked in the back seat, hammering on the window with his fists.

'Daddy!' cried a desperate voice from the depths of the abandoned Mercedes' trunk.

'Caroline!' Meigs stopped and dashed back to the car. He lifted the trunk lid and then reached in for the girls, gathering them both in a desperate embrace. He felt relieved and then devastated as he absorbed their near-nudity, the bruised faces, the duct tape. Then he heard the faint cry of a newborn from inside the car.

'I'll go after him,' said Mason, who had come up beside him, panting. 'You stay with the girls and the baby.'

Meigs hesitated. He couldn't send another officer alone on

a dangerous chase. He popped the cruiser's trunk, unlocked the back doors, and threw Paul a Swiss Army knife. 'Cut the tape off the girls and get them covered up,' he said brusquely. 'Blankets in the trunk. Call nine-one-one and get an ambulance here right away. Get two. And take care of the baby, too.'

He cradled Caroline's head between his hands. 'I'll be back soon,' he said fiercely. 'Your father will take care of you until then.'

Then he and Mason ran into the woods, keeping their flashlights pointed at the ground, listening for the sounds of the man and his hostage crashing through the bushes.

Rafe stabbed her between the shoulder blades with the muzzle of his gun and she ran faster, away from the McDonald's and the gas pumps that she had recognized as part of the highway rest stop, and into the woods. Her breath came in harsh gasps, her thigh and calf muscles burning. She slid on a patch of frozen leaves and felt the heel snap off her left boot. She stumbled and fell.

'Keep moving or I shoot you here,' Rafe shouted, grabbing her arm.

She scrambled up and started running again, lurching unevenly on the broken boot, branches snapping and tearing at the tender skin on her face. He forced her up and over a chain-link fence and she felt the fabric of her skirt rip almost to her waist. Then the jagged metal at the top of the fence caught on her tights and tore at her thigh. She fell to the ground on the other side and he jerked her to her feet again. Her breath came in short, harsh pants. She wasn't in shape for sprinting, but a fierce shot of adrenalin that had begun when they heard the sirens and pulled off the highway kept her going. They ran through a new townhouse development and crossed New Road to return to the crumbling, abandoned house.

'My car's behind the garage,' Rafe said, yanking her toward the outbuilding. 'You're driving. Do you have that cop's phone number?' he asked as they got into the white car, her in the driver's seat.

She nodded yes.

'Start the car, and here's what you say.' He poked her in the side with his gun to remind her who was in charge, and gave her the lines.

'This is Elizabeth,' she said, when the detective answered his cell. 'Elizabeth Brown? He told me to call and tell you—'

'Where are you?' Meigs barked. 'Put the man on the phone. He must turn himself in.'

'He told me to tell you that if you don't back off, he will shoot both of us.' She choked back a hysterical sob. The car began to beep a warning that all seat belts weren't fastened.

'Put him on the line,' said Meigs again.

Rafe grabbed her phone and threw it out into the snow. 'Screw them. Now go.'

She began to steer through the path in the trees toward the driveway, trying to imagine how this could end well. How could the police shoot at him without killing her too? They couldn't. She stomped on the accelerator and veered toward a massive oak fifty yards down the hill.

# THIRTY-EIGHT

They slammed into the tree, and the car flipped over. Elizabeth's air bag deployed and the nylon fabric smacked hard into her face and chest. She hung from the seatbelt like a bobblehead, too dazed to take any action. A grim-faced cop with his gun drawn appeared outside her window, yelling for her to unlock the door. With his help, she managed to unhook her seat belt and then crawl out, shaking crumbles of glass and white powder out of her hair. She trembled with fear and too much adrenalin, unable to believe it was over. Meanwhile, Meigs and another cop trained their guns on the man who'd taken her hostage. He was crumpled in a heap inside the car, next to the passenger side door. The gun had dropped to the ceiling and his head was canted at an awkward angle and dripping with blood. The windshield where he'd made impact after the collision had spidered into a million cracks.

'I've got him,' said Meigs. 'He's not going anywhere. You get the lady away from the car.'

The second cop helped Elizabeth stagger a few yards into the woods where she sank into the snow, her back against a tree. Within minutes, an ambulance and three more police cars had roared up the driveway.

Detective Meigs jogged over with a paramedic.

'We're going to take you to the hospital, get you checked over,' he said gently.

'What about the girls?'

'Everyone's fine, thanks to you,' Meigs said, his voice gruff.

She glanced at the crashed car, where more paramedics loaded Rafe's body onto a gurney. 'There's nothing wrong with me that a hot bath and a new pair of boots won't take care of.' She shuddered.

'You're bleeding,' the paramedic said. 'And you're probably in shock.'

She nodded, feeling a whoosh of relief that someone else was deciding.

'Where's Olivia?'

'Olivia?' Meigs asked.

Elizabeth frowned, then winced and grabbed her thigh as she stood up. 'She's the reporter who was following Addy for a story. That's how I ended up here – I thought the white car was hers. But when we were all in the trunk, this Georgia woman spoke up and I heard the baby cry. Then I heard Olivia's voice, trying to talk them into giving up. Then somebody got hit hard and there was a gunshot. More than one.'

She had started to blubber and repeat herself. Honestly, she had no idea what had really happened outside that trunk. She should have believed Olivia in the first place, that Addy was in serious danger. 'You've got to find them. Please.'

Meigs's eyes widened and he jogged over to the uniforms clustered around the crashed car. 'Patrol the area,' he said. 'Look for another attacker. And her hostage.'

From her seat in the back of the ambulance, Elizabeth watched them fan out across the deep snow in the overgrown yard and the woods behind the house. The shout came only minutes later from behind the ramshackle garage.

'Over here!' called one of the cops. 'We need another ambulance!'

# THIRTY-NINE

Once inside the emergency department at the Shoreline Medical Center, a doctor checked Elizabeth for signs of a concussion. Then a cheerful nurse cleaned up the cut on her thigh and administered a tetanus shot, before allowing Meigs and another officer to come into the cubicle.

'Thank you,' he said, holding his hand out to shake hers. He handed over her phone. 'It was in the snow, so who knows whether it will work. Do you feel well enough to walk us through the evening?'

She nodded, and began with how she'd received the texts from Olivia, and followed the white car but lost it even though she'd seen tire tracks leading to the old house. And then she was taken at gunpoint and forced to join the girls in the basement.

'He'd hit them and they were freezing and scared to death,' she said softly, blotting the moisture in the corner of one eye. 'I think your daughter's OK. She was very brave.'

'And you were too,' Meigs said.

Mason brought Elizabeth's parents, her aunt, and Wilma, her father's secretary, into the crowded room.

'Oh my God, you could have been killed,' said Videen, taking Elizabeth's face in her hands and kissing her over and over. Elizabeth had been stoic up to then, but Videen's words turned the faucet on.

'My God, what were you thinking going to that house by

yourself?' said her dad. But the usual critical bite wasn't in
his voice and he waited impatiently for his turn to hug her.
Then Aunt Susan squeezed her in a tight embrace.

'You were so, so brave,' she said. 'I'm so proud of you.'

Next Wilma moved in for a hug. 'We are so glad you're all
right.' Her eyes were shining with tears as she pulled away.
Elizabeth suddenly flashed on the loving look on Wilma's face
when she'd served tea the other day. And how they both had
the sturdy legs of a peasant. And hair that refused to stay
straight. She would think about this later.

'Where are the others?' Elizabeth asked Meigs.

'Rafe is dead,' he said. 'He wasn't wearing a seat belt.'
He paused to watch her face. 'Remember that you did what
you had to do to save yourself and the others, OK?' He
placed his hand on her shoulder and looked at her until she
nodded.

'They took Addy and the baby to Yale. It's complicated
because Child and Family Services will be involved. Olivia
went in too, because the paramedics were concerned about
possible concussion. She followed Rafe's car to that house
and saw him take the girls inside. She parked her car out of
sight and was going to walk up to the house when you arrived
on the scene. She considered going in after you, but when
you came out with Rafe she saw an opportunity to try to
rescue the girls. She searched the house from top to bottom,
but couldn't find anyone in there. It was dark in the cellar so
she went back to her car for a flashlight, but when she returned
Georgia had arrived. She said she was about to call for assistance when Georgia knocked her out.'

'And the dreadful Georgia?'

'Georgia is on her way to jail, once the ER patches up the
gunshot wound,' Meigs told her.

'What can you tell us about all this?' asked Elizabeth's
father.

'I'll say what we've pieced together from talking briefly
with Addy, but more of the story will unfold, I'm sure. Some
of this is still speculative.' Meigs explained how Addy had
escaped from the brothel at Rafe's urging.

'He had made arrangements to sell Addy's baby to a desperate couple,' said Meigs. 'Apparently, they'd already paid him a big chunk of dough. But Georgia, the woman who'd enslaved Addy, knew Senator Lester was the father. Blackmailing him would be a lot more lucrative than selling the kid. But she needed the baby, and the phone that Addy stole, and Addy too – at least until his paternity was proven and she'd squeezed as much as she could from him. Rafe realized all this and thought he'd enlist Addy to help him cut Georgia out of it. The stakes were high for all of them. The baby was worth a lot, Addy not so much. But they probably agreed on one thing – it was important to keep her quiet.'

'In the end, he left everything behind except for me,' Elizabeth said, shivering as she realized how close she'd come to disaster. 'I was his escape route.'

'He did have Lester's phone on him,' Meigs added. 'And that is safely locked away as evidence.'

'I hope that senator and his aide go to prison for a long time.' Elizabeth winced. 'I still can't believe a man in that position would take advantage of an underaged girl.'

'Believe it,' said Meigs. 'Lester appears to be a scumbag. We picked up his chief of staff at the airport. He was on his way back to Washington, but since we started questioning him and told him we had the phone in our possession, he's been squealing like a pig. Lester was also making a load of money trading his insider status in Congress to insurance companies. And his staffer was just as crooked. If justice prevails, they'll both go away for a long time.' He scratched his head and grimaced.

Susan said, 'Sometimes the people we elect to office, to work for us, are best at taking things for themselves.'

'What about Rafe's partner, did you catch him?' Elizabeth asked.

'He was working alone,' Meigs said. 'He acted like he had a partner to keep the girls and you in line. You came up to that house at the wrong time. Or the right time . . .'

'How's your daughter? How's Caroline?' Elizabeth asked.

'Coming along,' he said gruffly. 'Thank you. And thanks

for what you did. You kept cool and probably saved the girls' lives.'

'Instinct,' said Elizabeth with a shudder. 'I was scared out of my mind.'

# FORTY

The dog next door wheezed a few desultory barks as Meigs pulled into his driveway. The old mutt seemed to have lost his oomph in the two days since Caroline left. Truth was he had too. Maybe he'd take a road trip out to California next summer, just to say hello. Maybe Caroline would go with him for a few days to Disneyland. No, she would be too old, over all that. And over him too.

He went inside, locking the deadbolt behind him, then dropped his keys and wallet on the living room coffee table. The hide-a-bed was still unfolded, with Paul's sheets in a tangle. He and Caroline had stayed with him that last night until Caroline had gotten her stuff packed up and felt ready to travel. Now the house felt unbearably quiet. He knew it would be hard to lose Alice's girl, but was it possible that he even missed that annoying lunk, Paul? He snapped on the TV, just for some noise.

In the kitchen, he fished a frozen dinner from the freezer and stashed it on the counter for later. Swiss steak with mashed potatoes. It would taste like cardboard – but who cared? Everything tasted that way these days. He cracked open a nonalcoholic beer and walked back to the living room to watch the news. The neighbor's dog launched into a frenzy of barks and Meigs clicked the volume higher. The weatherman predicted a three-day span of perfect January thaw. Great weather for catching up on paperwork, he thought glumly. And planning better outreach to the high school kids.

His phone buzzed with a text message. From Caroline. His heart ticked faster.

*How wd u feel if I came bk to Guilford?*

*Can't w8,* he typed in clumsily. *Visit any time.*

*Sweet,* she wrote back.

*Keep me posted,* he typed.

*Open the door? I don't have a key.*

He took three quick steps to the front door, threw it open, and scooped her into a bear hug and rocked her like a baby. Paul waited down on the sidewalk, looking sheepish.

'I tried to talk her out of this, but she's stubborn, just like her mother. She thinks she made a mistake, going with me,' he said. 'Luckily, we had a couple of days in Hartford to figure this out before flying her all the way to California.' He rolled his eyes at Meigs, as if at the absurdity of teenagers. 'If it's OK with you, she'd like to stay here in Connecticut, finish up the school year living with you.'

'I know we have things to figure out,' said Caroline. 'I'm willing to live by your rules. Except the thing about being grounded for two months – that seems a little harsh.' She laughed, but she had a fragile look on her face, as if she feared he'd say no.

'Of course you can live here,' he said, grinning, and picked up the enormous duffle bag from the step below her.

'If that's set then, I'll be off,' said Paul. He blew a kiss to his daughter and trotted down the walk to his car. Meigs watched him go, wondering how he could bear to leave this little spitfire behind.

Once they had delivered Caroline's stuff to her room, she said: 'Mrs Brown has the baby. Addy was going over there today, too, with her DCF worker. She said I could come over to see her. And her worker says they can help Addy with the paperwork to become an emancipated minor. Can we go?'

'Mrs Brown has the baby?'

'She's the foster mother,' Caroline said.

Meigs figured all of this was a lot more complicated than Caroline had made it sound. But she looked so hopeful. And so happy.

'Sure,' he said. 'Do you mind if I give Mrs Brown a call first, make sure this is a good time?'

After a quick call, Meigs drove his girl across town and along the river to the Browns' house. A few Christmas lights were still strung through the downtown, but the thaw had melted most of the snow, leaving behind a carpet of withered grass and the remnants of any leaves that hadn't been raked.

Caroline pointed to a handsome Colonial across from the river. 'Isn't it pretty?' Lights sparkled in all of the windows downstairs, and the old-fashioned lamppost wound with more lights welcomed them to the front door. Addy and an older woman he didn't recognize were just disappearing inside.

'Maybe we could get them to help us decorate next year,' Caroline said. She was out of the car and up the walk before he got the engine turned off.

Addy remembered the last time she'd been here, after she had gotten off the train, exhausted and filthy from giving birth in the city. She felt a flush of embarrassment, thinking about how these people knew about the senator and Georgia and all the unspeakable things she'd done in the past year. And her new friend Caroline was probably furious, and had every right to be. Addy had dragged her into an awful mess and almost gotten them killed.

And Mrs Brown would be so disappointed now that she knew the truth about where Addy had come from and what she'd done. Sure, she'd said it was fine to come see the baby. But she didn't say the rest, how this should be the end of it. That little girl needed a real mother, not a runaway slut. Maybe she should take off, start somewhere new where no one knew anything about her.

Then Caroline came up behind her and squeezed her hand and grinned. 'Aren't you so excited to see the baby?' So the moment passed and she was hustled into the kitchen, where Elizabeth waited with a warm hug. The air was perfumed with cinnamon, and a rack of baby bottles sat on the counter next to the sink.

'We're so thrilled you're here. Come in, come in. We've made hot chocolate and snickerdoodles. Mom tried to add some chai spice to the dough, but I told her not to mess with perfection.' She took their coats and welcomed them into the living room, no longer crowded with wedding presents. Now it was cluttered with baby gear, a tiny rocking chair, a pile of pink and white clothing, and stuffed animals everywhere.

Addy lost her breath when Videen came into the living room carrying a pink bundle in the crook of her right arm, and a bottle in her other hand. 'You're just in time to feed the baby, sweetheart.'

Addie felt her heart freeze. 'I don't know how.' She could sense the other grown-ups lurking near the door to the kitchen, watching. The DCF worker who'd brought her over. Caroline's father, the cop. And Elizabeth. They'd see she was a fraud.

Videen laughed. 'It's easy, I'll show you. Remember what I said on the phone? No one is born knowing these things, but anyone can learn.' She perched on the couch and patted the seat beside her.

She tucked the baby into Addy's arms, then stood up and backed away, smiling. Caroline leaned over to nudge the white blanket out of the baby's face.

'Oh my gosh, she's so sweet, Addy. And I bet her eyes are going to be the same color as yours.' The baby started to whimper, her little brow puckering the way Addy remembered it had in the subway bathroom. Within seconds she worked herself into a piercing wail. Addy stiffened, feeling terrified. This was a terrible mistake. She couldn't do it. Rafe had been right to say she had no idea how to be a mother. That it was better to give her away.

Videen came back over with her arms out. 'May I take her for a minute?' Once Addy handed off the baby, Videen held her against her shoulder and began to jiggle her gently, patting her back in comforting circles. 'Like that,' she told Addy. 'And whispering shhhh, shhhh, as you rock her, that helps sometimes too.' She settled the baby back in Addy's arms. 'Walk and talk and jiggle, you can do it. No one is born knowing what to do,' she repeated.

Addy got to her feet and circled the room, whispering. The baby closed her eyes and melted into her shoulder. Addy grinned with relief.

'You're a natural,' said Videen.

Once Addy returned to the couch, Videen put the bottle in

her hand and showed her how to hold it close to the baby's lips. She began to suckle and Addy swore she looked right into her eyes.

'I was thinking of naming her Winifred,' she said. 'I know the new mother can change it. But maybe when she's older I can write her a letter and tell her about it.'

'Winifred's a lovely name,' said Videen.

'After my grandmother,' said Addy. 'I'm staying with Gram for now until I can figure things out. She wants to come and meet the baby too. If that's all right?' She cast a worried glance at Videen.

'Of course, you and she are always welcome,' Videen said.

'Did you see the article that Olivia Lovett wrote about the baby?' Elizabeth asked.

Addy shook her head. She hadn't wanted to read it; it would make her feel too sad.

'So many people offered to give her a home,' said Videen. 'But my husband and I have been talking, and I'd like to keep her here for a while. If that's OK with you.'

Addy couldn't speak; she could feel the tears sliding down her cheeks and dropping onto the baby's blanket.

'This way, you can come and visit when you're in town.'

'How often can she come?' asked Caroline, looking doubtful.

'Every day, if she wants. And if Addy decides she wants to help be the mother, she can. You know we have two spare rooms upstairs so you girls can always spend the night.'

Addy dabbed at the baby's chin and looked up at Elizabeth. 'I heard you say that you were adopted. Did you ever wonder who the real mother was?'

'Of course she did,' said Videen, briskly. 'Her mother loved her so much that she did what she thought would give her the best life. She didn't think she could take care of her alone, so she gave her to us.'

Addy looked at Elizabeth. 'You never wanted to find out who she was?'

'I did want to know – some day. I figured it out this week,' said Elizabeth, meeting her mother's eyes and smiling. 'I was lucky. She stayed close by so she could watch me grow up. I bet Winifred would love that too.'

# ACKNOWLEDGMENTS

The idea for this book was hatched in 2009, when I visited Project Lighthouse, a drop-in youth center in Key West, Florida. The staff helps runaway teens and homeless youth find food and shelter, and then make longer-term plans. I recently found notes from a conversation I'd overheard while talking with the director, Jai Somers. A teenage boy was talking to his mother. 'What do human beings really need? Just food,' he told her. 'What help?' he asked, before he got off the phone. 'She thinks I have mental problems,' he told us once he'd hung up. This conversation broke my heart. I began to think about a new character, Addison, wondering what her home was like, and how it might have been bad enough for her to decide to run away. Thank you Jai Somers for the important work you do, and for showing me around.

I'm grateful to my agent, Paige Wheeler, who persevered until she found a home for the book, and to Kate Lyall Grant, for welcoming me and the book to Severn House. I am so pleased with Sara Porter's thoughtful editing, and with copy-editor, Rachel Malig. And what an amazing cover! Thanks to all of the good folks at Severn House who brought this book to life in a most professional and thoughtful way.

Thanks go to Hallie Ephron, Susan Hubbard, and Hank Phillippi Ryan for reading early drafts and giving smart advice. More thanks to Ramona Long for her careful editing. The Key West Writers Guild also gave me support and encouragement on early drafts. Thanks to Detective Bernie Whalen for help with police procedure in New York City. My good friend Lyn McHugh scouted out subway stations until she found the perfect setting. Andrew Brady and Ben Fishel helped with plot brainstorming on the DC political scene. Thank you to midwife Gail Hardy, nurse Christine Falcone, and Dr Molly Brady for medical details – any mistakes are absolutely mine!

Thank you to Christine Falcone and Angelo Pompano, my

writers' group for so many years – you are intrepid readers, fine writers, and treasured friends! My Jungle Red Writers family is always there for advice and a comforting word – or congratulations. I'm so happy to have them along on this crazy journey. I'm grateful for my sister, Susan Cerulean, whose friendship and support are invaluable.

And as always, sincere thanks go to my dearest partner in life, John, who will brainstorm in a heartbeat, plus walk the puppy, and even clean the kitty litter, when I have a crazy deadline.

Finally, to bookstores, libraries, and readers who are giving this new book a chance, I am overwhelmed with gratitude. Thank you!